MANNING SCOPED THE AREA, THEN GAVE THE ALL-CLEAR

James, Hawkins and McCarter broke out of the tree line and cautiously moved toward the main building in the drug lab compound. Their weapons were at the ready, their fingers on the triggers, their eyes scanning for movement.

Suddenly the jungle exploded around them.

"Ambush!" Hawkins yelled as he dived for cover.

Automatic-weapons' fire slashed at them from four directions. They were caught in a professionally prepared kill zone and had walked into it like raw recruits on a training exercise. The bigger issue of how the enemy had known they were coming didn't occur to Hawkins right then.

He was too busy fighting for his life.

DON PENDLETON'S

MACK BOLAN®

STONY MAN™

REPRISAL

A GOLD EAGLE BOOK FROM

WORLDWIDE®

TORONTO • NEW YORK • LONDON
AMSTERDAM • PARIS • SYDNEY • HAMBURG
STOCKHOLM • ATHENS • TOKYO • MILAN
MADRID • WARSAW • BUDAPEST • AUCKLAND

First edition May 1998

ISBN 0-373-61918-9

Special thanks and acknowledgment to
Michael Kasner for his contribution to this work.

REPRISAL

REPRISAL

CHAPTER ONE

Colombia

Thomas Jefferson Hawkins was an ex–U.S. Army Ranger, and he had worked some near impenetrable bush in his life. But he had never seen anything like this before, and he was in no hurry to ever see it again. Nonetheless, he was stuck with it for another day or so, and he had been a soldier long enough to know that bitching about the mission didn't make it go any easier.

It was supposed to be the dry season in eastern Colombia, but it might as well have been the middle of the monsoon season in Southeast Asia. Everything was wet, sticky, steaming wet, and that included the floor of the jungle. He doubted seriously if the red clay sucking at his canvas-topped jungle boots had been dry since the end of the last Ice Age. Heading up the side of a mountain the way they were didn't make the going any easier. For every step he took forward, he slid back half a step.

He was supposed to be walking slack on this gig,

the guy who was supposed to back up the pointman if trouble arose. In better terrain, he would have been hanging back twenty yards or so behind the point, so as not to get caught short if the pointman tripped an ambush. In this terrain, though, if he dropped more than a dozen feet behind Calvin James, he'd lose him completely in this steaming green hell.

Hawkins glanced at his watch and instantly wished that he hadn't. They were still an hour away from their objective. If, that was, they were keeping to the schedule, which he seriously doubted. Taking one of the collapsible plastic canteens from his belt, he took a long drink of the tepid, stale water. With the humidity hovering around ninety-nine percent, he knew it was important to replace the fluids he was sweating away. A person could die of dehydration just as quickly in the jungle as in the desert.

David McCarter, as the middle man in the five-man team struggling up the hill, was trying to stay close behind Hawkins. But the one-time British Special Air Service commando was having a difficult time keeping up with the younger man in front of him. The jungles of the world were his least favorite places to play the game, but this was one of those times when his personal opinions didn't mean a hell of a lot. Since he was the leader of the Phoenix Force, his lot in life was to lead his counterterrorist team to its target and orchestrate its efforts to destroy.

The target this time was a major coca-paste processing facility on a remote mountaintop. The cartel moved its raw material in and the finished product out by helicopter. The combination of the remote location, the dense jungle and the impassable terrain was the facility's main defense. But there was no place on earth that determined men couldn't reach. McCarter wouldn't mind very much, however, if it wasn't so much of a struggle to reach it.

Behind McCarter was Rafael Encizo, who had been born in Cuba. This wasn't the first time he had ever been in the jungle, but even Encizo had never seen any terrain like this. He'd heard Vietnam veterans tell tales of the triple-canopy jungles of Southeast Asia, where the sun never shone, and of the battles they fought in its perpetual twilight. He had been in the Asian jungles himself, and while they were dense, they had been like well-tended public parks compared to this. The heat and humidity were familiar, however, and he hardly noticed the sweat pouring off him.

The Canadian, Gary Manning, had the drag position at the end of the five-man team. He was both an experienced woodsman and an ex-soldier and, like the rest of the men, he had never seen anything like this jungle. But he had to admit that it was the perfect place to hide a drug lab. There was no way that anyone could send in a large body of troops as a raiding party. In fact he wasn't at all sure that Phoenix Force was going to be able to fight its way through to it, either. At least not within the window that had been planned for the raid and their withdrawal.

He knew that the Stony Man team back in Virginia

had used the best information they'd had when they'd put the operation together, but sometimes even the best wasn't enough. Spy-satellite photos, radar maps and aerial recon had laid out the terrain for them, but they hadn't been able to get under the trees and show how dense it was on the ground.

No matter how long it took, though, they'd keep humping. No one on the team was a quitter.

THE JUNGLE WAS so thick that Calvin James almost didn't notice when he entered an area that had been partially cleared. But when he spotted the fresh-cut stump of a banana tree, he held up a clenched fist to signal a halt and instantly went to ground. Looking forward, he saw more cut brush and realized that they had finally reached their objective.

Making sure that he was well under cover, he keyed his throat mike. "Heads up, guys," he whispered over the team's com link. "We've arrived. I just hit the beginning of a cleared area."

"Thank you, Jesus," Encizo muttered as he shifted his shoulders under the straps of his heavy backpack.

"Hold there," McCarter radioed back. "I'm coming up."

As the slack man, Hawkins came up alongside James and slid into cover a few yards away. He saw the cut underbrush, but the foliage was still too thick for him to have a good field of fire or observation. There could be a platoon of hardened jungle fighters hiding ten yards away and he wouldn't see them.

With James and Hawkins scanning the jungle, McCarter checked his maps and saw that they were, in fact, approaching their objective. To make sure, he reached into the pouch on his equipment belt and took out his Global Positioning System—GPS—unit to take a positive fix on their location. The compact device wasn't much bigger than a hard-bound edition of a thriller and was a vast improvement on the earlier, bulky GPS units that had been in service as recently as the Gulf War.

Extending the antenna, he punched in their satcom access code, and the GPS unit transmitted a signal to space. GPS navigation worked by exchanging signals with the twenty-four NAVSTAR satellites orbiting the earth at a height of 10,900 miles. When the GPS receiver made contact with any three of the satellites, it triangulated its location on the ground by using the satellite's precise location in orbit at that particular split second. The grid location that read out on the digital screen was accurate to within three inches of wherever it happened to be on Earth.

Even with that kind of electronic precision, the GPS system was only as good as the map that was being used with it. But that wasn't a problem this time. The mission workup had included tasking the ultrasecret National Reconnaissance Office—NRO—to provide a radar map of the objective area. With that map in hand and the GPS readout, he saw that they were only eight hundred yards from the center of the drug-lab complex.

"Okay, lads," he whispered into his mike. "This is it. It's supposed to be about eight hundred yards almost due east. Let's find it."

"On the way," James answered.

HAWKINS STAYED on James's heels as the ex-SEAL carefully wove his way deeper into the vegetation, moving even more slowly than before. This was no time to miss a trip wire or the firing port of a bunker. Ever so gradually the jungle had been thinned out as if it had been done by nature rather than the hand of man.

Most of the trees had been left in place to provide overhead cover, but most of the underbrush had been cut back to allow free movement inside the compound. He didn't see any obvious gun emplacements, bunkers or other defenses, but that didn't mean that they weren't there.

The buildings in the clearing had been camouflage painted in varying shades of matt green and shadow gray and, under the trees, they would be invisible from the air. He noticed that the structures appeared to be made of wood and didn't even have sheet tin roofs. That would further aid the camouflage by not giving hard aerial or space radar returns. Even on a remote mountain top in the middle of the jungle, the cartel was taking no chances of the compound being discovered. The compound appeared to be deserted. All the windows were dark, no one was walking between the buildings and no smoke or chemical odors were in the air. There was no sign that anything was being refined in the long warehouselike buildings that had to be the reported production labs.

Hawkins bit back an angry curse. They had come a long way to hit a dry hole. They could still burn the buildings, but he had hoped that there would be a major stock of either coca paste or refined cocaine to add to the flames.

While the other four men kept a close watch on the compound, McCarter tried once more to report to Stony Man Farm on the team's satcom radio. But as had happened the last time he had tried to call, two hours before, he wasn't able to get through.

The Briton really didn't have time for this right now. The sooner they burned this place to the ground, the sooner they could get off the mountain and out of the jungle. Mack Bolan and Jack Grimaldi were standing by in Panama with the extraction chopper, and all they needed was a quick call and they would take to the air. If, that was, he could get through to them.

"You still can't get through?" Encizo asked.

McCarter shook his head. "Not a bloody damned thing."

"Maybe it'll work when we get back down on the flat land."

"If it doesn't, we'll be walking home," McCarter said as he put the radio into his backpack.

"Rafael," he said as he picked up his MP-5 subgun, "you and Gary stay here and cover us. We're going in anyway."

Manning slung his MP-5 and unlimbered the Remington Model 700 sniper's rifle. The Nikon twenty-power ranging scope on the rifle could be very useful in a situation like this. The powerful scope brought the jungle close enough for him to see into the shadows of the underbrush.

Stony Man Farm, Virginia

BARBARA PRICE COULD barely suppress the urge to pace the floor in Aaron Kurtzman's crowded domain on the first floor of the main house at Stony Man Farm. The pent-up energy needed a release, but she couldn't leave the Farm's computer room right then, and space was at a premium.

She also was trying hard not to ask Kurtzman yet again if he had anything new, but she lost that fight. "Do you have anything—?"

"No!" he snapped, cutting her off.

Price took the curt answer without offence. It wasn't for nothing that the man who ran the state-of-the-art cybernetic intelligence-gathering-and-analysis system for the Stony Man operation was known as "the Bear." Usually he was called that because of his bulk, but it also sometimes had to do with his temperament. When things weren't going well in Kurtzman's electronic cyber kingdom, he could get as snappish as a wounded grizzly.

As always, he had gone to every source he could access to provide background information to plan this strike. This time, though, most leads ran into a stone wall and he didn't quite know what to do about it. The frustration didn't sit well with him, but then it never did.

"Don't you think it's time that we let Striker know what's going on?" Price asked.

The honey-blond woman was the Stony Man Farm mission controller, which meant that she was the one who ran the show. Having a woman who looked like a high-fashion model run the nation's most secret counterterrorist organization might have surprised some people, but she hadn't been chosen for her looks. Price had a mind like a steel trap. But when a mission was going down, she knew when to stop giving orders and listen to the other people of the Stony Man team. And Aaron Kurtzman was always a man well worth listening to.

"What do you think?" she repeated. "Do you think we should call him?"

Kurtzman hated to admit defeat. Fighting to the last cyber round was his usual way of dealing with a difficult situation, but he was smart enough to know when the situation had the better of him and he needed to call for reinforcements. Phoenix Force was on the ground somewhere in Colombia, and since he had lost all communication with them, he had to get help to find them. For the kind of help that he needed, few people on earth were more suited for the job than Mack Bolan.

"Yeah. I guess it's time."

"You talk to him," she said. "And while you're doing that, I'll give Hal a briefing on this."

Kurtzman winced inwardly when she said that. "Thank you," he said. Admitting defeat to the man who oversaw the Stony Man operations was not something that he really wanted to have to do today.

Colombia

JAMES, HAWKINS and McCarter broke out of the tree line and cautiously moved toward the main building in the drug-lab compound. Their weapons were at the ready, their fingers on the triggers, their eyes scanning the compound for movement.

Suddenly the jungle exploded around them.

"Ambush!" Hawkins yelled as he dived for cover.

Automatic-weapons fire slashed at them from four different directions. They were caught in a professionally prepared kill zone and had walked into it like recruits on a training exercise. The bigger issue of how the enemy had known that they were coming didn't occur to Hawkins right then.

He was too busy trying to save his life.

CHAPTER TWO

Back in the tree line, Rafael Encizo snapped his over-and-under M-16/M-203 combo to his shoulder and triggered the grenade launcher. With a characteristic thump, the high-explosive shell arched into the clearing. Not waiting to see where the grenade landed, the Cuban slid the launcher open and loaded another cartridge into the breech and snapped it shut. The instant the second 40 mm round was in the air, he switched to the M-16 and sent a full magazine of 5.56 mm slugs after it. Dropping into a crouch, he dumped the empty clip and snapped a new one into place. Beside him, Gary Manning was up on one knee, his MP-5 smoking on full-auto fire. The Remington sniper rifle was a damned good weapon, but it was not the tool of choice to use to break up a jungle ambush. If the guys in the open were going to survive, he and Encizo had to do what was called *achieve fire superiority*. In plain English that meant throwing lead fast enough to make the other guy keep his head down.

The return fire was tearing up the jungle around

them, chunks of tree bark and branches flying, but that was the way Encizo wanted it. It meant that the ambushers were concentrating their fire on them instead of on the three men caught out in the open. And that was the name of the game. Until James, Hawkins and McCarter could get out of the kill zone, they had to keep drawing the enemy fire down on themselves.

FROM HIS FACEDOWN position in the middle of the clearing, McCarter quickly assessed the situation while he burned a 32-round magazine of 9 mm parabellum slugs through his H&K MP-5. They were in a tight situation, but the ambush had been sprung a few yards too early. Had the enemy waited for just another minute or two, it would have been all over for Phoenix Force.

Slamming another magazine into the well of his subgun, he started to crawl backward. Encizo and Manning were putting out a blaze of fire to cover his retreat. Rounds were snapping over his head going both ways.

HAWKINS WAS ALSO MOVING to the rear as fast as he could go when he felt a round slam into his thigh. He didn't have time to stop and see how badly he had been hit, but he wiggled his toes and tensed his muscles to see if everything still worked. So far, so good. All he had to do was to keep from getting hit again before he could get back into the bush. And there was nothing like a minor wound to keep your mind focused on the business at hand.

Raising his head, he burned off half a clip at a muzzle-flash and continued crawling backward. Getting to his feet would be a good way to commit suicide. Glancing behind him, he spotted a clump of brush to his left and headed toward it. He could support his two teammates from there until they could get to the tree line.

JAMES HAD BEEN on the right flank when the action started and had been able to find a depression in the ground to drop into. Glancing to his left, he saw McCarter and Hawkins frantically trying to clear the kill zone. He burned through half a magazine to try to cover them, but he saw a string of slugs chew into the ground past Hawkins, and it looked like his teammate had taken a hit.

Zeroing in on the muzzle-flash, James burned off the other half mag of 5.56 mm rounds and the gunner went silent. "T.J.!" he called over the team's com link. "You okay?"

"I'm fine," Hawkins radioed back. "See if you can get to the tree line and cover us. I'll stay here until David gets clear."

"On the way."

Since he had been on the far right, James was closer to the shelter of the tree line and was able to crawl to safety without drawing unwelcome attention. Once under cover, he joined Manning and Encizo in suppressing the enemy fire.

Hawkins keyed his mike. "David, it's your turn. Go for it!"

With four weapons concentrating on providing him covering fire, McCarter quickly crawled out of the kill zone, then turned to cover Hawkins, who didn't wait to be invited to clear the area.

ONCE THEY WERE all back in the tree line, the Phoenix Force commandos ran fifty yards back down the trail and regrouped. The mission was blown, but before they moved out, they had to figure out where they were going next, and they had to do it fast. Whoever they had come up against would be after them in no time.

"You're hit!" James said when he saw the blood soaking the leg of Hawkins's muddy fatigue pants.

In the press of the moment, Hawkins had been busy ignoring that little fact. The adrenaline shooting through his veins had a lot to do with his being able to do that. He knew that he still had a few minutes before the wound started to hurt and he was willing to wait until then before he started to worry about it.

"It'll keep," he snapped. "Let's get the hell out of here!"

"Let me put a pressure bandage on that so you don't bleed out, dammit!" James reached for the aid pack on his belt. He had taken combat medical training in the SEALs and served as the team's medic.

"Okay." Hawkins knew that James was right, and he stood still while the pressure bandage was tied around his thigh.

"Are you two finished?" McCarter looked up from his map.

"I'm okay," Hawkins replied.

"Let's move it, then," McCarter ordered. "I'll take point. Rafe, you cover me. Calvin, take drag with Gary. And T.J., you hump the bloody radio."

As THEY RAN, Hawkins tried the radio again, but had no better luck with it than McCarter had before the ambush. Where the hell was everybody? Why couldn't he get through to either the Farm or to Bolan and Grimaldi in Panama?

Stony Man was supposed to have the most sophisticated communications system in the world, or so Aaron Kurtzman always liked to brag. But if it was so good, why couldn't he reach anyone? Where were all of those satellite links and scramblers when they were needed?

MANNING AND JAMES hung back to give the others a chance to get a good head start. At James's signal, both took M-26 fragmentation grenades from their ammo pouches and pulled the pins. If they could deliver the explosive eggs on the target, frags were very effective in the jungle.

After lofting the grenades back along their path, they listened for the muffled thumps of the detonations and the sharp cries of pain that followed. After firing a magazine on full-auto into the kill zone of their mini-ambush, the two Phoenix Force warriors spun and ran through the jungle after the rest of the team.

A hundred yards farther on, the pair stopped again at James's signal. Reaching into his side pants pocket, he pulled out what looked like half a dozen wet green leaves six inches in diameter. With Manning covering him, James pulled a red tab on the bottom of each leaf and carefully placed them in the middle of the trail they had made in the jungle.

While the leaves blended in with the foliage, they hadn't grown on any tree. They were molded plastic explosive with touch-sensitive fuses and enough force to blow a man's foot off. As soon as the minimines had been placed, the two turned and again ran after the rest of the team.

THE MERCENARY LEADER known as El Machetero, "the Machete," listened to the reports coming in over the radio. He wasn't surprised to hear that the gringos had broken the ambush and were trying to get away. That was what happened when you tried to go up against professionals with a bunch of amateurs. Like it or not, the gringos were professional soldiers. And if they were who he thought they were, they were perhaps the best professionals in the world.

The veteran guerrilla leader had asked his paymaster to hire the best men that his U.S. dollars would buy for the mission, but he had been overruled. The CIA agent he knew as James Jordan had told him that he had to hire unknowns so that no one would notice that all of the well-known, high-profile Latin American mercenaries had suddenly disappeared from the market. It would jeopardize the mission, he had explained, by alerting the intelligence agencies who kept a close watch on the region's professional soldiers for hire.

Jordan had made up for the lack of quality, though, by hiring quantity, lots of it, and providing first-class American-made weapons and equipment for the force. It was a typical American solution: if it won't work, get a bigger hammer. But El Machetero had to admit that the hundred men he had been given should be able to track down and kill a five-man team no matter how good they were.

Tracing a track on the map, he sent orders to several of his tracking teams to move in on the targets as he had planned. As a man who had been a guerrilla fighter since he was a teenager, El Machetero had known better than to expect the ambush at the compound to completely take care of the situation. Even the best of plans were subject to the whims of the Gods of War.

That was particularly true when your opponents were as good as these particular five. Jordan hadn't told him who these men were, just that they were mercenaries contracted to the American DEA. But when he read through what little material the CIA man had provided on them, they both looked and sounded familiar. For years there had been a team of commandos

who had worked with the man who was best known
as the Soldier. Their leader had been a one-armed man
who was thought to be an Israeli. There were other
non-Americans on the team, as well, one of them a
British mercenary, and another who was believed to
be a Canadian.

These five men had been in action all over the world
against freedom fighters, Communists, drug lords and
other enemies of American imperialism, and their record was impressive. The fact that they were still alive
after so many years was proof enough that they were
good at what they did.

This team was usually believed to work for the CIA,
but El Machetero seriously doubted that for several
reasons. One of which was that, as they had just shown
at the ambush site, they were simply too good to be
CIA men. The American intelligence agency had been
an effective enemy back in the good old days, he had
to admit that. But it had never been half as good as
its legend had made it out to be. All too often, the
Company, as it was called, had failed to act in a de-
cisive manner because it was always subject to the
whims of political meddling.

From everything he had heard, this team operated
more like a Mossad or KGB unit. When they went
into action, they killed and destroyed without any evidence of inept political control. Who they really were
wasn't important anymore. He had them, and when
they had been run to ground and killed, he would have
photos of their faces taken and maybe someone would

be able to solve the mystery. But even then, it wouldn't matter because they would be dead. And he would be rich enough to permanently retire to his cattle ranch in Guatemala.

Jordan had promised that the targets wouldn't be able to use their radio to call for help, and that they would just be five men alone in the jungle.

The hawk-faced El Machetero had been born in the jungle. He had lived most of his life there, and he knew it better than most men knew their home towns. Even his favorite weapon was the jungle machete, hence his nom de guerre. Even if these men were who he thought they were, they were on his home ground and they were his to do with as he chose.

And he chose to run them to ground and kill them.

"After them!" he ordered over the radio.

Panama

MACK BOLAN FROWNED as he listened to Aaron Kurtzman explain Phoenix Force's situation in Colombia over the secure phone line. Losing communication with a team in the field wasn't uncommon; in fact it happened all the time. But from what Kurtzman was telling him, it sounded like something had knocked out the entire Stony Man communications system.

"We'll be airborne in five minutes," he stated. "And we'll check in with you as soon as we reach the target area."

"Jack!" Bolan called out as he ran for the Sikorsky

CH-53D Sea Stallion helicopter sitting in front of the hangar. "Get it in gear!"

Jack Grimaldi was Stony Man's ace pilot. The man could fly anything with wings or rotors and had done so at one time or the other. After ferrying Phoenix Force to its jungle landing zone, he and Bolan had returned to the American Army airfield in Panama City to wait for the extraction.

He glanced at his watch as he grabbed his flight bag and headed for his bird. The call was early, but maybe the mission had gone off without a hitch for a change.

"They're early," he said as he pushed past Bolan to enter the chopper.

"They're something," Bolan replied, "but we don't know what. Aaron called and said that they lost all communication with them."

"Oh, shit."

Bolan quickly strapped himself into the copilot's seat as Grimaldi started the preflight checklist.

The pilot had been flying choppers for so long that his eyes and hands went through the checklist without his even having to think about it. The CH-53D was a bigger brother to the old HH-3 Jolly Green Giant search-and-rescue chopper of Vietnam War fame. It was bigger, had more powerful turbines, had longer range and was faster. Though it was known officially as the Sea Stallion, in Grimaldi's mind, it was still a Jolly Green.

Checking over his shoulder to make sure that no one was standing too close to the chopper, he hit the starter button to the port side turbine. The 3,925 shaft horsepower General Electric T64-GE-413 turbine fired up with a whoosh. Overhead, the seventy-two foot, six-bladed rotor slowly started to turn.

Grimaldi kept an eye on the tachometer needle and, when the turbine's rpms rose into the green, he reached out and fired up its twin. With both turbines burning, the rotor came up to speed quickly.

With a last check of the instrument panel, he clicked in his throat mike. "Tower, this is Three Niner Four. Code name Green Ramparts. Request clearance for immediate takeoff."

"Roger, Three Niner Four," the flight controller answered. He didn't know who was flying the Green Ramparts machine, but the code name gave him priority over all other traffic. "You are cleared for immediate takeoff on runway One Eight Two. Be advised that there is traffic inbound at twelve thousand, vector two-three-niner. I will hold them until you're clear."

"Roger, copy," Grimaldi said as he twisted the throttle up against the stop and pulled up on the collective. "Taking off now."

The hulking Sea Stallion rose on her landing gear, and the pilot fed in enough pedal pressure to swing the nose around. When the ship was aimed in the right direction, he nudged the cyclic control forward, and the chopper started down the runway. Fifty yards farther on, he had enough forward speed to haul up on the collective and they were airborne. Once out of the traffic pattern, he headed southeast to the Gulf of Mexico.

The CH-53D was supposed to be capable of doing almost two hundred miles per hour. But with a good tailwind and by pegging the throttles up against the stops, Grimaldi was able to get over the maximum. His comrades-in-arms were on the ground and they were in trouble. The least he could do was get to them as quickly as possible.

CHAPTER THREE

Colombia

El Machetero smiled when he got the report from the survivors of the tracking team that had run into the leaf mines the targets had placed on the trail. He had lost three men to the mines, but he wasn't angry. He was pleased that they had been killed. It proved to him that the men they were chasing were the men he thought they were. Leaf mines were almost impossible to get in the world's black markets, and the fact that they were armed with them proved that they had high-level government sponsorship of some kind.

The mercenary felt his pulse increase. This hunt would be a crowning end to his long career. He had wanted to take these men down in his own backyard, and it had come to pass just as Jordan had promised. When this was over and he had the photos of their dead bodies, he would be the most celebrated guerrilla fighter of modern times since Che Guevara.

Bending over his map, he plotted the report of the leaf mines and studied the terrain downhill from the ambush site. He didn't have radar maps like the ones he knew his targets had, but this was his home turf and he could almost see the terrain in his mind without even having to look at the map.

Seeing all of the possible escape routes down the mountain, he used his experience to put himself into the mind of the team leader. The man wouldn't choose the most direct route out; that would be too obvious. He might not even take the second choice. He would, however, see the need for speed, and since his radio wasn't working, he would want to head for the coast or the nearest large town. That cut the choices down to two.

After studying both routes, El Machetero made his decision as to the one the targets would most likely take. Picking up the radio microphone, he started to move his teams into position to block them and turn them away from the coastal plains. He wanted to drive them to the south, to keep them in the mountains where it would be easier to contain them.

As soon as his forces had been properly deployed, the mercenary leader called for his helicopter to come in and pick him up. For this hunt to work as he had planned it, he needed to be in the air. The Americans might have proved themselves to be rank bumblers in Vietnam, but they had come up with a good idea when they had put their commanders in the air over their operations. The flying command post was the best way for him to keep track of the targets' movement and vector his forces in to block them. Jordan had made the small helicopter available to him, and it was proving to be very useful.

HAWKINS WAS COPING with his leg wound. So far, it wasn't affecting his movement through the jungle. But he knew that as soon as they stopped for any length of time, it would stiffen up and cause him a lot of trouble when they moved out again. He was thirsty, though. He knew that when the body lost blood, it kicked in the thirst responses to provide enough fluid to replace the blood.

But this seemed to be more than that. He was beginning to feel as if he was a bit feverish, but with the ambient air temperature hovering around the ninety-nine-degree mark, it was impossible for him to tell without a thermometer. Opening the first-aid pouch on his field belt, he palmed a pair of aspirin tablets and swallowed them dry. They would help if he did have a fever.

McCarter raised his hand to halt the team and whispered, "Quiet!" into his throat mike.

Jungles are the noisiest uninhabited places on Earth. Even with no humans contributing the unique din that is characteristic of their species, the local fauna was quite vocal and made up for it. Hunting cries, the wails of fallen prey, mating calls and all the other forms of animal communication made the jungle a discordant cacophony. It was only when the jungle creatures fell completely silent that a man needed to worry.

McCarter tried to filter out the background noise

around him to focus on something he thought he had heard in the sky. The thick canopy overhead kept him from searching the skies, but he thought he had heard the characteristic whupping sound of chopper rotors in the distance. He strained his ears, but heard nothing.

His desire to get out of there had to have started affecting his brain. Either that or it was the heat. Whatever it was, he had to get a grip. This was no time for him to start having hallucinations about helicopters he hadn't been able to contact.

But since he hadn't been able to call for the extraction, he couldn't expect Bolan and Grimaldi to come on their own for at least another day. Because of the difficulty of the terrain, the mission had been planned with a lot of slack built into the time frame. No one would know that they were in trouble until they failed to check in after another twenty-four hours.

Even then, it would be awhile longer before Stony Man gave up waiting for them and pushed the panic button. It would take a couple of more hours for Bolan and Grimaldi to have the Jolly Green chopper on station. Once it showed up, he should be able to contact them on the team's personal radios. But, with all of that taken into consideration, they were looking at having to hang on for at least another twenty-four hours that they might not have.

The ambush at the mountaintop lab hadn't been a fickle finger from fate. They had been set up and set up well by a real professional. Someone who knew what he was doing had gone to a lot of work to suck them in, and there was no reason to think that they were going to be allowed to escape unmolested. Whoever it was behind the scenes was out for blood, and he wasn't going to be happy that they hadn't been cut down in the kill zone. He would be coming after them.

"Let's go," McCarter growled.

JACK GRIMALDI CROSSED the coast of Colombia at wave-top height and at top speed. "Feet dry," he called back to Bolan on the intercom, using the Navy code word for crossing from a flight over water to one over dry land.

"Roger," Bolan answered curtly from his station at the communications console behind the flight deck.

The Stony Man pilot had chosen the wave-top approach to ensure that their penetration of Colombian airspace would go unnoticed by both the legal authorities in the country, as well as by the ever more sophisticated drug lords. The arms race in the war against drugs had taken a dramatic turn, and for the men on the front line of the battle, it was a turn for the worse. Since many drug lords had more money to spend than plenty of nations of the world, there was very little that their vast wealth couldn't buy.

Advanced security and radar systems and private communication satellites were becoming more and more common in the cartel's forces. There was even a report that one of the crime families had purchased a submarine from the Chinese and was outfitting it to transport drugs. Modern helicopter gunships were also showing up more and more in the skies over the jungles where the drug lords hid their labs and manufacturing facilities.

Grimaldi was in no position to go up against a hostile gunship, not this time and not in the aircraft he was flying. The Sikorsky choppers had earned undying fame over North Vietnam in the hands of the search-and-rescue crews who put their lives on the line to rescue downed pilots and endangered recon teams. There were a hundred tales where SAR crews had braved a storm of ground fire, prowling MiGs or even SAM missiles to pluck some poor soldier literally from the jaws of death on the ground. His ship was the best in the world to do what he had to do today, but it wasn't up to facing enemy gunships.

For one thing, this aircraft wasn't well armed. He had an M-60 machine gun mounted in the side door for Bolan to provide suppressive fire at the pickup zone, but it would be next to useless against an aerial attack. Also, while the CH-53D had good range and fair speed for a machine of its size, it wasn't very maneuverable. That marginal maneuverability was further diminished by the fact that this particular aircraft had a belly full of several thousand pounds of electronics and communications gear that had been added specifically for this mission.

In short, Grimaldi was flying an overloaded charter bus that hopefully would have to make only one stop and pick up five passengers. The fact that the stop would be made by hovering over a jungle and that the locals might be on hand to protest this special stop was the only thing that made the flight interesting. But before any of that could happen, he had to locate his prospective passengers.

And that was where this carefully planned program was going to fall apart. Without radio contact with McCarter and the others, there was simply no way to pick them up.

"Mack," he called back to Bolan, "do you have contact with them yet?"

"Negative. What's the ETA to the extraction area?"

"Twenty-eight minutes."

That was close enough to dash in for a quick snatch and to get out with no one being the wiser. But if the Phoenix Force warriors weren't waiting for them at the PZ, it might as well be on the far side of the moon. And until they made contact with the five men, they didn't know where they were waiting or even if they were.

"Phoenix One, Phoenix One," Bolan said, trying the satellite radio again. "This is Phoenix Bird, Phoenix Bird on Satcom One. Over."

When Bolan listened for an answer, he didn't hear static on the frequency as he normally would have expected. Instead, there was an odd, hollow sound as if he were standing inside a huge empty building. In all his years of using military FM radios, he had never heard that kind of sound before. But all of his instruments indicated that his radios were transmitting properly.

"Phoenix One, Phoenix One, this is Phoenix Bird. I am switching to Tac One and will try to contact you on that frequency. Out."

Tac One was the frequency of the team's com links, their personal radios. Even if the chopper was out of the range of the small radio's transmitters, they should still be able to receive his stronger transmission.

"Phoenix One, this is Phoenix Bird on Tac One. If you hear me, change to the alternate push on your satcom radio and try to contact me."

After receiving no answer, he repeated his message several times, switching to all of the frequencies the Phoenix Force communications equipment could receive. Each frequency had the same odd, empty sound on it.

"Jack," he called up to the cockpit on the intercom, "either they're all dead or Aaron's right. There's been some kind of total communications blackout on their equipment."

"Could it be some kind of localized EM pulse?" the pilot asked.

It was well-known that an electromagnetic-energy burst could burn out a solid-state circuit, and all modern radios used solid-state circuits. But a burst of energy great enough to do that kind of damage would have been detected back at the Farm.

"I don't think so," Bolan replied. "The jump scanner is picking up other local radio transmissions in

Spanish, but there's nothing on any of our satcom or tactical radio frequencies.''

"I'll head toward the objective area and see if it gets any better."

"Roger."

As Grimaldi banked the chopper to the west, Bolan switched back to the team's main frequency again and listened to the hollow sound. He had no idea what he was listening to, but it was an ominous sound—how he would expect death to sound.

DAVID MCCARTER WAS on point again as the Phoenix Force commandos headed downhill as fast as they could. It was much easier going down the mountain than it had been going up, but the jungle was still as thick, and it hindered their retreat just as much as it had their advance. Like any professional soldier, McCarter didn't particularly like the word *retreat,* but that's what they were doing. Cut off without communication and outnumbered more than they could count, they had no choice but to clear the area.

HAWKINS HAD no problem with getting out of the area. Normally he might have wanted to turn around and fight, but not this time. He hadn't said anything to James about how he was feeling, but he wasn't sure how much longer he could keep up the brutal pace. He was sure now that he was running a fever, and the most likely cause was that his leg wound had become infected.

He wasn't as experienced in jungle warfare as some of the others were, but he knew how quickly an infection could take a man out of action. And if he went down, it would take the rest of the team with him.

Making his decision, he keyed his throat mike. "Calvin, T.J. Do you have any antibiotics in your kit bag? I think I'm running a fever."

"Oh, shit!"

"See to it, Cal," McCarter said. Since their team radios were voice activated, all of them could hear what any single man said. There were no secrets on a mission like this. They would all live or they would all die, but they would do it together.

JACK GRIMALDI HAD crisscrossed the pickup zone several times, but Bolan hadn't been able to make radio contact with the five men on the ground. Visual contact was impossible, as well. All he could see was a thick, tangled sea of green below them. Not even a trace of the red earth of the jungle floor showed through the canopy.

Once they made contact and Phoenix Force marked its location with a smoke grenade, he could lower the jungle penetrator into the tangle and get them out in just a couple of minutes. But until there was contact, nothing was going to happen and he was running low on fuel.

"We're going to need a gas station in another hour," Grimaldi called back. "So do you want to go back to Panama or call for a refueling bird?"

"Let me check in with the Farm first. I have another idea."

"What's that?"

"Rather than go all the way back to Panama, I want to set down somewhere closer to the extraction area until we can get this communication glitch sorted out. I don't like the way this looks, and I don't want to be too far away."

"You've got that right," the pilot responded. "What do you have in mind?"

"I know a place here in Colombia where we can get refueled and maybe even pick up some heavy armament."

"Sounds good to me. I was getting tired of that Panamanian beer anyway."

"Head out on a bearing of zero-eight-nine, and I'll come up to guide you in after I talk to Barbara."

"Roger," the pilot answered as he banked away to the southwest.

CHAPTER FOUR

Northern Mexico

Hermann "Gadgets" Schwarz wasn't having a good day. The temperature of the northern Mexican desert was hovering just under a hundred degrees, and the sun was burning the back of his neck. A fine dust was blowing into his eyes and coating the lenses of his field glasses. Worse than the mere physical discomfort, though, was the situation at the small cluster of buildings three hundred yards in front of him.

Removing the field glasses from his eyes, he blew the dust from the lenses and went back to studying his objective. The tractor-trailer rigs he had been told to expect were backed up to the warehouse with their rear doors open, waiting to be loaded. Through the open loading doors of the building, he could see the fifty-five-gallon steel drums labeled Molasses that half of a ton of cocaine was supposed to be packed in.

What he didn't see was anyone loading the drums into the waiting trucks, or even standing around waiting to load the trucks.

According to the Stony Man mission briefing, there should have been a dozen or so Mexicans down there, sweating in the midafternoon sun as they rolled the drums into the open trucks. But there was no one on the loading dock and no one anywhere else around the cluster of ramshackle buildings. It was a setup. And that was what he hated more than anything in the world.

"Ironman," Schwarz whispered into his com link, "we're getting sucked in. There's supposed to be a bunch of guys down there, and I see squat. The place looks completely deserted, and I don't like the feel of it. Let's call in and make sure this is the right day."

Carl Lyons wasn't as suspicious of the objective as was his Able Team teammate. The ex-LAPD cop's Ironman nickname had to do with the way he dealt with obstacles. To him, every mission was an obstacle that was to be met head-on, balls out, and damn anything that got in his way. This time though, he didn't see what the obstacle was.

If there weren't any Mexican drug traffickers down there, they wouldn't have to spend the time to take them out of the play. They could just go down, rig the drums for demolition, burn the warehouse and split.

"Don't sweat it, Gadgets," he answered. "The goods are there, and that's what we came for. As for the mules, maybe they're taking a siesta or something."

Rosario Blancanales, the third member of Able Team, agreed with Schwarz. He had to admit that it looked good down there, but maybe a little too good. Barbara Price had told them that there should be people at the site, at least a half-dozen men loading the trucks and another half-dozen standing guard over the operation.

He also would have expected to see a limousine or four-wheel-drive, the local kingpin's personal ride, parked somewhere close by while the transfer took place. No drug runner would trust that much of his valuable product to minimum-wage laborers unless he was on-site, gun in hand, to make sure that none of it got stolen.

Schwarz was right. This was a setup.

"Ironman," Blancanales said, turning to Lyons, "Let's give it a little more time. We're not on a clock here. We've got the rest of the day to take care of business."

While that was true, it had taken the three men longer than they had planned to get into position on the rise overlooking the buildings in the valley below. Even though they were in the middle of the desert some twenty miles from the nearest town and a hundred more from the border with Arizona, there had been a lot of traffic on the dirt roads around the remote compound. To make sure that they weren't spotted moving in, they'd had to lie low to let the traffic clear.

"Okay," Lyons said reluctantly. "We'll give it a few more minutes."

"Let's make it at least an hour?" Schwarz suggested, cutting in.

"Okay, an hour."

Schwarz was every bit as anxious to get out of the sun as Lyons was, but he had a very high regard for the sanctity of his skin. He had learned a long time ago that patience was the best armor he could have. He was willing to sit and watch the objective for the rest of the day and all through the night if that's what it took to figure what was going on down there. Or more accurately, what wasn't going on and why it was not.

Able Team usually acted as the domestic-action arm of the Stony Man operation, including Central and South America. While the Phoenix Force commandos handled most of the overseas assignments, Schwarz, Lyons and Blancanales usually took care of business in the United States, Canada and Latin America. They were targeted against terrorists, drug lords and the other dregs of society bent on destroying civilization in the Western Hemisphere.

This time Hal Brognola had sent Able Team into action based on information gathered from a number of sources both domestic and foreign. The DEA, CIA and the intelligence services of Mexico and several other Latin American governments had contributed to the planning phase of the mission. Their objective was to take out one of the new drug-shipment points that had sprung up after the relaxing of Mexican trade regulations under the provisions of NAFTA, the North American Free Trade Agreement.

While NAFTA was supposed to be good for business, both Mexican and American, it had been a disaster for the never ending war on drug traffickers. Mexican trucks were being allowed across border checkpoints in greater numbers than ever before, and the problems of searching them for drugs had increased proportionately. There was no way that the understaffed and overworked U.S. border police could completely check all of the cargo that crossed into the States.

The best way to cut down on this new method of smuggling cocaine was to strike at the source of the shipments in Mexico. But with the Mexican government still unable or unwilling to get serious with drug traffickers, the only thing left to do was to hit the shipment points.

Hal Brognola had sent Able Team to destroy this place for two reasons. First, if they did it instead of the DEA or the Mexican authorities, word of the raid wouldn't leak out and the drugs would be destroyed instead of disappearing while in custody. Second, it was hoped that the aftermath of the destruction of so much cocaine would shake the rafters in both Mexico and the United States. He wanted to see what kind of rats would fall out so they could be targeted next.

The big Fed also knew that the cartel got frantic every time they took a hit from unknown attackers, such as the Stony Man team. It always sent them into a panic, since there was no way they could know when or where the commandos were going to strike next. Even with their vast wealth, money couldn't buy that information the way it could purchase advance warning of DEA or FBI raids.

GADGETS SCHWARZ SAW a figure dash out from the rear of a small building off to one side of the main warehouse.

"Heads up," he whispered into his throat mike. "We've got a live one down there."

"Got him," Rosario Blancanales replied.

The lone man raced across the open ground and disappeared behind the door at the end of the warehouse. For several more long minutes, nothing else happened. Then three heavily armed men stepped out of the warehouse and lit up cigarettes in the shade of the loading dock.

"Oh, my," Schwarz said over his radio. "Look what we have here. The rats are coming out of their holes because the cats didn't show up on time."

Even Lyons had to admit now that something was going down. Taking the SPAS-12 assault shotgun from the ground beside him, he jacked a buckshot round in the chamber.

As the three Able Team warriors watched, a dozen more Mexicans came out of their hiding places and started to walk around the compound as if they were taking a break. All of the men were heavily armed: AK-47 assault rifles were slung over their shoulders, and they all carried automatic pistols holstered on their belts.

Now that the doors of the outbuildings were open,

Schwarz could see more men sitting in the unlit rooms inside. If they had moved in instead of waiting, they would have been caught in a cross fire before they reached the front bumpers of the parked semi trucks.

"I've got over a dozen of them strolling around," Schwarz reported.

"Roger that," Blancanales confirmed. "And I've got a half-dozen more approaching from the outbuildings. We'd better get out of here while we still can."

Lyons wasn't willing to retreat simply because they were outnumbered four or five to one. On the other hand, he wasn't about to go charging down there, his Colt Python blazing in one hand and the SPAS-12 in the other. He might be hardheaded, but he wasn't suicidal. There was, however, another alternative.

The rise they stood on was about three hundred yards from the warehouse, a perfect position from which to fire on the men milling below. They'd been suckered, but Lyons wasn't going to leave until he had registered his complaint with someone, and they would do nicely.

"We're leaving," Lyons confirmed. "But before we go, I want to send someone a message."

"Oh, shit," Schwarz said as he reached for the M-16 on the ground beside him.

"On three," Lyons directed. "One, two, three!"

Three weapons opened up, discharging a storm of lead on the Mexicans caught in the open. The stunned gunmen had to dive for cover before they could return fire.

It took only a couple of seconds for the gunmen to get out of the line of fire, but four of them lay where they had fallen, their blood soaking into the sand.

Though taken by surprise, the Mexicans responded quickly, and Able Team had a real fight on its hands. While a dozen Mexicans set up a base of fire from the warehouse, the rest charged the rise.

Most of them were on foot, but two Jeeps full of gunmen pulled out from behind the warehouse and raced across the sand. There was strength in numbers, and the Mexicans had the numbers on their side. At least for the time being.

Laying down suppressing fire with his M-16, Schwarz started picking up hits two hundred yards out. His first targets were the two vehicles. Tracking the lead Jeep, he drilled a 3-round burst into the driver's side of the windshield before switching aim to the radiator for a longer burst. The vehicle veered to the right with a dead man at the wheel, a cloud of steam enveloping the front end.

He gave the second Jeep the same treatment, but it managed to roll over, throwing the gunmen onto the sand.

Even with the vehicles out of action, though, the men on foot kept coming, and Lyons slung his H&K subgun in favor of his SPAS-12 assault shotgun. The SPAS was short ranged, but it was good in a target-rich environment like the one he was in now. He could do more damage to a man with one double-aught Magnum buckshot round than he could with a handful of 9 mm slugs from a subgun.

The man in the lead was so busy firing on full-auto on the run that he didn't see the danger he faced until it was too late. He paused when his AK cycled dry, and Lyons brought his own weapon into target acquisition.

The Mexican's eyes grew wide when he saw his death swinging toward him. He frantically scrambled at his pants pocket for another magazine for his weapon, but came up empty. He was still trying to figure out what to do when Lyons tripped the SPAS's trigger.

The load of double-aught lead balls caught the gunman in the center of his chest and slammed him backward off his feet. With several of the balls driving through his heart, he was dead before he hit the ground.

Not bothering to wait to see if he had scored, Lyons swung onto the next target. This time he caught a gunman taking aim at Blancanales. Two rounds from the SPAS turned the hardman into a bloody ruin as he was slammed to the ground.

Whatever the cartel was paying these men, it wasn't enough for them to charge up a hill into the face of certain death. First the men at the rear started to back away instead of charging after their buddies. Then, as the men in the front rank kept going down, they turned and ran.

"Gadgets!" Lyons shouted as he sent round after round into their fleeing backs. "Get the truck!"

Running in a crouch, Schwarz sprinted to the dusty Land Rover in the arroyo behind their hill. He slid behind the wheel and turned the key. When the engine fired up, he keyed his com link and shouted, "Go! Go! Go!"

Slamming the gearshift into first and four-wheel-drive, Schwarz cranked the wheel and hit the gas. The Land Rover took off like a gut-shot rabbit. Keeping below the crest of the ridge, Schwarz pulled up behind Blancanales and Lyons. "Get on!"

Still firing as they retreated, the two men jumped aboard, and Schwarz floored the accelerator. They were away before the Mexicans could react.

Since they had left the two Jeeps with their radiators shot out, Schwarz wasn't worried about being followed. More important was getting away from the scene of destruction without being spotted by the civilian traffic on the highway and reported. Getting pulled over by the *federales* wasn't part of the plan.

Setting out across the desert, he planned to make a wide swing to the west before heading back to the highway some twenty miles north. They hadn't travelled more than five miles when they heard the unmistakable sound of helicopter rotor blades cutting the air.

Before they could turn to see where the sound was coming from, the chopper flashed past them not fifty feet off the ground. Two men in the open side door sprayed sustained bursts of lead at their vehicle. Flying that close to the ground, the chopper was hitting air turbulence caused by the wind, and the machine wasn't a stable firing platform. The shots went wild.

"Watch him!" Schwarz shouted as he instinctively ducked.

"I got him!" Lyons stood up in the passenger's seat, the H&K subgun in his hands blazing fire. Since the helicopter had come up on them from behind and was flying so low, Lyons scored several hits before it flew out of range.

"I got the bastard!" he growled with satisfaction when he saw a thin tendril of smoke start from the chopper's turbine exhaust.

"Not good enough, Carl," Blancanales said. "He's coming around again."

As they watched, the thin tendril of smoke trailing from the chopper's turbine thickened to a steady stream. The Mexican pilot either didn't know that he had a turbine fire or, in his desire to destroy his target, he simply didn't care. Taking the Bell 222 in a tight one-eighty, he came straight at them again.

Schwarz pointed the grille of the Land Rover at the oncoming aircraft and slammed the pedal to the floor. The vehicle shot forward, presenting the smallest possible target to the enemy aircraft.

Lyons steadied himself as he fired at the nose of the rapidly closing ship. Behind him Blancanales added his firepower, dumping a full magazine from his subgun into the pilot's position.

The Plexiglas canopy shattered, and chunks of the plastic blew away in the slipstream. Some of the pieces were streaked with crimson. With a dead pilot at the controls, the chopper abruptly veered to the left and drilled straight into the ground.

Schwarz saw one of the gunmen try to jump clear before the aircraft impacted, but he didn't make it. The detonation of JP-4 fuel that instantly followed the crash engulfed him.

"I'm going to have someone's ass for this," Lyons growled as he watched the fireball of exploding fuel rocket into the clear, blue Mexican sky. "This was supposed to be a clean operation."

"I've seen cleaner public toilets in a Tijuana bus station," Schwarz snorted. "We were completely set up, man. Someone was told that we were coming and exactly when we were coming. We'd better tell the Farm ASAP that someone's been reading our mail."

"Except, of course," Blancanales added, "we're talking about E-mail this time. And that's a completely different matter, I'd say."

As the Able Team's technological wizard, Gadgets Schwarz didn't need to have that fact pointed out to him. All of their electronic communications with the Farm were encoded and secure. The only way their communications could be intercepted was if the codes had been broken. The only way Stony Man could survive was if its security was unbreakable and remained that way.

And if Stony Man couldn't survive, neither could they.

CHAPTER FIVE

Northern Colombia

The DEA outpost in Colombia that Mack Bolan and Jack Grimaldi were approaching looked for all the world like a Vietnam-era firebase. It was built on top of a low hill in the middle of a broad valley. The trees and underbrush had been cut back for at least five hundred yards in all directions to clear the fields of fire. The hundred-yard perimeter was an earthen berm faced with barbed wire, which was familiar to both men. They saw that fighting bunkers had been built into the berm every ten yards or so.

The buildings inside the perimeter were all low, squat sandbag-and-perforated-steel-plate structures designed to withstand mortar and fire from rocket-propelled grenades. A tall wooden tower stood in the center of the compound next to the largest of the bunkers. The tower had a searchlight on the top, with what looked like an old .50-caliber machine gun behind sandbags, and it was festooned with radio antennae.

"It sure as hell looks like home down there, doesn't it?" Grimaldi asked, grinning.

"That it does," Bolan agreed. "It's businesslike, but it should be a lot quieter here than it was back in the good old days when we lived in similar camps. Even so, it's a good idea to build a camp like that to make sure that the other guys know that you mean business."

"It looks like they're ready for damned near anything," the pilot agreed. "And if they have enough people to man all of those bunkers, they should be able to hold off a good-sized attack."

"They have a cadre of a dozen American DEA people and a couple of companies of local Indian troops who cycle in and out between operations in the hills."

"We have landing clearance," Grimaldi said as he fed in enough rudder pedal to turn the Sea Stallion downwind to set it down on the chopper pad outside the wire. "I'm going in."

He landed the helicopter without raising too much dust and killed the fuel feed to the turbines. As the two men unbuckled their shoulder harnesses, a delegation of three well-armed men dressed in faded jungle fatigues walked up to the chopper.

A deeply tanned young man approached with his hand out when Bolan stepped out of the aircraft. "I'm Dave Nesbit," he stated, "DEA station chief."

"Mike Belasko." Bolan took the DEA man's hand. "I'm glad you could help us on such short notice."

Nesbit grinned. "I'm glad to do anything I can for a Green Ramparts team."

Bolan didn't know exactly what Brognola had put out as their cover this time, but the code name was getting a lot of positive response.

"I'm Jack Neilson," Grimaldi said, using his cover name for the mission. "This is some station you've got here."

Nesbit grinned proudly. "Isn't it? We call it Fort Apache."

"How are the local Indians?"

"Most of them work for me," the DEA man explained. "Our opposition is working with the local coca farmers. The Indians were in their way, so they came to work for me."

"I've heard that story before."

"Come on inside," Nesbit offered. "I'll show you around."

After a quick walk past some of the fighting positions, the DEA man led Bolan and Grimaldi directly to the largest of the sandbagged buildings, his command bunker. The operations center inside was a state-of-the-art facility. Along with the expected UHF and VHF radios for tactical communications, they had a satcom radio and a bank of computers, faxes and printers satellite-linked to DEA headquarters in Washington.

"Do you have secure-transmission capability?" Bolan asked as Nesbit showed him around.

"If you need to make a call, you can use this console."

"Thanks," Bolan said.

Taking the hint, Nesbit nodded for the radio operator to go outside and followed him to give Bolan privacy for his call. He was able to patch right into Barbara Price at Stony Man Farm on the first ring.

"I'm on a secure line," he said when she answered. "And we're at a DEA firebase in northern Colombia named Fort Apache."

"What's going on down there?" she asked. "Aaron is bouncing off the walls here trying to figure out what's happened to Phoenix."

"I don't know," Bolan answered. "We overflew their entire AO and weren't able to make contact with them on any frequency. There's some kind of complete communications breakdown on all of our field frequencies. And I don't think that it's equipment failure. Something is jamming our radios, including the team com links."

"That's the same conclusion Aaron came to," she said. "And he's concerned about a breach in security."

"More importantly, though," Bolan said bluntly, "we have five men in the jungle and we don't have any way to get them out because we can't talk to them."

"I know," she replied, and Bolan could hear the sincere concern in her voice.

One of the side benefits of having a woman as the

Stony Man operations officer was that she brought a woman's unique viewpoint to the brutal realities of clandestine warfare. The men of Phoenix Force and Able Team placed their lives on the line every day they went to work. And, while they were ready to die for their belief that some things were worth dying for, they could go into battle knowing that their lives wouldn't be callously thrown away. Barbara Price would make sure of that.

"Since they can't talk to us on the radio," Bolan went on, "David would have figured that he was cut off and he should have headed downhill to try to make it to the coast. That's standard operating procedure. He'll be counting on finding some way to get in touch with you through commercial communications, so you need to be alert for that."

"Aaron's already monitoring all those channels."

"But since we don't know what happened to them at the objective, I don't think we can afford to wait until he finds a phone. If this radio blackout is part of an operation against us, they might have gotten into serious trouble."

"What do you want to do?"

Bolan quickly briefed her on his plan. "The DEA station chief here has good contacts with the local Indians. I think I can convince him to let me borrow some of his men to give us a hand with this. I'm going to have Jack fly in some search teams to check their planned routes and try to find them or find out what happened to them."

"I guess that's all you can do," she said. "But be advised that this might be part of a larger problem. Carl ran into a similar situation when they tried to hit a cocaine-shipment point in northern Mexico. They got cut off, as well, and didn't get back in contact with us until they crossed back into the States and called from a motel."

"I'm going to talk to the DEA man here and I might need confirmation of our Green Ramparts status, so stand by in case he calls to clear the mission."

"Will do."

Washington, D.C.

THE MAN WHO WAS KNOWN in most of Latin America as James Jordan listened intently to the "secure" communication between a man who went by the name Mike Belasko and a woman named Barbara Price at a place he had learned was called Stony Man Farm. He didn't know its location yet, but it shouldn't pose much of a problem to a man with his connections and resources. He had people working on it. But what he did know from the various transmissions from Stony Man Farm was that it was run by a man called Hal Brognola, who worked in the Justice Department.

For an operation that prided itself on being beyond the cutting edge of high technology, the Stony Man staff was seriously overrated. Clipper chips like the one he was using to decode their supposedly secure transmission were old hat now. It was true that the particular clipper chip he was using was the latest issue from the lab of a cybernetics firm on an exclusive 'black' contract to the CIA. And it was also true that the only example of this particular clip in existence was the one that he was using.

But if the Stony Man crew was so good, they would have made plans to counter clipper-chip technology. As he well knew, though, doing that took more than merely wanting it to happen. Computer and communications security was one of the top concerns of every nation in the world right now. And for every advance in security some cybertech could think up, another one would make a corresponding breakthrough in defeating it.

It was the oldest game in the world, and it was working to his advantage this time. His operation to destroy Stony Man Farm was proceeding on the schedule he had proposed to the cartel a little over a year earlier. It had taken that much time to put all of the pieces in place, and even though he could now see that much of his caution had been wasted, he didn't regret having planned for every possible contingency.

Destroying the nation's premier clandestine agency wasn't something to be undertaken lightly. From what he'd garnered from various communiqués, Stony Man was small, but it had a long reach and, more important, it had bottomless funding. The latter factor was the reason that he'd been forced to tap into the Cali cartel to finance its downfall.

The Central Intelligence Agency had fallen on hard

times in the nineties. Founded in the aftermath of World War II to counter the expansionist plans of Soviet Russia and Red China, the Company, as it was known to insiders, had been the major player during the Cold War. Now that the statues of Lenin and Stalin had been taken down all over Eastern Europe and China had been granted most-favored-nation trading status, many people wanted to put an end to the CIA, as well. Far too many of those who thought that way were in the halls of Congress.

The waves of budget cuts, moles and internal scandals of the past few years had reduced the once feared intelligence agency to a toothless tiger, but even that wasn't enough for the Company's enemies. There was a movement in Congress to abolish the CIA completely and turn its dwindling resources and mission over to the military-intelligence services. Some of the CIA's top brass were resigned to their fate, as they saw it, but not the man known as James Jordan.

He had given his life to the CIA in the same way that a Catholic priest gave his life to the church. He had been recruited right out of the university where he had majored in political science and foreign affairs. He had originally intended to go into the Foreign Service of the State Department, but when he was given a chance to become a Cold War warrior, he had jumped at it.

He graduated the year of JFK's assassination and went into training as a field agent. A year later, he was in the tunnels under the Berlin Wall helping defectors escape the Communist bosses of the East. When the Vietnam War went white-hot, he transferred to Southeast Asia and received his baptism by fire while leading indigenous troops in Laos as part of Project White Star, the real hidden war in Indochina.

With the winding down of CIA involvement in Southeast Asia, Jordan requested an assignment in Latin America and finally found his home. Like all Americans, he had been a stranger in Indochina, a Long Nose. South of the border, he was a gringo, but after learning to speak Spanish, he fit in as he had never done in Laos and Vietnam. He'd been a major player in everything that had happened in the region since the early seventies and had built a spotless record.

After a thirty-year career on the cutting edge of the war against communism, he should have been in line to be at least the CIA deputy director for foreign operations, if not the director of the Company itself. With the very existence of the CIA in doubt now, that wasn't going to happen. He was stuck in a desk job as the director of communications, and unless he made his move, he would retire there.

He was a warrior and, unfortunately, warriors were out of fashion in the post–Soviet Union era of Washington politics. Men like him were seen as an embarrassment in the politically correct nineties and were being passed over for promotion or being forced into early retirement. Jordan had given his life to the cause, and he wasn't about to quit now. Even with the Soviet

Union gone, he knew that there was still a need for warriors. America still had enemies that had to be crushed, and anyone who thought that the Cold War was over was deluded.

There was still a war to be fought against the new enemies of American civilization, but it wasn't being conducted by the Company. More and more it was being handed over to the military and closet clandestine groups while the experienced men of the CIA sat idle.

He couldn't believe his luck when more than a year earlier he'd been approached by an old acquaintance who had once been a member of Delta Force. His son had been arrested in Mexico on drug charges, and here was the father, hat in hand, offering to barter information with the only Fed he knew in order to get the boy out of a sticky situation. The commando had rotated into a facility known as the Farm and had become what was known as a "blacksuit." He had detailed information of the operation. The CIA man knew a good deal when he saw one. The youth was freed, the commando debriefed. Three months later father and son died in a tragic car accident.

As soon as Stony Man Farm was out of the way, the CIA would regain the position of authority and importance it had once known. Once more, the Company would be the guardian of the nation, and he would take his rightful place as its director.

The fact that he'd had to go to the cartel to finance this operation was unfortunate but unavoidable. As far as he was concerned, though, drug trafficking and use was a concern for the police and the DEA, not the CIA. The so-called War against Drugs was little more than a political shell game pumped up for election years and then immediately put on the back burner as soon as the votes had been counted.

Anytime that the United States seriously wanted to end the drug trade, it could be crushed in a few months. The fact that it was allowed to exist was evidence to him that it was politically useful to both parties. For one thing, drugs gave the underclasses of American society something to do with their otherwise empty lives. For another, and more important reason, drug abuse gave the government a convenient excuse to increase its influence over even more aspects of American life. Jordan didn't see that as necessarily a bad thing.

To run a powerful empire, the government needed to be strong.

NOW THAT the Stony Man air arm was on the ground at that DEA outpost, it was time to take them out of action, as well. The DEA man in charge was good at what he did, but he had been playing a nickel-and-dime game until now.

Like most of the DEA flunkies stumbling around in Latin America, Nesbit had no idea what a real war was all about. He should have been in some of the Laotian or Cambodian mountaintop camps back in the good old days of the secret war in Southeast Asia. That had been a real war back then. The North Vietnamese army hadn't been the poorly armed pushovers that most of the so-called drug lord troops were. They had been real pros.

Jordan smiled. Nesbit was just about to find out what a real war was like, and he wouldn't enjoy it very much. Not all of the drug lords' troops were amateurs. As with everything else, the cartels had enough money to buy anything they wanted, and that included mercenaries. Fort Apache was about to fall because the DEA hadn't brought the CIA into their Colombian operations.

As far as James Jordan was concerned, anyone who wasn't with him was against him, and that included the DEA.

Along with Stony Man's Phoenix Force, he had its Able Team to deal with. But he had a completely different plan to take them out of action. They were back in the States now, and they would stay there until he was ready to confront them. He had sent their photos and particulars to every airport and border crossing, alerting federal, state and local authorities to be on the watch for them.

The documents indicated that the three were wanted narcoterrorists, a cartel-connected hit team, and were to be considered armed and dangerous. If they tried to leave the country, they were to be apprehended and taken into custody.

Knowing their record, however, Jordan knew that when the three were confronted, they wouldn't go along quietly. That didn't concern him. In fact it would be better if they died in a hail of gunfire. It would further show that the Stony Man operatives were rogues and not to be trusted.

CHAPTER SIX

Stony Man Farm, Virginia

Hal Brognola stared out of the front of the speeding helicopter and absentmindedly chewed on the end of the unlit cigar stuck in one side of his mouth. It had been a while since he had smoked, but he was still addicted to the taste, and the nicotine, of his favorite cigars, lighted or not. Right now he could have used a stiff shot of bourbon to go with the nicotine chew, but he was on duty.

In the files of Washington officialdom, Brognola was listed as a high-ranking official of the Justice Department assigned as liaison to the White House. In the shadow world of covert operations, however, he was the director of the Sensitive Operations Group based out of Stony Man Farm, Virginia. The ultra-secret organization's title meant exactly what it suggested: when the operation was too sensitive to be handled through normal channels, Stony Man Farm was given the job.

In this instance, the word *sensitive* was applied to

any situation that was brutal, nasty, dangerous and required the skills of people who could kill, if that's what was needed. Since killing people, even people who needed to be taken out for the greater good of humankind, was such a delicate issue, it had to be done with the utmost secrecy and expertise. When an operation of this kind needed doing, the work was carried out by the Stony Man Farm action teams, Phoenix Force and Able Team, and Hal Brognola was the man who passed the President's orders down to the people who would undertake the mission.

He had sent the Phoenix Force Warriors to Colombia to take out the drug lab, and the fact that the mission hadn't gone well was troubling to him. A great deal of intel had gone into planning that mission, and it should have gone down without a hitch. That it hadn't could only mean that something was seriously wrong.

"ETA zero-five," the pilot reported over the intercom. "We're on the screen and I'm transmitting our IFF."

Brognola merely grunted in reply.

A minute later, the Farm appeared through the canopy. As always, it was a picture-postcard scene of rural tranquillity. The setting sun washed the hills with blazing gold and touched the leaves with cold fire. The fact that they were being tracked on radar and followed by a first-rate antiaircraft weapons system didn't diminish the spectacular view. But the beauty of the Shenandoah Valley hardly registered on Brognola's brain. He had seen it many times before, and it always meant trouble.

BARBARA PRICE BRIEFLY turned her back to the rotor wash as the unmarked Bell JetRanger helicopter approached the camouflaged landing pad at Stony Man Farm and touched down lightly on its skids. When she turned back, she saw that Hal Brognola looked worried as he stepped down from the aircraft. Apparently the ninety-mile flight from Washington, D.C., to the serenity of the Shenandoah Valley hadn't lightened his mood, as it often did.

"Anything new?" he asked without preamble.

Price shook her head. "Not yet."

When he didn't reply, she added, "Everyone's waiting in the War Room."

"Let's go."

As Brognola turned to follow Price to the farmhouse, he saw the ground-support people moving in behind him to service the helicopter for his return flight to Washington, D.C. If he could get frequent-flyer-miles credit for all the time he spent in the aircraft, he'd never have to buy an airline ticket for the rest of his life.

He silently followed Price to the front door of the three-story main house and waited while she keyed the door's security system. Once inside, he headed directly for the elevator leading down to the basement War Room.

THE ATMOSPHERE in the War Room was tense when Brognola walked in. The entire Farm crew was waiting around the big table to brief him on the situation, and no one was smiling.

Aaron Kurtzman often wore a frown, so that didn't bother him very much. His frown remained the same if the coffeepot was broken or the end of the world was imminent. However, Yakov Katzenelenbogen, the Farm's tactical adviser, looked concerned, and that gave Brognola pause. Katz's long career fighting terrorists and other hardforces, first as an officer in the Israeli army and then as Phoenix Force's original leader, had given him a rather jaundiced outlook on life. He wasn't prone to panic, so the situation had to be grave for him to look so grim.

Huntington Wethers was a tall, distinguished-looking black man who had been a professor of advanced cybernetics at Berkeley before Kurtzman asked him to join the Stony Man Farm team. He had jumped at the chance to work with one of the nation's most advanced artificial-intelligence systems.

Carmen Delahunt was a former FBI agent who brought a long career of fighting crime to the staff. The vivacious redhead was usually unflappable, but she also looked worried.

Akira Tokaido had his ever present stereo headset off his ears for a change and hanging around his neck. As the junior member of the computer team, he was trying to put on a good front in front of the big boss.

The washed-out Planet Hollywood T-shirt and ragged jeans, however, blunted the effect.

Even the Farm's security chief was present this time, so this had to be big.

"Where's Striker?" Brognola asked when he saw that the one man he most wanted to talk to wasn't seated at the table.

"He's with Grimaldi in Colombia," Price answered.

That answer satisfied Brognola for the moment. It meant that the Executioner was in the game, and he knew he'd get the details later. Although Mack Bolan took part in many of the Stony Man missions, there was no hard and fast rule that said he had to go on any of them. While he used the Farm's facilities as his home base, he retained his complete independence of action.

That wasn't the situation Brognola would have chosen, but it hadn't been his choice to make. This loose arrangement was the price he'd had to pay to keep the Executioner involved with Stony Man after the disaster of the attack on the Farm shortly after it had been established.

"Okay, people," Brognola said as he took his seat at the head of the table and opened his briefcase, "Let's do it."

He listened intently as Price quickly recounted the beginning of the Phoenix Force mission up to the time contact had been lost. The mission had been strongly promoted by the President, and the Man was keeping

a close eye on its progress. That meant that Brognola
had to understand exactly what had gone wrong in
complete detail so he could report the failure to the
Oval Office.

Failure wasn't a topic that anyone liked to bring to
the President's attention, but it was a fact of life, even
for Stony Man. What it did to Brognola's stomach was
another matter entirely.

"You're sure," he asked when she finished, "that
this communications breakdown wasn't equipment related?"

"I'm positive," Kurtzman said. "Our satcom
uplink read out completely operational and the satellite
itself was working properly. But I was still getting this
strange jamming, almost like it was white noise. Whatever it is, it overrides all of our tactical frequencies."

"What effect do you think that had on the mission?"

"I feel," Katzenelenbogen interjected, "that even
though they had a communications blackout, McCarter
would have continued on to the objective."

Brognola had to agree with that. The British leader
of Phoenix wouldn't let a minor inconvenience such
as not being able to talk to anyone get in the way of
completing a mission.

"What happened after that," the Israeli stated,
shrugging, "is open to conjecture."

"I'm picking up a lot of tactical-radio chatter in
Spanish in their AO," Kurtzman explained. "And
while no one is using any names, it sounds like some-

one is operating a large force in the area, and they're hunting someone or something using frequencies common to cartel communications."

"What does that tell you, Katz?" Brognola turned back to the resident tactical wizard.

"The most likely scenario is that they ran into heavy opposition at the objective, were forced to pull back and are now being pursued."

"When we had been twenty-four hours without contact," Price said, "I sent Striker and Grimaldi over the AO in the chopper, but they weren't able to make contact, either. All of our frequencies were still jammed, and they still are. It isn't the equipment, and nor do I think that it's accidental."

"So you're saying that someone set it up so Phoenix would hit a dummy lab and be ambushed?" Brognola frowned. "To do that, they would have had to know that the mission was being planned."

"That's exactly my point," Katz said. "I think that we've been seriously compromised and probably at a very high level. This mission came from outside the Farm, and only you know how many other people knew about it."

"Unless, of course," Price broke in, "Lyons is right and someone has broken our communications security."

"What do you mean by that?" Brognola asked. "I thought Able Team had its own mission, a drug raid in Mexico."

Price's jaw was clenched. "The Able Team mission went bad, too."

That was the last thing Brognola wanted to hear. His hand automatically went to the pocket of his jacket to search for a roll of antacid tablets. "What the hell happened there?"

"Again we lost all tactical communications with them before they reached the objective."

"The same thing that happened to Phoenix?"

"Yes. The same unexplained jamming on our frequencies. Carl got through to us on an unsecure phone after they withdrew from the objective area just long enough to give me an outline."

"What happened at their objective?"

She quickly recounted the high points of the failed ambush in Mexico. "Carl's convinced that someone set them up. The number of armed men and the heavy guns at the compound, the chopper that chased them and the attempt to make it look like the site was deserted. As he bluntly put it, someone had been reading his mail."

Brognola instantly forgot his other concerns. "Are you telling me that you really think that Stony Man's security has been compromised?"

Price met his gaze squarely and nodded. "I'm afraid that's what it looks like at this point in time, Hal."

For a moment, there was silence in the room. A breach in security at Stony Man Farm was serious. Not only lives were on the line. The confidentiality of the information Kurtzman had stored in his cyberspace kingdom was at risk. What he had amassed there over the years could bring a government down, and not just the U.S. government.

"What are your recommendations at this time?" Brognola asked formally. While this was the last thing in the world he wanted to hear, he had to trust his team as he had never trusted them before. This touched on foreign policy and economic affairs, as well as national defense and the war on terrorism.

"I don't want to go into a complete lockdown at this point," Price replied. "We still have Phoenix in the field and we have to recover them first."

"You don't want to go into Operation Drawbridge?"

The Drawbridge procedure would isolate Stony Man Farm as much as any piece of ground in the middle of Virginia could be isolated. They would go on full-alert status. Nothing would get in, not as much as a fly, and nothing would go out until the crisis had passed.

"Not yet. But I want to limit our outside lines until we find the penetrator. In fact I have already put that procedure into action. Except for Striker, Phoenix and Able, we're locked down until we can figure out what's going on."

"You should have talked to me about that first," Brognola said ominously.

"There was no time," she replied. "I saw a threat and I acted on it."

"I see."

There was an awkward silence for a moment. "I'll need to inform the President about this," he said.

"You can use the scrambled satcom line. It's still open."

"What is the state of your alert?"

"We're still at a stage two, but I want to go to a stage three as soon as possible."

Brognola looked at the people seated around the table. "All of you are convinced that the situation is serious enough to warrant this action?"

"Something is wrong," Katz stated. "There is no doubt about that, and it's seriously wrong. I feel that we have to take all possible precautions until we can find out what is going on. In short, we need to pull our heads in and button up."

Brognola had to take the Israeli's assessment without argument. Katz had more combat operations under his belt than anyone else he knew. If he said it was serious, it was. Nonetheless, he didn't look forward to telling the President of the United States that the nation's most secret organization had been compromised. The fallout would be horrendous, and heads would roll.

"What's your plan to recover Phoenix Force?" he asked Katz.

"Striker and Grimaldi are working on that in Colombia right now."

"Brief them on what you are doing here and tell them to expedite. I want Phoenix Force recovered and available for action as soon as possible."

"Will do."

Brognola stood. "Now, I need to talk to the President."

He turned to Price. "Barb, tell my pilot that I'll be staying here until further notice, so he can return to Washington."

WHEN BROGNOLA returned from the communications room, his face was even grimmer. "The President has ordered Drawbridge procedures to go into effect immediately. Until further notice, Stony Man will have no contact with the outside world."

"But Hal," Price said, "did you tell him that Phoenix is still in the field?"

"I did."

"And he's willing to write them off?"

"'The good of the many outweighs the good of the few,'" he said gruffly, not letting his eyes meet hers.

CHAPTER SEVEN

Southern California

It had been late afternoon when Able Team hit the border checkpoint at Mexicali and reentered the United States. Even with the hardware in the back and a couple of bullet holes in the Land Rover's bodywork, they hadn't had to fear the border police. Their ID cards showed them to be DEA agents working a high-priority operation, and the border police were accustomed to seeing shot-up DEA rigs returning from south of the border.

All the way in, Lyons had kept trying to raise Stony Man on their radio, but without success. As soon as they crossed back into the States, he had placed his unsecured phone call to Barbara Price at the Farm and explained what had happened. She had told him to hole up until she could get back to them.

"We'd better find a place to ditch this rig," Schwarz commented. "Even in California, I don't think that bullet holes are appropriate automotive accessories."

"That depends on what neighborhood you live in, Gadgets," Blancanales said. "According to *People* magazine, bullet holes can be chic in L.A."

It was easy enough for them to pick up a Dodge van with the big V-8 at a rental agency. After transferring their belongings to it, they parked the four-wheel-drive rig on a side street minus its plates and registration. From there, it was a quick drive to a motel in nearby El Centro.

CARL LYONS PACED the floor of the motel room like a caged tiger.

Schwarz looked up from his computer monitor. "Carl, will you please park it somewhere? You're driving me bat shit with that walking back and forth. I can't concentrate on what I'm doing."

"I can't just sit around here, dammit. I want to know what's going on. She should have gotten back to us by now."

"Maybe they're busy," Schwarz offered. "After all, we're not the only people they've got in the field right now."

"What are we, chopped liver?"

"Pol," Schwarz announced on the team com link, "I'm sending Ironman down early."

"What's the matter?" Blancanales called back.

"I need a break."

"I understand," Blancanales replied with a chuckle. "Send him down."

"Carl, why don't you go downstairs and spell Pol? He says he needs a break."

Lyons grabbed his windbreaker and was out the door in a flash.

When Blancanales walked in a moment later, he went straight for the minibar. "It's like an oven out there," he said as he peered inside the small refrigerator. "It must be at least a hundred and it's not even noon yet."

He looked over when Schwarz didn't reply. The smaller man was intently bent over his keyboard hacking his way into some system. It wasn't for nothing that Schwarz was known as "Gadgets." Give him something with more than three parts to it, and he was happy either taking it apart and putting it back together or trying to make it work.

Blancanales was called "the Politician" because he was more comfortable working with people than machines. But he had to admit that there had been little so far for him to do in the way of manipulating people on this mission. The only people they had met so far had been intent on killing them, and that was a hard crowd to work with anything other than hot lead.

Beer in hand, he walked up to stand behind his teammate and look over his shoulder. Once more the message on the monitor read, "This line is not secure. Go to alternate communication."

"What do you think is happening?"

"I'll be damned if I know." Schwarz leaned his head back and closed his eyes for a moment to ease his muscles. "That's the last satcom link, and it isn't working, either. For some reason, the Farm's gone completely off-line. There's no way for us to contact them."

Blancanales glanced over to the phone on the nightstand between the two beds. "How about good old Ma Bell? The phone's still working, isn't it?"

"When they're under alert?" Schwarz shook his head. "No way."

"It's the one thing you haven't tried yet."

If there was anything that Schwarz hated, it was the old-fashioned direct approach. Half of the fun of working with Able Team was getting the chance to play with cutting-edge technological gadgets. But when the high-tech failed, maybe a landline would get through. At this stage, it was at least worth a try.

Walking over to the phone, he picked up the handset and punched in a number. It was picked up on the second ring.

"Martha's Knit Shop," the voice on the other end of the line said. "May I help you?"

Schwarz looked stunned. He had dialed a number known to less than a dozen people in the world, and he had been connected with an old lady in a knitting shop?

"Who am I speaking to, please?"

"This is Martha," the woman replied. "May I help you?"

"And where are you located, Martha?" he asked.

"I'm in Hampton, Virginia," the woman replied. "May I help you?"

"I think you already have. I must have the wrong number, sorry."

"We're screwed," Schwarz almost whispered as he carefully put the phone back in its cradle. "I got a little old lady in Hampton."

"Try it again," Blancanales suggested. "Maybe you misdialed."

Schwarz shook his head. "No way. I got the right number. Stony Man's shut down, and we're on our own. You'd better get Carl back up here. We need to talk."

Blancanales didn't want to push the panic button, but it had been quite a while since he had seen the wisecracking Schwarz this shaken up. And if Gadgets was concerned, he should be, as well.

LYONS LISTENED to Schwarz's tale before asking, "What's the number of that answering service we use?"

"What answering service?"

"The one we call to get our messages when we can't call the Farm directly."

"Jeez, I forgot all about that," Schwarz said as he reached for the phone.

"My turn, Gadgets," Lyons told him, taking the phone from his hand. "You get all bent around the axle and forget the easy way to do things. Like you said, they're probably tied up with Phoenix, but I'm sure they've left us a message. They always do."

Lyons quickly dialed the number, and the line connected after one ring. At the beep, he entered a four-digit number followed by three letters and another number. After another short ring, a woman's voice came on the line.

"If you see Butch," she said, "tell him that Sundance needs to get out of town."

The voice abruptly ended, and the dial tone came back.

Now Lyons had a shocked look on his face as he put the phone back on its cradle. "Barbara just gave us the Butch Cassidy code."

When those words sunk in, Schwarz's expression mirrored the shock on his partner's face. "Oh, shit."

Blancanales came out of the chair in their room and headed for the door.

"Where are you going?" Lyons asked.

"Like the lady said," he replied, "we need to get out of Dodge. We've been static for almost twelve hours now. I'm going down to settle the bill."

"Good point." Lyons snapped out of his lethargy. "We'll get packed up here."

Now he had something to do.

IT TOOK ONLY a few minutes for Able Team to clean out the room and be gone. They always traveled light, and they were well practiced in the art of the quick getaway.

Schwarz pulled the big Dodge van out into the stream of traffic. "Where to, Carl?"

For once Lyons looked to be at a complete loss for words. "Damned if I know, Gadgets. Just drive while I think."

"Which way?"

"North."

"I know a cabin we can go to until we can sort this out," Blancanales offered. "It belongs to a friend of mine, and I know where he hides the key."

"Who else knows about it?" Lyons asked.

"I don't know," Blancanales replied.

"Is it in Alaska?" Schwarz inquired.

"We can't go to Alaska," Lyons said. "We'd be limiting our escape routes to the Alcan highway or an airliner. We have to stay mobile."

"You've got a point there," Schwarz admitted. "So what do you want to do, get lost in the crowd? L.A. maybe?"

Lyons turned to Blancanales. "Where's this cabin, Pol?"

"It's not far from Sonoma."

Lyons was ex-LAPD, but he knew the region around Sonoma. The town itself had once been a gold rush community. It had almost disappeared in the modern era, but had been rediscovered in time to save it. Now the town was a favorite with the New Agers and trendy baby boomers who wanted to get away from the Bay Area for a long weekend. It was in the mountains and had good access routes in all directions,

"Let's take a look at it."

"Sonoma it is," Schwarz said.

"Pull over at the next phone booth you see," Lyons instructed when they approached the edge of town. "I want to make a quick call."

"No," Schwarz said. "Use the cell phone."

"Why's that?"

"If the situation's bad enough that Barb had to give us the Butch Cassidy number, I don't want anyone to get a phone fix on us. I don't think we want anyone to know where we're calling from until we know more about what's going on."

"Good point,"

Picking up the cell phone, Lyons punched in a number from memory. "Jim," he said when the phone was picked up, "this is—"

"Yeah, Jake," the man abruptly broke in. "I was just thinking about you, big guy. I got a call this morning from a guy who was asking questions about my old buddy Carl Lyons. You remember him. He was with the LAPD before he went freelance. Anyway, there's some people who really want to talk to him in the worst of ways. I hope he isn't in trouble or anything like that."

"Beats the hell out of me," Lyons replied, keeping his voice calm. "I haven't seen him in years."

"Well, if you hear from him, tell him to give me a ring at home."

"Will do."

"Someone's looking for us big-time," Lyons announced as he put the phone back ito the cradle. "I called an old friend at LAPD, and he said the dogs are after us."

"It's nice to have our worst fears confirmed," Schwarz said. "Do you still want to try to hole up at Pol's friend's cabin?"

"Yeah. We might as well take a look at it."

Schwarz took the lane for the northbound freeway and nosed out into the high-speed traffic. They had a full tank of gas and should be able to make the trip with only one stop.

Colombia

DAVE NESBIT LIKED Mike Belasko's plan to use his DEA troops to look for the missing men. He was too young to have gone to Vietnam, but his favorite reading material had always been Vietnam War fiction. Going on a rescue mission like this was like something straight out of the Vietnam novels he had read. He had no idea who these two hardcases were, but the one who called himself Belasko looked and talked like he had seen it all and had seen it more than once. His hard-core professionalism was undeniable. Nesbit envied him his experience and was happy to have a chance for some of it to rub off on him.

"My second platoon is ready to go out tomorrow morning on a routine sweep," Nesbit said. "So, it'll be no problem to divert them, and I'll just let the sweep go till after you find your people."

"Good," Bolan said. "You have JP-4 here, right?"

Nesbit nodded. "At least seven or eight hundred gallons, and I can get more in a hurry if I need it."

"Good. If we can refuel from that, we can use our chopper to airlift your people in to cut down on the movement time."

"No problem. You're welcome to anything I have. Washington told me to cooperate in any way that I can."

"Think that'll extend to my borrowing you, as well?" Bolan asked. "I'll get more out of your men if they're working with their own commander."

Nesbit's face broke out in a big grin. "I was hoping you'd ask. I'll turn the camp over to my deputy and get my gear ready."

"I'd like to start at first light."

"No sweat. We stand to at dawn anyway."

CHAPTER EIGHT

Night fell at the DEA outpost abruptly, as it always did in the tropics. One minute it was light enough to read a newspaper, and five minutes later it was night. With the darkness, the camp changed as Dave Nesbit put his people on nighttime alert. The DEA man wasn't a veteran jungle fighter, but he didn't need to be to know that the night always favored the attacker. One of the main reasons that Fort Apache hadn't been taken out by either the drug armies or the roving guerrilla bands in the area was that Nesbit never let his guard down, especially not at night.

Bolan was impressed with what he had witnessed of the operation so far. He had seen more than one American military firebase that wasn't run as well as this place. But the field operations of the DEA in Colombia were military operations in all but the name. They stayed very low profile, though, because the last thing that anyone in the government wanted was to draw media attention to what was really going on south of the border.

Even though the DEA hadn't even existed in the

sixties, the organization had learned the number-one lesson of the Vietnam War—never try to fight a war in front of a TV camera crew. Beyond the occasional news-special update on the War against Drugs, the DEA's activities didn't often make the news.

That meant that the majority of the American public was completely unaware that its country had troops in action in South America. But that was the way the DEA wanted it, and it was the only way the organization could be at all effective.

After finalizing the plans for the morning, Bolan and Grimaldi went over their personal gear before seeking their bunks for the night. It had been a long day, and the following one would be even longer.

José Hernando studied Fort Apache through his night-vision glasses from the tree line five hundred yards from the DEA camp. With the exception of the big helicopter parked outside the wire, nothing he saw was different from the aerial photographs of the camp Jordan had given him the previous day. Everything from the bunker positions to the defenses was as he had been told to expect, and that meant that the attack could proceed as he had planned.

It had been a logistical nightmare trying to get his men, weapons and equipment into the area on such short notice, but everyone was in place now. It was time to earn his money, and the money was good. Jordan always paid well.

Keying the mike of his radio, Hernando spoke one word in Spanish. Go.

At his command, two teams of three men started out from the edge of the jungle, moving toward the DEA camp. It would take them half an hour to reach their objective, the wire perimeter around the camp, but Hernando was in no hurry. He had all night if he needed it and all of the next day, as well, if it came to that. His mission was to destroy the DEA camp and everyone inside of it, and he wouldn't leave until he had accomplished that mission.

Even with the rush to reach the area on such short notice, Jordan had provided him with more than enough experienced men and up-to-date weaponry to ensure his success. That was typical of Jordan's operations—the gringo always had enough money, and in the mercenary business, money meant success.

It was a little over the half-hour mark when Hernando heard the click code on his radio from the demolitions team poised in front of the camp's wire defenses. It was time to start phase two of the operation.

"Mortars," he spoke into the microphone. "Fire!"

The first 81 mm mortar round rocketed from its tube before the word finished leaving his lips.

MACK BOLAN'S combat trained responses were still razor sharp. They had been honed on so many battlefields that they could never be dulled. The first hollow thump of a mortar round leaving the tube was all it took to have him come completely awake.

"Incoming!" he shouted as he dived out of bed to pull on his boots. Snatching up his Heckler & Koch assault rifle, he raced for the door of the bunker Nesbit had assigned them to sleep in. Grimaldi was right on his heels as they ran for the camp's tactical operations center. Nesbit was already in the TOC.

"What's the sitrep?" Bolan asked.

"We're taking mortar fire," Nesbit said, working hard to keep his voice under control. "They've never done that to us before. They've always used RPGs."

"Tell your bunker line to keep a sharp eye out. It could be diversionary fire to cover a ground assault."

The DEA man was on the landline to the men in the perimeter bunkers almost before Bolan had stopped speaking. He was young, but he learned fast.

"Do you have an extra radio?" Bolan asked. "I want to go out and take a look. If this is what I think it is, I'll let you know. I'm also going to have Jack try to get the chopper into the air. It's too big a target where it's parked, and I don't want to lose it."

Grabbing a small walkie-talkie-type radio from a shelf in front of him, Nesbit handed it to Bolan. "There's a communications bunker by the main gate, and it has a good view of the northern sector of the perimeter."

"I'll call you from there."

ONCE HE REACHED the perimeter, Bolan saw that he was right. The mortar attack was a feint. Through his night-vision glasses, he saw three men crawling through the grass toward the main gate. From the packs on their backs, they had to be demolitions men. Their mission would be to blow the defenses at the gate to create an avenue of approach for a ground assault.

The men packed dangerous cargo. A single round in the wrong place could create havoc.

Reading the range to the lead man from the night-vision goggles, he zeroed in on him and triggered a short burst of 5.56 mm from his H&K assault rifle.

The night suddenly turned bright with a double thump. The flash showed that the first man's detonating satchel charge had taken out a second man and his explosive package, as well. That still left the third man, and he was coming on strong. Dropping into a hollow in the ground, the attacker pulled the fuse lighter on his satchel and lobbed the explosive package at the gate.

"Get down!" Bolan yelled as the satchel arched through the air. It landed right next to the left-hand gate post and detonated with a blinding flash. The thundering blast sent chunks of the concrete and wooden beams flying through the air.

Before the sound of the explosion had time to echo away, another blast erupted in front of the main machine-gun bunker to the right of the gate. This time the screams of the wounded could be heard over the blast.

"They're coming," Bolan shouted in Spanish.

Keying the mike of his radio, he tried to get through to the operations center. "This is Belasko," he said when Nesbit answered. "You've got a ground attack coming in toward the main gate. Satchel charges took out most of the barricades and the machine-gun bunker."

Just then, he heard the explosions from the other side of the camp. "They're hitting the other side of the perimeter, too. I don't know which one is the main attack yet, so you're just going to have tell your perimeter to hold on until we can sort this out."

"Will do," Nesbit replied calmly.

JACK GRIMALDI WAS having a hard time trying to get to his ride. Fortunately the chopper was parked on the far side of the camp away from most of the action, but the air was still full of lead. And when he ran up behind the bunker line, several of the defenders spun their M-16s to track him.

"I'm the pilot!" he shouted in Spanish. "Let me through!"

The Indians heard his shouts and backed off to let him get to his machine. Grimaldi's fingers were hitting the switches before he hit the seat cushion. It was difficult to fast-start a Sea Stallion the way you could a JetRanger or a Huey, but he had no choice. He had to try it. Every second he was on the ground was another second that someone could put an RPG rocket in his lap or put an AK slug into something that couldn't take the hit.

When the port-side turbine lit off with a whoosh, he didn't even give it time to spool up before he fired up the starboard jet. He had to be careful not to advance the throttles too fast and cause a flameout, but once he saw the needle pass sixty percent on the tachs, he knew he would make it.

He didn't know what he could do to help Bolan once he was in the air, but at least he could get their ride safely out of the line of fire. No matter what else happened here this night, they'd need the chopper in the morning. If for nothing else, simply to get them out of the area and back to Panama City.

As soon as both tachs showed that he had minimum rotor rpm, he eased up on the collective to start feathering in pitch to the blades. As the blades bit the night air, he saw the rpm falter before starting to climb again. The mountain air was cool, and that lowered the air density, which in turn made the rotors lift better. He was counting on that slight margin to make this work.

Only a pilot as experienced as Jack Grimaldi could have lifted the fully fueled chopper off of the ground that quickly. Handling the cyclic and collective controls like they were fragile glass rods, he balanced the turbine rpm and rotor pitch against the weight of the craft.

It was only when he reached a thousand feet that he had enough rpm and airspeed to fly the chopper the way Sikorsky had intended it to be flown. Now the question was, what could he do to aid the situation down there?

The Sea Stallion was rigged for a SAR mission, and beyond the M-60 door gun, it wasn't carrying any armament. He was a hotshot pilot, but the laws of physics made it impossible for him to be in two places at once. He could either fly the chopper or he could fire the door gun. There was no way he could possibly do both at the same time.

He suddenly remembered that the SAR ship had a remote-controlled searchlight in a housing under the nose. Maybe he could use that to point out targets for the men on the ground like the LAPD did. It was worth a try, but he needed to get a little more altitude before he tried it. The instant he turned it on, every bad guy down there would start shooting at him with everything he had.

ONCE BOLAN HEARD the aircraft take off, he put the chopper out of his mind. Grimaldi was safe, and since the Sea Stallion wasn't armed, he was out of the game. And that was just as well. Things weren't going too well for the defenders of Fort Apache. The storm of fire from the waves of attackers had everyone under cover. Bolan left cover to put in a burst whenever he could, but it wasn't making any difference.

The only bright spot was that while the enemy's mortar rounds were dropping all around the big tower, the structure was still standing and Old Ma Deuce was still having her say at the rate of 600 .50-caliber rounds per minute. It was always comforting to hear the heavy-throated chugging of the big machine gun.

The attackers had made the mistake of putting their mortars inside the tree line about eight hundred yards away. It made for easy shooting because the gunners could adjust their own fire without having to use forward observers. But it also meant that the tubes were well within range of the .50-caliber gun. Any time you pitted a direct-fire weapon like the big gun against an indirect fire piece, well aimed, direct fire always won out.

With the enemy mortars well within the tracer burnout point of the big gun, Bolan could see the .50-caliber fire arching out and slashing into the mortar positions. It wouldn't be long now before the gun crews were out of the play.

But even in an unequal contest, the losing side could occasionally get lucky. An 81 mm round detonated at the base of one of the tower's legs, the blast and razor-sharp shrapnel splintering the wooden beam like a matchstick. When the smoke cleared, Bolan saw the tower topple to the ground with a crash.

With the big gun out of action, the mortars turned their attention back to the perimeter of the camp. But it seemed to Bolan as if the rounds weren't falling as fast as before. Maybe the machine gun had taken out one of the tubes after all.

He keyed his radio and called Nesbit. "Call the

bunkers by the main gate and tell them to turn it on. The Fifty's out of action, and they're rushing us.''

Not waiting for the DEA man to answer, Bolan snapped a fresh magazine into his assault rifle and started pumping out single shots on rapid fire, raking the front ranks of the attackers. Several of the Indian DEA troops followed his lead, but it wasn't enough. For every man that went down, two more came out of the darkness to take his place.

Suddenly Bolan heard Grimaldi's chopper, and a three-hundred-yard circle in front of the blasted main gate lit up like someone had turned on the lights of a football stadium at midnight. The flashes of grenades and the flames from the burning structures had provided some battlefield illumination, but this was as if the midday sun blazed in the sky.

Many of the attackers looked up at the light, immediately blinding themselves. The defenders, however, were too busy shooting the suddenly illuminated targets to pay any attention to where the much-needed light was coming from.

Flying at the edge of small-arms range, Grimaldi played his light like a traffic cop on speed. He kept moving from one group of attackers to the next, keeping them in the beam long enough for the defenders to take them under fire before moving on to the next group. By the time the third bunch of enemy gunners was illuminated, the attackers were pulling back.

One of the fleeing hardmen stopped long enough to raise an RPG rocket launcher to his shoulder and aim it into the sky. Before he could pull the trigger, though, a burst of fire from the perimeter cut him down where he stood. A dying reflex tightened his finger on the rocket launcher's trigger, but the round flew off to the side harmlessly.

HERNANDO CURSED as he watched his carefully planned attack fall apart. He was so angry that he completely ignored the bullet wound he had taken to his right shoulder.

The attack was a failure, but there was no way that Jordan could hold him responsible for this debacle. Hernando was a craftsman, but one of the basic tools he needed to practice his trade was information, and he hadn't been told that the helicopter was carrying that kind of light. Had he known what kind of danger the chopper represented, he would have brought a Stinger antiaircraft missile or two to take it out.

As it was, with the thing flying outside of rifle range, he had no choice but to pull back while some of his men were still on their feet. To try to keep this up was simply a waste of good men, and Jordan hadn't paid these men to commit suicide.

AFTER FIRING the last of his magazine in well-paced bursts at the retreating enemy, Bolan keyed the microphone on his radio. "They're running," he told Nesbit. "You might want to call a cease-fire to save ammo in case they come back."

"Good idea," the DEA man responded.

CHAPTER NINE

Stony Man Farm, Virginia

John "Cowboy" Kissinger frowned as he studied the readout from the diagnostic test on the targeting radar of the number-two Phalanx 20 mm antiaircraft defense system, realizing that guns were easier to maintain when he didn't have to diddle around with add-on electronics. The weapons system was a simple enough 20 mm Vulcan Gatling gun cannon hooked up with a fire-control radar that had an IFF—Identification Friends or Foe—feature and a computer. The 20 mm gun was easy enough to work on, but its fire-control component was a nightmare.

The Phalanx *would* choose not to work properly when he needed it the most. And in accordance with Murphy's Law, it was the IFF module that had failed. That meant that the gun would track and shoot at anything it saw on the radar instead of waiting for a microsecond to determine if the target was a friend or a foe before it automatically unleashed its 20 mm fury and blew the aircraft out of the sky.

Since the Farm was well off the normal flight paths, it was rare for private planes to fly over the area. But if some Sunday flyer in a Cessna strayed overhead before the gun was fixed, he'd be blasted out of the sky.

Clicking on to his spare-parts menu in his laptop, Kissinger found that he had a serviceable spare IFF module in his stores, and the maintenance note indicated that it required four hours to change out the defective unit, install and test the new one. That meant that he could do it in three, but he was a bit short on time.

The problem with being the Farm's weapons smith was that he was *the* weapons smith for the entire operation. He was a one-man band, and while that usually meant that he stayed fairly busy, now he was frantic. Stony Man hadn't been at this stage of alert for a long time, and he kept finding things in the defense systems that were operating less than perfectly. And less than perfect was simply not going to cut it right now.

Unplugging the diagnostic computer, he took the Phalanx off-line for independent automatic fire, but he kept it up for directed fire by slaving it to the number-three gun mount. The other two Phalanxes should be enough to guard the skies over Stony Man until he could find the three hours that was required to replace the IFF module and bring the unit fully back on-line.

"I'm done up here," Kissinger called in to Price at the command center. "Be advised that the number-two Phalanx has been slaved to number three and is on direct-fire mode only until I have more time to fix what's wrong with it. What's next?''

"The Alpha Seven surveillance camera on the north corner of the orchard is coming in fuzzy. We need to have it changed out ASAP.''

"I'll get right on it," he replied. "Can you have someone meet me there to give me a hand with it?''

"Will do," she promised.

Heading for the outbuilding where he kept his stash of surveillance equipment, Kissinger noticed more evidence of the increased security Price had ordered. Along with the usual number of blacksuits in their everyday farmhand civilian clothing and concealed weapons, he saw that several of the camouflaged heavy-weapons positions were now fully manned by men in camouflage uniforms, helmets and body armor.

He was still fuzzy on the details of exactly what had hit the fan this time. But whatever it was, Price wasn't taking any chances. The only man busier than he was right now was the security chief in charge of the blacksuits. The chief had every man who could handle a gun on rotating eighteen-hour duty.

After finding the right video camera unit in his storeroom, Kissinger tossed it into the back of his Jeep and headed for the peach orchard. As he had requested, two of the Farm's blacksuit farmhands were waiting to help him.

Since they were close to the civilian highway that ran through the valley, both of the men were in their "work" clothes, washed-out shirts and jeans, with boots. The only thing that made them any different than the other agricultural workers in the area were the Heckler & Koch assault rifles slung over their shoulders and the Glock auto pistols holstered on their belts.

With the two men helping him, it took Kissinger only fifteen minutes to change the surveillance camera and get the new one back on-line.

"How's the picture now?" Kissinger called in to the command post.

"It's fine," Price replied.

"What's next?" he asked.

"The chief says that he doesn't like the night-scope mount on one of the Fifties and would like you to take a look at it at your earliest convenience."

At least that was something that didn't require him to mess around with any electronics; guns he could fix in his sleep. "Tell him that I'll meet him in the armory in zero-five."

"Will do."

AARON KURTZMAN SAT at his keyboard and stared at a blank screen. A tall cup of cold coffee sat next to his left hand, and he automatically reached for it before remembering that it was hours old. A minute later, he reached for the cup again and took a shot anyway. Almost gagging on the stale, cold brew, he backed his wheelchair out of its slot and wheeled himself over to the industrial-size coffeemaker that was as much a fixture of the computer center as he was.

Dumping the cold dregs from his cup, he filled it with his particular brand of high-test coffee. There were those who claimed that his coffee was more battery acid than anything that could be brewed from a roasted bean.

Placing the cup in the holder in his chair, he wheeled back to his workstation to continue staring at the blank screen. He had been over the problem time after time, but he simply couldn't figure out how someone had been able to access all of their communications, break the security codes, read their secure transmissions and land them in the situation they were in now.

There was no doubt, however, that it had been done. Now that he knew what to look for, the signs were there. Blanking their communications channels to the field teams had been the easiest part of the job. The Stony Man satellite-communications radios operated on a specific set of frequencies that had been reserved for their exclusive use. After breaking the communications security codes, all it took to render their radios unusable was to somehow transmit a stronger masking signal on those frequencies.

Under normal circumstances, all the Farm would have to do to reestablish communications would be to go to their alternate frequencies. But since they couldn't talk to the teams to tell them to switch frequencies on their radios, they were very effectively cut off.

He knew what had been done to them; he just

couldn't find out how it had been done, much less who had done it. He had been over everything a hundred times already, and still nothing came to him.

Wethers, Tokaido and Delahunt were also immersed in trying to solve the problem. Stony Man existed only because of the power of cyberspace, and until they could restore their secure communications, they were out of business. Even though restoring secure communications to the teams was the top priority, it wasn't going to be as easy as that. The problem was that if someone was reading their mail, as Lyons had so succinctly put it, any new security code they installed could be read as it was being installed.

That meant that before they could become secure again, they had to find out who the culprit was and how he or she had breached the system. Anything they did to try to find the infiltrator could be intercepted and countered because they weren't secure. It was a circular problem, and it was frustrating Kurtzman.

Barbara Price stuck her head around the corner of the door to the computer room. "Hal wants to have another brain session in the War Room," she told Kurtzman. "And he wants everyone there this time."

Barbara's hair was pulled back in a ponytail and Kurtzman noticed that she looked ragged. Although this was a computer room screwup and belonged squarely in his lap, she was taking it as personally as he was.

Kurtzman was of two minds about sitting through another damned meeting. On the one hand, he was desperate for anything to take him away from staring at a blank screen. But, at the same time, he hated meetings when he had work to do. Even when he didn't have the slightest idea in what direction he should focus it.

In the end, he did not want to cause Barbara any more trouble than she already had and he wheeled his way out of his lair, down the hall to the elevator.

HAL BROGNOLA WAS seated at his customary place at the head of the big conference table. As soon as everyone was present, he started around the table. Everyone reported on his or her area, and most of the news was bad.

"There's one thing that bothers me about this situation," Hunt Wethers said when it came his turn to speak. "Because I don't have the necessary military background, I'd like to bounce it off you."

"Only one thing?" Kurtzman asked. "If that's all that's bothering you, then I must be cut out of the loop. From where I sit, we're in major trouble all the way around."

"That we are," Wethers agreed. "But I'm still looking for a motive."

"What do you mean?" Brognola asked from around the stub of the cold cigar in his mouth. "It's obvious that someone is trying to destroy this operation."

"I agree, but the question is still why are they doing this? It has been my experience that people rarely do anything without having a reason. Look at it this way. We all agree that our unknown adversary has demonstrated his ability to render our electronic-security systems useless, correct?"

Everyone nodded their assent.

"And," he continued, "if that's the case, why didn't he just quietly infiltrate us through cyberspace, sit back and use the information he can access to counter our moves. Why did he tip his hand by letting us know that he was inside by blanking our communications to the field teams? That doesn't look smart from where I sit."

"Because we're not the target." Price instantly saw where Wethers was going with his long, somewhat academic argument. The man was good, but his long spell in academia hadn't entirely left him. Coming directly to the point was still a struggle for him sometimes.

Brognola frowned. "What do you mean? Of course we're the target. We're the nation's top counterterrorist and clandestine operation."

"What allows us to do what we do, Hal?" Price asked rhetorically. "As you so rightly said, we're the nation's weapon of last resort against the enemies who can hurt the nation the most. We're the only organization that can act effectively and decisively to do something positive about a critical situation the instant it shows up."

"But as Hunt just reminded us, our man's not after us here at the Farm. He's after Phoenix Force and Able

Team. Without them, we're little more than an intelligence-gathering organization, and there are dozens of them on the federal payroll."

The truth of what Price said stuck everyone at the same time. Kurtzman let out a muffled oath, Brognola reached into his pocket for his roll of antacid tablets and a new cigar to chew on. He had just bitten his old one in two.

"Look at it this way," Price continued. "Our mystery man hasn't really hurt us here at the Farm. But he has Phoenix cut off in the jungle, and God only knows where Able Team is right now. We can assume that he has forces moving against Phoenix in Colombia, and I'll bet that he's posted a Wanted bulletin on Able Team, as well."

She paused before concluding, "Our action teams are in trouble, but no one's attacking us."

"Do you want me to take the blacksuits off alert?" the overworked security chief asked.

"No!" Brognola snapped before Price could answer.

"I agree with Barbara's assessment," he went on to explain. "But that doesn't mean that they won't try to hit us here sooner or later. I don't want as much as a gnat getting in here until we can get to the bottom of this."

"I agree," Price stated. "But our first priority has to be recovering Phoenix from the field and making sure that Able Team is safe. As far as I am concerned, until that has been taken care of, nothing else matters as long as we hold the Farm. Once we know that our field teams are secure, we can worry about how all of this happened. To say nothing of making sure that it doesn't happen again.''

Kurtzman started to grumble. His personal priority was to discover how his electronic empire had been invaded and his files violated. But he realized that once again Price was right. Until Phoenix Force and Able Team were out of danger, it didn't really matter how they had been put in danger in the first place.

That, however, would be nothing compared to what would happen if the Farm's action teams were lost. It was true that they were just men, but they weren't the kind of men whom you could find on every street corner.

The formation of Phoenix Force had required a search of the world's elite counterterrorist units to find the right five men to make up the team. Able Team had come together in a much more casual manner, but they, too, would be difficult, if not impossible, to replace.

Too many times, the men of Phoenix Force and Able Team had put their lives on the line to stop a national disaster, and they had to be saved at all costs.

''Okay,'' Brognola stated. ''What's the plan to recover our field teams?''

''I can't say that we really have a plan at this time,'' Katz admitted. ''Striker and Grimaldi are on the ground at a DEA base in Colombia, and they're going to try to locate Phoenix from the air. Until I hear back from them, we're not planning anything.''

That sat well with Brognola. Bolan had a way of solving problems like this on his own.

"The real problem," Katz continued, "is with Able Team. Since we are completely out of contact with them, we don't know where they are, much less if they're even still alive. Worse than that, with our opponent apparently knowing as much about the situation as we do, there's no way for us to contact Able without giving away their location. So, I don't plan to contact them. If they're to have any chance at all, Carl, Rosario and Gadgets are going to have to get out of this one on their own."

That wasn't what Brognola wanted to hear, but he also knew the truth when he heard it. The men of the Stony Man teams were supposed to be the world's best, and their skills alone would have to pull them through this time. He hated the feeling of helplessness, but if Katz couldn't find anything to do to help them, no one could.

"Keep working on it," he replied unnecessarily.

CHAPTER TEN

Sonoma, California

Sonoma was a good place for Able Team to go un-
derground for the next couple of days while they tried
to get this mess sorted out. Even though the town was
small, when they drove in they saw that the streets
were jammed with people and most of the cars parked
along the main street wore out-of-state plates. Anyone
seeing them would think that they were just more
trendy tourists escaping the insanity of the Bay Area.

"If we're going to fit in around this place," Blancanales commented as he scoped out the crowds,
"we're going to have to ditch our cowboy clothes and
buy some pastel-colored stuff."

The team was still in cowboy gear, well-worn blue
jeans, wide belts, Western shirts and boots. While
many of the locals wore a version of that garb, it was
plain that most of the visitors were into a trendier,
upscale look. This year, that included pastel colors
heavy on the mauves, dark pinks and baby blues.

"I don't care where in the hell we are," Schwarz

snorted. "I'll be damned if you're going to get me into clothes designed for toddlers and grannies."

"You want us to blend in with the rest of the Sunday tourists, don't you?" Blancanales asked.

"I'll just keep what I'm wearing and pass as a local shit kicker."

"Not driving this van, you won't," Blancanales stated. "The locals aren't driving rigs like this."

"Maybe I made a killing on the lottery. It happens, you know."

"Not to us, it doesn't."

Pulling into the parking lot of a local bank, Lyons got out of the van and walked over to the ATM. Slipping his credit card into the slot, he punched in the code number and rang up five hundred dollars in twenties. They would need a little walking-around money as long as they were in town.

"Okay," Lyons said to Blancanales when he got back in the van, "how do we get to this cabin of yours?"

"Head north out of town on the main drag. It's ten or twelve miles out."

It took a while to work their way through the traffic on the two-lane main street to get to the edge of town and the road leading northeast. Outside of town, the road was almost free of traffic as it ran through the gently rolling hills. This was good country to hide out in.

"Heads up, guys," Schwarz said, glancing into his

rearview mirror. "We've got a black-and-white coming up on us fast."

Lyons looked out his side mirror and saw another highway-patrol car appear around the corner behind the first one. "Make that a pair of them."

"What's the drill?"

As an ex-cop, Lyons had always tried to not get in a situation where he would have to fire on peace officers. Unless, of course, they were part of the problem he was trying to fix. This time, he had no idea what had gone wrong, and he didn't want to start popping caps on anyone until he had more information to go on.

"Pull into that dirt road off to the right up there," he told Schwarz.

Schwarz signaled for the turn and pulled off the road. As he stopped at the closed gate, the two CHP cars raced past them, their lights flashing.

"What do you want to bet that they're going to your friend's cabin?" Schwarz asked as he watched them disappear around the next turn in the road.

Blancanales didn't think that was possible, but stranger things had happened to them in the past couple of days. "But," he asked, "how would they have known that we were here, much less about the cabin?"

"Let's get real paranoid here for a minute," Schwarz said.

"What do you mean?"

"First we've had something go real bad at the Farm, and they gave us the Butch Cassidy drill. Then Carl calls his old LAPD buddy and finds out that someone has been asking questions about him at his old place of work. What if someone's also been asking questions about you and me, as well? Let's say that they talked to your old buddy and found out that he has a cabin up here in the hills."

"But that isn't enough," Lyons protested. "They wouldn't send a black-and-white racing up there unless they were positive that we were in the area."

"But they are." Schwarz smiled grimly. "You just used your ATM card back in town."

"But I used one of our Stony Man cards," Lyons said. "Kurtzman has always said that they're untraceable."

"Maybe they were at one time," Schwarz replied. "But I'm not sure about that anymore. Look, if someone was able to find out that we were supposed to hit that place in Mexico, they might know about all the rest of the Stony Man operation. And that could include our bank accounts, our IDs, the whole nine yards."

There was complete silence in the van for a couple of long moments. No one wanted to be the first to ask the question that all three of them were thinking.

"So," Blancanales asked, "what do we do?"

"I'd say that we have two choices," Schwarz answered. "We can either run for it, and I mean run all the way out of the country. Or we can keep on the move and try to get back in contact with the Farm."

"I want to take a little drive back to Virginia myself," Lyons stated. "I understand the Shenandoah Valley is real nice this time of year."

"That'll take us three or four days," Blancanales said. "Why don't we just ditch the truck and fly?"

"We don't want to be picked off at the airport," Lyons answered. "It's too easy to nail us there where there's no place to run."

"Let's get the hell out of here now—" Schwarz found reverse and started backing out "—and we'll talk about it while we're going somewhere else."

Back out on the road, Schwarz headed south at the speed limit.

"Make a left at the next junction," Lyons said, reading the map. "That'll put us on the way back to Modesto, and we can pick up the freeway from there."

"First, though," Schwarz said to Lyons, "how did you pay for this van?"

Lyons realized immediately what Schwarz was getting at. "I used the card."

Schwarz eased the van off the road and turned around. "We need to go back to Oakland or someplace like that and dump this thing. If they've got the ATMs wired to look for us, they'll be getting to the rental agencies next. And from there, it takes only a few minutes for them to put out an APB on this rig."

"Damn!"

It was a nerve-racking three-hour drive to Oakland and every eye was watching their rear.

Washington, D.C.

JAMES JORDAN DIDN'T panic when he got word that the attack on Fort Apache had failed. Or rather, had only been partially successful. If nothing else, though, the attack had shown the DEA that their intelligence gathering wasn't up to par.

When the CIA had offered to handle intelligence gathering for the drug agency's Latin American operations, DEA had firmly turned the Company down. They explained that they were hesitant to use information from CIA sources because it was believed to be "tainted"—that was how they had put it. The DEA didn't want anything to do with agents who might have been involved in the Iran-Contra affair or any of the other operations where the Company had used its connections with the cartel or other underworld figures to gain their objectives.

That kind of puritanical, holier-than-thou short-sightedness had just cost the drug agency a major base camp, and it could cost them even more before this was all over. In the end, though, the DEA would come running to the CIA, hat in hand, to beg to use their sources and information. That would be the beginning of the rebirth of the Company, and Jordan was ready to take advantage of it.

There was no room in the real world of intelligence gathering for the intellectually prissy attitude the DEA had shown. In the hard reality of the business, information was where you could find it or develop it. If that meant that you had to get down in the mud to get what you needed, you were bound to get some of it on you. All that mattered in the end was that you got the information you needed, no matter what you had to do to get it.

As gratifying as it was, though, the DEA's situation in Colombia wasn't on the top of his mind at the moment. First and foremost, he had to put an end to the Stony Man operation. With the exception of the attack on Fort Apache, so far the operation was going well. El Machetero had the vaunted Phoenix Force trapped in the jungle, a cartel wet team was ready to move in on Able Team, and the Farm itself was locked down tight.

For now, he would let Hal Brognola and his people continue to play their little games inside the Stony Man base. They weren't going anywhere, and they were a paper tiger without their action teams to protect them. He wouldn't show them how helpless they really were, however, until he had closure on their muscle.

Then he would put paid to Stony Man itself by taking Brognola out of the picture first. With him gone, the group's single link to the Oval Office would be cut, and their high-level protection would cease to exist. Then he would tip the ATF off about the weapons they had stored there and see how that shook out. Jordan thought the ATF was a bunch of low-grade clowns good for little more than busting down doors, but sometimes they had their uses.

That would be the one time that he would invite the media in to watch one of his operations. In Jordan's mind, the media ranked only slightly higher than dog shit on his shoes, but the media, too, had its uses. And considering that it had been instrumental in the CIA's demotion to its current lowly status, it was only fitting that the media should be instrumental in the Company's rebirth.

When his plan went down, Jordan would alert the media to the terrorist threat that had existed in the deepest levels of government in the form of Stony Man and its action teams.

When he was done, the TV news broadcasts would scream about a rogue secret agency gone mad. There would also be rumors about how they had tried to take over the government by infiltrating the White House.

He would see that the camera crews got into whatever was left of the Farm, and there would be slow video pans over the Farm's weapons and surveillance systems. For CNN, there would be the cameras tracking over the dead bodies on the premises. When the smoke finally cleared, the President would realize that the only people he could really depend on belonged to the old tried-and-true, the Central Intelligence Agency.

Jordan didn't think that he would be able to recreate the halcyon days of Eisenhower and Kennedy when the Company had been the premier arm of American foreign policy, but he would come damned close.

One of the first things on his agenda after this happened would be to put paid to Fidel Castro once and for all. The Bearded Bastard had started the long decline of the Company when the Kennedy brothers lost their guts at the Bay of Pigs and turned their backs on the CIA operation. They had paid the price for their failures long ago, and that left only Castro who was still owed for that debacle. Bringing him down would be a glorious first act for a revitalized CIA and would show the world that they were back. After him, Saddam Hussein would be next, followed by Moammar Khaddafi, or perhaps whatever holy man was in charge of Iran these days.

The list was long, but the Company would be up to it.

For a long time, the President had used Hal Brognola's private army for all of his dirty work. Now he would be forced to turn to the CIA when someone needed to be killed for the good of humanity and the American way of life.

In their day, the CIA wet teams had been damned good. Jordan felt that they had been even better than the KGB and Mossad hit teams. They had been so good, in fact, that most of their actions had never made the papers. It was only on the odd occasion when one of their operations went bad, as a certain percentage of operations always did, that they had made the headlines.

In the new CIA as he envisioned it, the American media wouldn't play any part in their operations after they exposed Stony Man. The one thing that the Soviets had done well was to keep the KGB under wraps the way the Israelis did with the Mossad. That's how it would be with the new CIA. The so-called public's right to know everything was so much political bullshit, and the existence of Stony Man Farm was proof of that. The White House had kept it secret from the entire nation, Congress and all, and Jordan would move to do the same with the new Company.

For all that to happen, though, he had to get back to the operation in Colombia. In mythology, the phoenix was a bird that could rise from the ashes of its own funeral pyre. In the real world, this was one Phoenix that was going to stay dead after he burned them. Then he would turn his attention to permanently disabling Able Team.

California

IT WAS EASY ENOUGH for Able Team to dump the van in Oakland. First, though, they went across the bridge and hit several ATMs in San Francisco. Since their opponent had already picked up their trail in California, they used the Farm's cards up to their very high limits, then they emptied their own personal accounts. When they were done, they had quite a stash, but they would need it the way they would have to travel.

Before dumping the rental van at the airport parking lot, they picked up a local paper and sent Blancanales auto shopping in another rental paid for with cash. Even though they had several thousand dollars in traveling money, he bought wisely and ended up with a six-year-old Chevy van that was wearing a new set of tires. After Blancanales bought the vehicle with cash, he drove it to a Chevy service center and had it completely serviced, again paying with untraceable cash.

It was the end of the day by the time they were on the road, but now they had a ride that should take a while to trace.

"Where to?" Schwarz asked as soon as all their gear had been stored in their vehicle.

Lyons looked up from the map in his lap. "Hit the freeway heading south, and we'll turn east when we reach L.A."

CHAPTER ELEVEN

Fort Apache, Colombia

The tropical sun rose over the DEA camp. The fires that had burned through much of the night had all been extinguished, but thin tendrils of smoke still rose from smoldering timbers and supplies. The scorched smell blended with the odors of burned cordite and spilled blood. Several of the sandbag bunkers had been blasted apart by the rain of mortar rounds and RPG rockets, scattering their contents. Discarded ammo boxes and bandoliers added to the clutter of war.

Mack Bolan found the camp's commander, Dave Nesbit, standing on top of the berm line by the destroyed main gate, looking out over what had been a battlefield a few short hours earlier. It was an old story to Bolan, both the sights and the smells. But this was the first time that the DEA man had ever witnessed anything even close to this, and it showed on his face. Fort Apache had been attacked several times before, but never on such a large scale.

Nesbit's face showed his disbelief, as well as the

expected fatigue. He was dirty, stained with both blood and smoke, and looked as though he could use several hours' sleep.

"It might be a good idea to start rebuilding your defenses first," Bolan suggested. "Whoever was behind this might want to come back and finish the job."

Nesbit nodded. After the previous night, it came naturally for him to take the older man's suggestions as orders. He still didn't have the slightest idea who Belasko was, but the man sure as hell knew how to fight. That was enough to make him the man of the hour, and the DEA officer was willing to listen to anything he had to say. Had it not been for Belasko and his pilot, he would probably be dead now.

"I'll get right on that," he said. "As soon as the men have had a chance to get some breakfast."

"You might want to send a couple of patrols out, as well," Bolan suggested, "to cover your avenues of approach. This wouldn't be a good time to get caught with your guard down."

Nesbit nodded his agreement.

"And if you can spare a couple of your better troops, I'd like to sweep the tree line where they had those mortars set up and see what I can find that might tell us who they were."

"Good idea," Nesbit agreed. Faced with the utter destruction of his camp, he was glad to have the more experienced man take care of some of these chores for him. "I'll give you a couple of my best scouts. When do you want to go?"

"Right now, before it gets too hot."

"Just as long as it doesn't get any hotter than it did last night," Nesbit replied grimly.

"You'll get used to it," Bolan said.

"God, I hope not."

WITH THE TWO SCOUTS flanking him on either side, Bolan moved through the ruins of the camp's main gate. As he had expected, the bodies of the attackers were gone. But he could see the pools of coagulated blood where they had lain and could see the trails where they had been dragged off. Motioning to the scouts, he followed the trails.

Inside the tree line, he saw more signs of the attackers. Empty 5.56 mm cartridge cases littered the ground under the trees. Stooping, he picked one up and, looking at the head stamp on the base, saw that it was U.S. Army issue made at Lake City Arsenal in 1983. Though he had expected to see 7.62 mm AK-47 cases, it wasn't unusual to see American ammunition in this part of the world. The Latin American guerrillas who weren't armed with AK-47s usually carried U.S.-made M-16s because they were so easy to get.

Next to a pile of 5.56 mm brass, he saw empty cases for the U.S.-made 40 mm M-79 grenade launcher, the well-known Thumper. Like the M-16s, they were a common weapon in this part of the world and might not indicate anything in particular. Farther into the trees, he located the firing positions for the mortars that had bombarded the camp. Searching through the grass, he recovered a safety clip from one of the 81 mm mortar rounds and instantly recognized it as American-made, as well.

Once was happenstance, twice was coincidence, but three times was enemy action. He didn't want to jump to a conclusion here, but he didn't like the picture that was developing. The only things he had seen so far from what was considered to be traditional guerrilla weaponry were empty prop-charge canisters for RPG rockets. But since the American Army still didn't have an equivalent weapon to the Russian-designed RPG, that was to be expected.

Motioning to the scouts that he wanted to sweep through the enemy position from flank to flank, Bolan moved out again. He was halfway through the sweep when, on the far left flank, one of the scouts signaled that he had found something. When Bolan walked over, he saw the Indian standing over a body that had been missed when the attackers pulled back.

The corpse wore standard U.S. Army woodland-pattern BDUs, had an Alice pack on his back, U.S.-style jungle boots on his feet and an American pistol belt around his waist with the expected matching ammo pouches and canteens. Had it not been for the Mexican-made maroon beret the man had been wearing, he could easily have been an American soldier with Hispanic heritage.

Bolan knew, though, that the man had never been closer to the United States than the southern border of

Panama. He was a little too skinny and had the distinctive features of a Meso-American Indian. Nonetheless, this find only increased his sense of unease. He could discount the evidence of the M-16s, the M-79s and maybe even the U.S. mortars. But when the American weaponry was added to the U.S.-issue uniforms and equipments of the attackers, the alarm bells started going off in Bolan's mind.

When tallied up, it meant that whoever was behind this had good contacts in the United States. This wasn't to say that the equipment, uniforms and weapons couldn't have been bought on the black market almost anywhere in the world, but it would have been cheaper to outfit a force from almost any other source. There were cheaper uniforms, cheaper sets of personal equipment and cheaper weapons more easily available. You could get three brand-new Chinese AKs for the price of a well-used M-16.

What this meant to Bolan was that the backer of the force had gone with American products because he knew them best. Also it meant that he either had a lot of money to spend, he had an inside to a source inside the U.S. or, more simply, that he was an American.

Some of the cartel's armies he had crossed paths with had been well armed and equipped. They often bought U.S. because it was easier to spend drug money in the States than it was to go to the trouble of getting it out of the country. But most drug lords went for more exotic weaponry than the old M-16. The assault rifle was a good weapon, but it didn't have the killer look of the bullpup designs that were so popular with European arms manufacturers. Since the look was as important as the function to the drug lords, he was inclined to count them out as being behind this one.

Signaling for the two scouts, he left the body where it was and started back for the camp.

"WHAT DID YOU FIND?" Nesbit asked when Bolan walked into the command bunker.

"In case you didn't notice it," Bolan replied, "you got hit by a well armed force. Along with a couple of RPGs, they had three tubes of U.S. 81 mm mortar, several M-79 grenade launchers and M-16s. Who do you know in the area who's armed that way?"

"That almost sounds like government troops." Nesbit frowned. "The Marxists are more into AKs and RPGs, and the druggies rarely use heavy weapons like mortars. They're not flashy enough."

"Are there any renegade government units operating in the area?"

"None that I know of," Nesbit said with quiet confidence. "And I would know."

"So," Bolan stated, "that means that an unknown force was moved into the area with enough strength to try to take you out. What do you have going on here that would warrant that kind of an attack?"

Nesbit looked Bolan directly in the eyes and shook his head. "Honest to God, mister, I don't know. I thought I knew what was going down around here, but

I haven't the slightest idea what's behind this. Apparently I've been getting to someone big-time."

Bolan didn't have enough information to go on yet, but he knew that there was also a possibility that he and Grimaldi's presence in the camp was the reason it had been attacked. But that wasn't something that the DEA man needed to know.

"I know this is a bad time for you," Bolan said, "but I'd still like to borrow that tracking team and a couple of squads to help me like we talked about yesterday."

Nesbit blinked. "Yeah, I forgot about that. You can still have them, but I'm afraid that I won't be able to go with you. I need to stick around here and try to explain what happened to the agency big shots who are flying in from Florida. I just got a call to expect them."

"If they give you a hard time," Bolan said, "you tell them to talk to me. You run a good camp here, and your men put up a good fight last night. If you hadn't been good, you'd have all died."

Nesbit met his eyes squarely. "You and your helicopter had a lot to do with our being that good."

"We helped," Bolan told him, "but that doesn't take anything away from what you and your men did. If they hadn't stood their ground, we wouldn't have made any difference."

WHEN BOLAN TRIED to call the Farm on Nesbit's secure radio, he got no reply. He quickly ran through all the frequencies they used, but the response was the same; no one was answering. Without mentioning anything to Nesbit, he went looking for Jack Grimaldi.

"We've got a problem, Jack."

"Do tell," the pilot said. "We've got our guys somewhere out there and we can't talk to them. Someone tried to kill us last night, and now I can't get this damned fuel nozzle to work right. Which one of these particular problems did you have in mind, Mack?"

"I mean a bigger problem. The Farm has gone completely off the air."

"Say what!"

"They are completely out of communication on all frequencies."

"Oh, shit," the pilot said. "Do you want to break contact here?"

Bolan's eyes took on a faraway look. "No. We're going to finish up this before we do anything else, even look into what's gone wrong at Stony Man. Whatever it is, it started here with Phoenix Force, and I want to finish this first. How soon can we get out of here?"

"I'll be done as soon as I get this fuel transferred."

"I'll go get our tracking team."

WHEN THE SUN came up over the jungle, David McCarter and the Phoenix Force commandos were still running. Since the first shot had been fired at the drug lab, he had been reacting blindly, playing another man's game. And if there was anything the ex-SAS commando hated, it was not being in charge of the game.

So far, they had been lucky in that they had been able to break the ambush with the only cost being T.J. Hawkins's wound, and they had been able to evade their pursuers. But he couldn't count on luck to keep dealing them aces. He had to get control of the situation before they stumbled into something they couldn't handle.

"Gary," he radioed up to Manning, who was taking his turn on point, "try to find us someplace we can hole up for an hour or two. We've got to stop to rest and bloody well get organized."

"That might not be easy." McCarter had to strain to hear his pointman because the Canadian was whispering. "I've got at least two bunches of the enemy blocking us, and I'm going to have to break off to the south."

McCarter pulled out his map and studied the terrain in that direction. From what he could see, it was worse there than where they were right then, and that was saying a lot. Plus turning to the south would put another range of mountains in the way of their breaking out onto the coastal plains and civilization.

"Hold where you are until I come up."

"Make it fast."

A few minutes later, McCarter slid in beside Manning. The pointman laid his hand on the team leader's shoulder to caution him not to speak. When McCarter nodded his understanding, Manning pointed out the location of the two blocking forces and passed him his field glasses.

They were heading down a small draw, and through the foliage, he saw movement on the ridge to the left, as well as a thin tendril of smoke from a breakfast fire two hundred yards in front of them. Handing the glasses back, the Briton swore under his breath. He jerked his thumb to the south, and Manning nodded.

As silently as they had advanced, the two men crept back to the rest of the team.

MCCARTER HAD Manning head south long enough to find a place for them to hole up for a while. When he called the halt, all of Phoenix Force was showing signs of the strain of the past day and night. Of them all, Hawkins should have been the least fatigued simply because he was the youngest. Instead, his eyes had black circles under them and his skin had a sickly pallor under a sheen of sweat.

McCarter knelt beside the young American. "How're you doing, mate?" he asked.

"He's not in good shape," James answered for him. "I've got him on antibiotics, but his wound's infected and there's not a hell of a lot I can do for him as long as we're on the run like this."

"I can keep up," Hawkins said firmly. "You don't have to worry about me."

McCarter knew that the ex-Ranger would keep going on guts alone until he went facefirst into the ground. But he also knew that if he didn't get control of that infection ASAP, Hawkins would end up face-first sooner rather than later.

"How far are we from the coast?" Encizo asked. He, too, knew that an infection in the jungle would take a man out of action as swiftly as a bullet. Hawkins needed medical attention, and that, as well as communications, would only be found when they reached the coast.

"They're not letting us go east," McCarter said. "Gary ran into blocking forces to the east and north of our route again. It's obvious that they're trying to push us south to make us stay in the hills."

"To try to keep us from reaching the plains," Encizo concluded.

"That's what it looks like."

"But why?" James asked.

"Damned if I know." McCarter shook his head.

"I vote that we go for it," Encizo said, "and try to punch through them instead of letting the bastards dictate our movements. We're on a time crunch here—" he glanced over at Hawkins "—and we need to put a quick end to this."

"I'm for that," Manning agreed.

"Me, too," James added.

Hawkins grinned. "It beats the hell out of sitting around here waiting for my leg to fall off."

"We'll rest here first," McCarter decided. "Get something to eat and sleep in turns for a couple of hours. Then we'll have another look. If they're still trying to block us, we'll take them out."

CHAPTER TWELVE

El Machetero let a trace of a smile cross his thin face. Once more his Yankee prey had taken the path he wanted them to. All he had to do now was to keep the pressure on them, keep dogging them throughout the night, keep them moving, and they would soon be finished. Men, even men like these, could keep going only so long without sleep before they collapsed of fatigue.

He had enough men that he could rotate them on the chase, give them time to eat and rest before putting them back on the trail. The Yankees didn't have that luxury, and it would start telling on them sooner or later. If they were able to break out and make it to the cooler coastal plains, they could keep going a little longer. But with the heat and humidity of the jungle sapping their strength, as well as the difficult terrain, this would be over very soon.

Picking up the radio, he sent more of his teams in to cover the flank of the fleeing Americans to guard against their breaking out to the east. On the coastal plains, they would be more difficult to control. But as long as he kept them confined to the ridges and valleys of the highlands, they were his to deal with as he wished.

But since the hunt was almost as pleasurable as the kill, he was in no great hurry to put an end to it. He would let them continue to try to break out. He might even give them an opening. And when they took it, he would let them run for a couple of hours. Then, just when they thought they were free, he would block their path again and turn them back toward his planned killing ground. By then they would be completely demoralized, and it should be child's play to finish them off.

He had told Jordan that he would need at least three days to take care of these Yankees, but he had overestimated them. The way it was going so far, he would do it sooner than that. Jordan would be pleased, and the man usually showed his pleasure with a bonus. He had already been promised enough money to live like a king, but a little more was always better.

CALVIN JAMES TOOK the opportunity of the break to check Hawkins's leg wound. Unwrapping the bandage, he caught the unmistakable smell of a wound going bad. It wasn't gangrenous yet, but that horror wouldn't be far behind if they stayed in this green hell much longer. The tropical jungles of the world didn't like mankind very much and they went out of their way to kill a man every chance they could.

Since many of those ways involved microscopic organisms, an open wound in the jungle was a one way ticket to death if it wasn't treated properly.

The medic cleaned the wound with the chlorinated water from his canteen, powdered it with antibiotic again and put on a fresh field bandage. After tying it off, he shook out two aspirin tablets and four anti-biotics capsules and handed them to Hawkins with his canteen. "Here, take these."

Hawkins put the pills in his mouth and chased them with the water. "Damn, those big ones are nasty."

"They're not as nasty as what's got into your leg," James told him. "You picked up an infection with that bullet, and I need to try to keep it under control."

Hawkins didn't really want to hear that piece of news, but he had a nose, too, and the situation had to be faced. "How much longer do you think I'll be able to keep going?"

"That's going to depend mostly on you," James replied honestly. "If you're as healthy as you look and can fight it off, you should be good for a couple more days. You'll be feverish, but that's okay. That just means that your system is fighting the infection. If your vision starts getting blurry, though, let me know immediately."

"What if I start seeing green everywhere I look?"

It took James a few seconds to catch that one. "Smart-ass."

Hawkins grinned weakly.

WHILE MCCARTER, ENCIZO, Manning and James took turns standing guard, they let Hawkins sleep all the way through the break. Since they couldn't give him the medical attention he needed, food and rest were the next-best things for him. They all knew that exhaustion would only cause the infection to spread that much faster.

When they moved out again, McCarter changed their order of march. It had become obvious that they didn't have to be as concerned about the troops behind them as they did the ones who kept popping up in front. The men tracking them were merely driving them as hunters drove game and radioing their position to the blocking forces in front.

He and Encizo took the point with Manning following close behind them while James and Hawkins brought up the rear. Less than a mile farther on, they ran into another blocking force preventing them from going east. This time, though, McCarter decided to fight instead of run. He had run far enough for the past twenty-four hours.

A quick council of war had Manning reaching for the matt green fiberglass case strapped to his backpack. Even though they were in the jungle, McCarter's plan called for a little long-range fire this time. He had the Remington sniper's rifle unlimbered and ready for action. Since his camouflage face paint had long since been sweated off, he took a mesh sniper's veil from his backpack and put it over his head. It wasn't as good as a full gullie rig, but it would break the outline of his upper body. In jungle this thick, it should be enough.

While the others moved in closer to the enemy, Manning took off on his own, moving through the jungle like a green shadow. A silent half hour later, he was in a good firing position on the right flank of the blocking force.

Looking through the twenty-power ranging scope, he swept the target area and spotted seven men. He expected that there were more that he couldn't see, but these seven would do for a start. "I've got seven targets," he radioed to McCarter. "And I'm ready when you are."

"Go for it."

Manning focused the crosshairs of his scope on the man farthest from him, took a deep breath, held it and stroked the trigger. The 7.62 mm NATO round took the man at the juncture of the neck and shoulders, drilling all the way through his body. He threw his hands up and spun around.

Without waiting to see his man fall, Manning shifted his scope to the next target. A bullet in the center of the chest put him down, as well. The third shot was directed at a man diving for cover, and Manning wasn't sure that he'd hit him. But the good thing about the heavy 7.62 mm slug was that it would drill through the jungle foliage and hit even if he didn't have a clear line of sight.

He hadn't brought the bulky sound suppressor for the Remington on this mission, and by now the gunmen knew the direction he was firing from. Return fire was slashing at the jungle around him, the M-16 rounds tearing up brush and leaves. Since most of the rounds weren't coming even close, Manning kept shooting. The enemy gunmen had secured good cover, so he was reduced to shooting at their muzzle-flashes.

Suddenly a burst of full-auto fire tore through the brush right in front of him. They had worked a couple of gunmen around on his left flank, and they were closing in.

"They've taken the bait," he radioed to McCarter as he shifted to face the new threat, "and they're maneuvering against me. This would be a real good time for you guys to make your play before I get my ass shot off."

"We're coming in," the Briton radioed back.

Over the clatter of small-arms fire coming his way, Manning heard his teammates hit the gunmen from the rear. The thump of a grenade launcher was followed closely by the crack of the 40 mm shell detonating and screams of pain. The men who were flanking Manning turned in panic to help their comrades. The sniper snapped off a fleeting shot at them before leaving his hiding place. It was time for him to rejoin the others.

McCarter and James had led the charge, their weapons spitting flame. Encizo kept his launcher thumping, dropping the 40 mm grenades like minimortar rounds, their wire shrapnel cutting a bloody swath through the opposition.

At the rear of the formation, Hawkins did his best to make a contribution to the party. His H&K subgun was spitting short bursts at anything that moved. Manning caught up with him and yelled, "Get it in gear, T.J.!"

Raking the brush on either side of them with full-auto fire, the two men caught up with the others. Once they were in the clear, the five commandos took off at a dead run to put some distance between them and pursuit.

Ever mindful of Hawkins's condition, McCarter called a halt after they had only gone a thousand yards from the ambush site. Normally he would have put a mile or so between him and the firefight, but he wanted to give the wounded man a break to recover from the run before they moved out again.

EL MACHETERO COULDN'T believe his ears when the leader of the blocking force called up to his helicopter and said that the Yankees had fought their way out of his net. They were good—he had to admit that—but in his heart of hearts, he knew that he was better. The problem wasn't with him, but with the men Jordan had given him. They weren't as good as he was, and a craftsman was only as good as his tools.

He now saw that another part of the problem was that he had been trying to control the operation from the air. In the helicopter, he couldn't smell and feel the jungle, and he couldn't hear the faint changes in the background noises that told him so much. He couldn't become one with the jungle when he was flying two thousand feet above it. He also couldn't keep the close eye on his men that was required. He knew that if he had been at the blocking position, the Yankees wouldn't have broken through.

"Pilot," he called over on the intercom, "put me on the ground close to the tracking team."

"It will take a while to find a suitable place to land, boss," the pilot replied.

"Do it as fast as you can."

"Yes, sir."

Knowing what was good for him, the pilot wasted no time getting in contact with the tracking team and having the men find a break in the canopy large enough for the chopper to land. The rotors barely had clearance, but he put the ship down anyway.

After joining up with his tracking team, El Machetero hurried through the jungle to the ambush site. He could smell the gunpowder in the air and the spilled blood before he saw the first body. The few survivors of the blocking force were standing around smoking and tending their wounds. Their leader had been wounded in the shoulder, and his eyes were glazed with pain and fear.

El Machetero understood the man's pain, he had been wounded many times himself and he knew pain very well. The fear he didn't understand unless it was a sign that the man had somehow failed to do as he had been told. If that was the case, he would pay for it. El Machetero didn't allow failure in the men he led any more than he allowed it in himself. He hadn't gotten where he was by becoming familiar with failure.

"How did the Yankees get past you?"

The man's eyes darted to his men. "They split up, and one group came at us from the flank. When we turned to deal with them, the others came in from behind us."

"You are trying to tell me that you and a dozen men could not keep five men from breaking through your position?"

"But, Chief," the man said, "we were—"

Reaching over his left shoulder, El Machetero's hand found the worn, familiar grip of the machete slung across his back. With one smooth, powerful move, he cleared the jungle knife from its scabbard and sent it arching around in a slash. The razor-sharp blade bit into the man's neck, right under his jaw, and continued through to the other side.

The man's eyes went wide with shock, and his mouth froze in a scream that he hadn't had time to voice as his head rolled forward and landed at his feet.

The headless torso stood for a moment, its heart pumping blood in a crimson fountain before crashing to the ground to join its head.

Bending, El Machetero wiped the blade of his namesake on the corpse's fatigue jacket before resheathing it across his back.

"You—" he pointed at the leader of the tracking team "—come here."

"Yes, sir." The man met his eyes as he stepped forward. If El Machetero was going to kill him, too, at least it would be quick.

"Your name?"

"Paco."

El Machetero glanced at the headless body at his feet. "Can you do a better job for me than that fool did, Paco?"

Paco nodded. "Yes, sir."

"If you do not, you will join him. Understand?"

"Yes."

"Move out and find those damned Yankees for me."

"Yes."

"First," El Machetero said, looking at the survivors of the failed ambush, "kill them."

WHEN BOLAN GOT BACK to the command post, Dave Nesbit was having second thoughts about the help he had offered him. He didn't want to go back on his word, but after going over the final results of the attack, the thought of losing a couple of squads of his troops made him more than a little nervous. His casualties from the battle hadn't been extensive—only three killed and another dozen wounded—but if the attackers came back for another round, he'd need every rifle he could get on the perimeter.

"Mr. Belasko," he said when he saw Bolan, "I think we need to talk."

When Nesbit explained his problem, Bolan instantly

understood. "Can you spare a couple of your scouts instead?" he asked. "I can actually move faster with them than I can with a larger group."

Relieved to be let off the hook, Nesbit checked his updated strength roster. "I can offer five scouts, and one of them speaks pretty good English."

"That's perfect."

"When do you want to leave?"

"Right away. Jack is finishing up on the chopper, and I'd like to get moving as soon as we can."

"I'll get them."

By the time Bolan retrieved the rest of his gear from the bunker and returned to the helicopter, Nesbit and five of his scouts were waiting for him with their weapons and packs.

"This is Carlos," the DEA man said, introducing one of the Indians. "He's my lead scout, and his English is pretty good."

The Indian looked Bolan in the eyes and nodded his head in acknowledgment. *"Señor."*

"Carlos, get your men on board."

Bolan thanked Nesbit, and Grimaldi fired up the turbines as the scouts boarded the chopper. As soon as they were belted into their seats, he pulled pitch to the twin rotors and the big aircraft lifted off. The scouts were used to riding in DEA helicopters and took the opportunity to doze off on the flight. They were veterans at this game and knew to always take advantage of an opportunity to sleep.

Bolan rode the copilot's seat beside Grimaldi. All

the way into the search area, he again tried to raise Phoenix Force on the radio, but to no avail. "I was hoping that it was just a temporary problem and had cleared up," he told the pilot.

"I'm beginning to think that this is anything but temporary," Grimaldi said. "And I don't think that it's local, either. Somebody's messing with us big time."

"I think you're right," Bolan replied. "But we have to take care of our situation here before we see what's happening at the Farm."

CHAPTER THIRTEEN

Stony Man Farm, Virginia

Barbara Price looked dead tired, but so did everyone else at the Farm. They had all been running at full speed for a long time now, and the pace was starting to take its toll. No one had seen a bed for more than a couple of hours at a time. A meal was something grabbed on the fly and even then it was little more than a cold sandwich.

"Is there anything at all we can do to help Able Team?" Price asked Kurtzman. Lyons and his teammates were on her mind more and more since they didn't have Bolan and Grimaldi looking for them.

"I don't know what it would be," Kurtzman answered honestly.

She'd known what his answer would be before she asked the question, but she'd wanted to hear him say it one more time so she could quit worrying about it.

"What do you think Carl is likely to be doing right now?" she asked.

That question gave Kurtzman pause. The Ironman

was well-known for his impulsive actions, but he was also cunning like a fox. His gut instincts, while appearing impulsive, more often than not were well thought out on a subconscious level. "There's only two things they can do that have any chance of success," he replied. "They can hole up somewhere and try to wait this out, or they can try to make it back here. My vote is that they'll try to come here."

"How?"

"Air is out," he said firmly. "It's too easy to track an airline ticket and grab them at the airport. My bet is that they'll try to drive."

"I know," he said, raising a hand. "That leaves them exposed for four or five days. Overall, though, it's still their best bet of not being spotted."

"What if there's been an APB put out on them or something like that?"

"A federal All Points Bulletin would be a real problem if they were stopped, yes. But Carl knows all the tricks to keep from attracting attention to himself. He knows that he can't afford to be pulled over for speeding or not wearing his seat belt."

"Is there any way we can lay a false trail for them that might throw the dogs off the scent?"

"Normally I'd say yes, piece of cake. But don't forget that we've got someone intercepting our cyberspace communications. I don't think I can e-mail out for pizza without them knowing what kind of toppings I ordered."

"Do you think that you're going to be able to find a way to get around these guys, whoever they are?"

Kurtzman sat silent for a moment, staring at the keyboard under his fingers. "You know," he said, "it was different back in the old days. I can remember when the Internet first got cranked up. It was, if I remember correctly, just three university mainframes connected to a mainframe somewhere in the Pentagon. They were testing to see if they could maintain some kind of computer capability for national defense if Washington got nuked. When the system worked out, they expanded it, but it stayed low key until fairly recently."

"Right now, though, every kid and his pet frog has Internet access and it's cluttered up cyberspace with horny guys and gals looking for cyberdates, kids playing stupid games and all that other crap. There's millions of computers operating on the Internet now and it makes it almost impossible to determine who is messing with us."

"As you know, we don't have a presence in cyberspace because I cut all our lines when we went into Drawbridge. I can go back in, but I have to be careful. For instance, I can safely listen in to everything that's going on in cyberspace anywhere in the world. I have to be careful, though, about downloading because anything I pull in to read, our opponents will know about it. If I try to upload anything, such as instructions to Lyons or a change in our cyber-encryption system, I have to expect that they'll be reading it as I'm sending it out.

"To make a long story brutally short, I honestly don't know what I can do to help those guys. Once they get back here, we can work up some new codes and reprogram their computer and communications gear. But they have to be here in person before I can do anything for them."

She shook her head slowly. "I was afraid that you were going to say that."

"I'm sorry."

"Don't be, Aaron. This isn't the time to indulge in wishful thinking. We have to work with the real situation, no matter how bad it is."

Nevada

LYONS, SCHWARZ and Blancanales all breathed a collective sigh of relief when they crossed the California border into Nevada on the interstate. So far, they had kept to the freeways because the interstate highway system offered the best place to hide a car in the western states. Taking to the less-traveled back roads would have only drawn unwelcome attention to themselves.

Even though the Nevada speed limit signs read 70 mph, Schwarz hit the gas to keep up with the stream of traffic that was running almost eighty. In California, he'd had to be careful not to speed and run the risk of being pulled over. In Nevada, however, he knew that the highway patrol rarely stopped anyone with an out-of-state plate who was heading in the direction of Tahoe, Reno or Vegas. They didn't want to anger a potential gambler and lose the revenue. They simply waited until the speeder left the gambling tables and was headed back home. Then they would pop him for as little as five miles per hour over the limit and take anything he happened to have left.

The three stopped for gas right inside the state line. While Lyons and Schwarz were servicing and fueling the van, Blancanales went into the station's convenience store to stock up on cold meals and drinks.

When they pulled out onto the highway again, Lyons took his turn at the wheel. None of the three paid much attention to the four-door sedan that pulled out a few minutes later, traveling in the same direction.

Colombia

THE AREA Bolan had chosen to search first was a band of jungle running north-south about halfway between Phoenix Force's original target and the coastal plains. He knew that if David McCarter was still alive, he would have headed for the coast instead of trying to hide in the mountains.

When Grimaldi reached the southern end of the search zone, he dropped down low and looked for a thin spot in the jungle canopy. Even though they had the jungle penetrator, it worked best when the canopy wasn't so thick.

"How does that look?" he asked Bolan, pointing to a low hill off to their left front. The hill was wooded, but the trees on top were thinned out enough that the ground between them was visible.

Bolan surveyed the area with a practiced eye. "That should do it. Bring us to a hover, and I'll break out the jungle penetrator."

The scouts had woken instantly with the change in the rotor pitch and were getting into their gear. Bolan opened the port-side door behind the cockpit and freed the retractable rescue-winch arm from its stowage clips inside the fuselage. After snapping the jungle-penetrator bucket to the end of the steel cable, he swung it out into the slipstream and locked it into place.

"Let's go," he shouted to the scouts over the rotor blast.

Since the scouts were so small in stature, two of them could ride the penetrator down at the same time. Though the device had been designed to pick up downed pilots, it worked well as an elevator. Standing on the floor of the basket, they held on to the cable for the short trip to the ground.

When the penetrator came up the last time, Bolan unlocked the arm and retracted it back inside the ship.

"Jack," he called up to the pilot, "I'm going down now."

"Be careful."

Holding on to the side of the open door, Bolan threw out a roll of nylon rope and watched it trail down through the green canopy below. Hooking the nylon line into the carabiner on his assault harness, he turned his back to the chopper's open door and stepped out. From there, it was a fast rappel to the jungle floor through the opening the penetrator had made.

"I'm clear," he radioed up to the chopper.

"Roger," Grimaldi answered. "I'll be monitoring your frequency, and I'll be back in twenty-four hours if I haven't heard from you."

"See you later."

It took only a few seconds for the DEA scouts to orient themselves on the map and the terrain. After talking among themselves for a moment, the lead scout told Bolan that he wanted to go south. When Bolan nodded his assent, the pointman took off at a trot.

HAWKINS HAD GIVEN IT his all. He had kept up with the others in the attack on the blocking position and had stayed with them after the breakout. Rather than taking a route through the valley again, McCarter had chosen to keep to the ridge lines. It was harder going that way, particularly for Hawkins, but it gave them better protection by taking them out of the ambush zone.

He had kept up on the grueling mountain route, but only at the cost of the last of his reserves. By the third hour, he could barely put one foot in front of the other, and his vision was starting to go fuzzy around the edges.

"Calvin," he finally called to the medic over the com link, "I think I'm going to pass out."

McCarter monitored the transmission and clicked in his own mike. "We'll hold it up here, lads. Calvin, check out T.J. Gary, you pull security for them while Rafe and I scout up ahead."

At the west end of the ridge they had been following was a valley with a low cleared hill in the middle. Crowded in the clearing was a cluster of small huts with what looked like nearly naked people walking around. This wasn't the last place in the world that they had expected to find an Indian village, but it was close.

"This looks like something out of a *National Geographic* magazine," Encizo said.

The vista in front of them did have that overly green, every-leaf-in-place look of the magazine. The huts in the clearing and the naked Indian children looked as if they had been placed there for a wide-angle shot.

"Does it look legitimate to you?" McCarter asked, handing him his field glasses. "We need to find a place for Hawkins to take a break."

Encizo slowly scanned the village below. One of the buildings was twice the size of the others and had a Christian cross on top of it. "That big hut with the cross looks like a missionary's headquarters, so I'd guess that they're used to seeing white men.''

''Let's give it a try, then.''

FATHER JOHN FULLERTON looked out from under the porch of his all-in-one chapel, dispensary and home in the jungle as the five men broke out of the tree line and approached the Indian village. One of them was being helped along, which meant that he was either sick or wounded.

For the most part, the missionary ran an equal-opportunity mission. All were welcome to come, to listen to the word of God and to be treated for whatever ailed them. Though he was a man dedicated to helping his fellow man, his preference wasn't to treat gunmen from any of the armed bands who drifted through the jungle around his small enclave.

Sometimes, though, he had no choice; guns in the hands of men all too ready to use them was a powerful argument. He had a feeling that this would be one of those times. He could see that these five men weren't the usual gunmen who came across the little village hidden in the jungle. One of them was black, one hispanic and the other three were probably Americans. He had been an American once, and he was always suspicious when he saw his compatriots, particularly armed ones, south of the California border. It always meant trouble for him and his people.

Most of the Americans he saw were hired guns working for one of the drug lords, or they were adventurers working for one of the armed political bands or the other. While these men were dangerous, they weren't as dangerous as the ones who worked for the CIA. They were dangerous because of their arrogance and their belief that, with the stroke of a pen or a sword, they could untangle situations that had existed for hundreds of years. But whichever type these men were, for the safety of his flock, Fullerton had to try to convince them to move on.

The priest walked up to them and stopped, his arms held at his sides. "This is a peaceful village," he said in Spanish. "We do not allow guns in here."

"We need to stay here for a little while," Encizo answered in the same language. "This man has been shot, and he is running a fever because the wound has become infected. Can you help him?"

"I don't treat gunshot wounds," the priest said stiffly. "I have very few medicines here, and I need to keep what little I have for my people."

McCarter started forward when Encizo translated the answer, but let himself be held back.

"We'll make you a trade, Father," James said in his Chicago street Spanish. "If you can help our man, we'll leave you everything we have in our first-aid pouches and my aid bag, and we'll pay you well for your services so you can buy even more supplies."

This wasn't the way these arguments usually went, so the priest backed off. "Have you any vitamins?"

"I have some C and a B complex," James said, digging into his pouch. "Here—" he held out two plastic bottles of high-potency pills "—take these."

Vitamin pills were a luxury that Father Fullerton

could rarely afford. Most of his medicine came from bartering native handicrafts, but the traders rarely gave him much for them and he had to spend his credits on essentials like aspirin and antibiotics.

"Bring him in," the priest said stiffly in English. "I will take a look at him."

James and Manning carried a comatose Hawkins into the hut and laid him on the table in the back of the room. From the contents of the shelves on the rear wall, it was obvious that this was the dispensary part of the building. The priest started by checking Hawkins's vital signs, taking his temperature and all the basic medical checks. When he had that information, he removed the muddy, blood-soaked field bandage from his wound.

"This isn't too bad," he said as he sniffed at the bandage he had removed from the wound on Hawkins's thigh. "He doesn't have gangrene yet."

James was glad to have his diagnosis confirmed. In his jungle clinic, the priest would have more experience with gangrene than he did. He watched as the priest cleaned the wound and washed it with water sterilized with iodine. When he was done, he brought out a clay pot containing what looked like a purple paste.

"What's that?" James asked when he saw that the priest was about to slather some of it on the wound.

"It is a poultice the Indians use on infected wounds, and I have seen it work wonders on infections like this."

James didn't like the looks of the stuff, but he knew that native herbal medicines were often very effective.

"I have done all I can for him right now," the priest said as he tied the field bandage loosely around Hawkins's leg. "I will check him again this evening. In the meantime, he must rest and I suggest that you give him some of your vitamin C and any antibiotics that you have left. He needs that more than anything else right now."

CHAPTER FOURTEEN

"You can call your people back," Rafael Encizo said when he realized that the Indians had taken to the brush when they arrived. "We won't hurt them."

"That's what all of you gunmen say," the priest said bitterly. "But the villagers have learned the hard way not to trust white men who come here with guns in their hands. There are not very many of them left here now, and they are rightly afraid."

"What happened to them?" James asked.

"There is a man called El Machetero..."

"'The machete,'" Encizo translated.

The missionary nodded. "He is a cold-blooded killer, and the last time he came though here, he took both men and young women with him and they never came back."

"Who does this guy work for?"

"He is a mercenary," the priest said, "and he has worked for both the Yankees and the cartel. Sometimes he works for both of them at the same time."

"By Yankees," McCarter asked, "do you mean the CIA?"

"Yes."

"I wonder if he's the bastard who's chasing us," Manning mused.

"You are being followed by El Machetero?" the priest almost shouted.

"We really don't know who's after us," McCarter answered honestly. "But he's good, I must give him that, and he has a lot of men with him. We keep trying to break out to the east so we can reach the coast and go home, but he keeps blocking us."

"That could be him," the priest said. "He has been recruiting men for some time now, and it is said that he has almost a hundred men in this region. All of them have new guns and plenty of ammunition for them."

"How do you know about things like that?" Manning asked. "You're not exactly in the middle of civilization."

"I stay here in the jungle because the people need me," the priest said, "but that does not mean that I am ignorant about what is going on in the rest of the region. These are dangerous times, and if I am to keep my people alive, I must know what is going on around us."

"How did you end up here anyway, Father?" Encizo asked.

"It is penance, my son, for my sins."

The Cuban looked around at the jungle. "They must have been big sins for you to have come to a place like this."

"They were."

Encizo didn't want to pry, and changed the subject. "Is there anything we can do for you or your people while we're waiting for our friend to get better?" he asked.

The priest wasn't accustomed to having the gunmen who passed through the village ask to help, and he hesitated for a moment.

"We can hunt game for them," Encizo suggested. "Do light construction, that sort of thing."

"You have explosives?"

The Cuban nodded. "Some."

"Our water supply has been blocked by a fallen tree that is too big to cut with our hand tools. If you could blast it out of the way, the women would not have to walk all the way to the valley to get water."

Encizo frowned. An explosion was the last thing he wanted to set off right now. It would let everyone within a ten-mile radius know where they were. "That may not be a wise thing to do right now, Father. The sound of a blast carries. But I'll make sure that we do it right before we leave."

Washington, D.C.

JAMES JORDAN WASN'T pleased to hear that El Machetero had lost contact with Phoenix Force. The hatchet-faced mercenary was good, one of the best the CIA man had ever worked with in his long career in Latin America, and he had expected better from him.

He grudgingly had to give Phoenix Force its due, though. Even against the overpowering odds he had stacked against them, they had still managed to break out of the cordon and escape. But no matter how good they were, they were still only five men against a hundred, and he had complete confidence in El Machetero.

In another era, the mercenary leader would have been able to carve out a nation with his blade. In the nineties, however, the best he could hope for was to gain fame in the shadow world of clandestine warfare and personal wealth. Jordan was aware that El Machetero was double-dipping on this operation by working for the cartel, as well as for him. But if he could put an end to Phoenix Force, he would have earned every dollar, or peso, of it.

Jordan's relationship with the cartel had started out as a marriage of convenience, and it went back many years. After the debacle in Vietnam ended, CIA operations in Latin America had almost been shut down, as well. The American public had been weary of its government in general and of its foreign involvement in particular. While America was consumed with Watergate and its aftermath, no one was minding the store in Latin America.

Cuba's Che Guevara had been dead by then, along with Allende of Chile, but that didn't mean that the Marxists had given up their plans of Communist domination of the region. Communist insurgencies kept sprouting up all over Latin America, and the Company had been hard-pressed to deal with them. In the face of budget and personnel cuts for covert operations, the CIA had been forced to make an unholy alliance with the emerging drug cartels. The Company didn't get involved in the drug trade as such, but they had been forced to rely heavily on the cartel's information resources.

Jordan was one of the Company men who made the original contacts with the Medellín cartel and created the cooperation that had lasted until today. Many Medellín drug lords were now either dead or imprisoned, and the Cali families controlled the Colombian cocaine concession. But Jordan's cartel contacts had remained intact. The Cali drug lords knew the value of having a high-level CIA contact.

Those contacts had been used to send his most recent message to El Machetero. In that message, he had made it abundantly clear what would happen to him if Phoenix Force wasn't dealt with promptly. He also made arrangements with the cartel to carry out his threat if the mercenary didn't come through as he had been instructed.

Colombia

EL MACHETERO HAD BEEN in the business far too long to panic when he received Jordan's message that morning. The gringo hadn't been happy that Phoenix Force had been able to break out of his trap. In fact he had actually threatened him, and he knew that Jordan's threat wasn't to be taken lightly.

The CIA man had a long reach in Latin America. It would be all too easy for him to make good on the threat, and there would be little he could do to protect himself. Jordan had contacts on all sides of the Latin American political arena: the governments, the guerrillas and the drug lords. Any of the three parties would be happy to do the job for the Yankee's gold or just for future considerations.

That was how Jordan had built his wide-reaching power base in the region—considerations, as he called them. A consideration could be tipping off a drug lord that the *federales* were coming to bust them, or it could be tipping the government where a drug lord was hiding. Either thing put people in his debt, and Jordan had a network of people who owed him everything they had. El Machetero was one of those who owed the Yankee big time.

This operation was supposed to have cleared the books for him with the CIA man. But if Jordan turned against him, it wouldn't matter what they had agreed on. Someone else would clear a debt by killing him for failing to carry out his mission.

It was too early for him to be thinking that way, though. The Yankees were still in the mountains, and there was no way that they could stay hidden for long. Now that the men of Phoenix Force thought that they had broken out, they would probably run all night to try to put more distance between them and their pursuers. But that didn't bother El Machetero. For one, it would tire them even more, and no matter how fast they ran, they couldn't outrun his helicopter.

Already it was ferrying his men to new blocking positions along the likely escape routes to the coast and safety. In another hour, all the avenues would be blocked. Even though he was moving a large part of his force, he really didn't think that the Yankees had escaped to the east. More and more, it was feeling like they had disappeared into the vast green maze of the jungle.

Since he always followed his instincts, El Machetero decided to go back to the last place that he could definitely place the Americans, the place where they had ambushed his blocking force, and see how it felt to him.

THE STENCH of the unburied bodies was strong over the normal smells of decaying vegetation of the jungle when El Machetero reached the ambush area. This time he wasn't going to rely on his trackers and would look for a trail himself. Stripping off his equipment down to his sweat rag, a pistol and his ever present machete, he had his men stand aside as he examined the site.

Starting at the center of the blocking position, he started to walk in an ever widening spiral. He paid close attention to the barely visible empty cartridge cases littering the jungle floor. The AK and M-16 empties he saw he knew were from his own men. But when he found a small group of 5.56 mm casings twenty yards in front of the blocking position, he reached down and picked one up.

Flipping it around to look at the head stamp, he noticed that it wasn't marked; it was a complete blank. He paused for a moment and thought back. The ammunition he had issued to his troops had come from an American Army depot and bore normal military-issue head stamps. From his experience, he knew that ammunition that was manufactured without head stamps was for special-operation issue, the CIA, Special Forces or one of the other Yankee special-operation units. Putting the casing in his pocket, he continued his search.

On the far right flank of the blocking position, he found half a dozen 7.62 mm NATO cases with black head stamps. Since there was no sign of the two indentations that would have indicated that an M-60 bipod had been set up, he figured that the ammunition had come from a sniper's rifle instead of a machine gun.

He closed his eyes and instantly saw what had happened here.

The Yankees had sent a sniper off to the flank to draw fire and inflict casualties. When his blocking force reacted to the fire and were off balance, the others hit them in a frontal attack. It had been a smart move, one of the few choices that a smaller force had against a larger one, and it had worked.

Now that he knew what had taken place, he went back to the location where he had found the first of the unmarked brass. Examining the ground carefully, he slowly walked toward the blocking position. Even though the area had been badly disturbed, he still saw enough signs to determine that three or four men had attacked along that axis.

When he reached his men's empty positions, he stood stock-still, his eyes closed and his nostrils flared, breathing in deeply the smells of the jungle. This was his home, and he knew it the way a dirt farmer knew the collection of hovels that made up his home village. Now that he knew what the Yankees commandos had done here, he started to put himself in the mind of their leader. Without consciously telling himself to do it, the guerrilla leader took off at a dead run, putting distance between him and the ambush site.

He wasn't following tracks as much as he was taking the easiest route through the undergrowth, the route the Yankees would have taken. After running for almost half a mile, he stopped cold and looked around. The Yankees had stopped here instead of running farther, but why? Had he been leading them, he would have continued on. If they had stopped here, there had to be a reason.

Looking around, he saw the foliage mashed down as if a man had lain there. Walking over, he sniffed the air in that area and smiled. "One of them is wounded," he said aloud.

Backing away, he ferreted out the faint traces of the resting places of three more men. He had them!

When he straightened from the last position, his head snapped to the south. Without saying a word, he got to his feet and took off running again.

El Machetero's second-in-command silently ran behind his leader. He had seen his boss do this before, and it always made him uneasy. It was almost as if the man had become possessed with the evil spirits that dwelled in the jungle. He followed him, though, because he had seen the results many times before. El Machetero was on the track of the Yankees and he would find them.

Texas

CARL LYONS WALKED into the motel room on the outskirts of El Paso and tossed his bag on the bed. They had been on the road for several days now, and he was long past due for a hot shower. The urgent need for the shower had been accentuated by the fact that for the past several hundred miles, they had been followed by a series of plain, unmarked, four-door sedans.

Whoever was following them had been doing it by the book. None of the cars had stayed in sight for more than an hour, and the passoffs to a new vehicle had been done professionally. But the men of Able Team had done more than one car surveillance themselves, and they knew all the tricks. For one thing, the cars that were being used were a dead giveaway. They were the four-door, fleet-sale American sedans that every federal agency drove.

Lyons had first spotted them between Phoenix and Tucson, and they had stayed with them all the way into El Paso. There was even one of the cars parked across the street from their motel.

"I'm tired of running," Lyons stated. "If someone's after us, I want to know who in the hell they are so we can take care of them. And since the Farm can't help me, I'm going to find out on my own."

Schwarz usually was cautious of the Ironman's bull 'em and bust 'em ideas, but this one sat well with him. It had been a long time since the three of them had been out in the cold like this and he was starting to get frostbite. Before they could even start to correct whatever had gone wrong, they had to have information and right now they didn't know zip except that they were in it deep.

"What do you have in mind?" he asked.

"How would you like to play target?"

Schwarz shook his head. "Why is it always me?" he muttered.

"Because you and your gadgets can make it sound like there are three of us in the room so Pol and I can break out of here without spooking the opposition."

"You're going to do a snatch-and-grab, right?"

"I don't know any other way to find out what we're

up against. We need information, and this time it means that we have to talk to someone face-to-face.''

Schwarz shrugged. "Let me get my recorder and I'll start making some background tapes."

While Schwarz recorded background noise Lyons got his long awaited shower. "There," he said as he towel dried his hair. "I'm ready to go out there and kick me some surveillance butt."

CHAPTER FIFTEEN

CIA Agent Bob Bailey had started out on this assignment being cautious. Any man with any sense would be cautious about going up against hit men connected to the cartel. But so far his three targets weren't doing much more than running like whipped dogs with their tails between their legs. All the way across the Southwest, they had done nothing more than stop for gas a couple of times. They were even buying food to go and were eating in their van. They were also not making any attempts to evade being spotted. They hadn't even changed plates on their van, something that any teenage car thief knew enough to do.

After seeing this kind of behavior, Bailey didn't know why he had been called up from his counterterrorist assignment in Panama to do something that any state cop could have easily done, to say nothing of the FBI. But Bailey was a good Company man, and that meant following orders even if he didn't understand them. The CIA wasn't supposed to be involved in domestic affairs, though Bailey knew it happened all the time. While he had no idea what was going down on this operation, if it was important to Geoffrey Whitworth, it sure as hell was important to him. The director of communications wouldn't have put this many men on this job if it wasn't.

He also couldn't figure out why, if these three guys were such bad actors, they were being allowed to run free instead of being picked up. He could only assume that it had to do with their leading the surveillance teams to a hideout or to other accomplices before the bust was made. But if that was the case, he didn't understand why he hadn't been briefed on the full plan.

He was also a little foggy about why the CIA was involved in this operation in the first place. Domestic terrorism was usually an FBI or ATF area of interest. These guys were reported to be American citizens, and simply having a cartel connection shouldn't be enough to call in the Company to deal with them.

Nonetheless, Senior Agent Bailey had learned a long time ago that it wasn't wise to ask too many questions about what his superiors told him to do. A good agent did exactly what he was told and lived long enough to retire.

ABLE TEAM'S TAKEDOWN went like clockwork. Since there was only one guy in the surveillance car, Carl Lyons could have taken him by himself. Having Blancanales on hand just ensured that nothing could go wrong. They were in Texas now, and Texas was a bad place to have something go wrong that would draw attention to themselves. An encounter with a Texas Ranger wasn't on their agenda this night.

It took them a while to work their way into position to take their man. But when Blancanales went into his drunk act in front of the car, drawing their target's attention, Lyons slid up into the target's blind spot and snatched open the driver's-side door.

"Don't even think about it," he snapped as he slammed the muzzle of his Colt Python into the man's side. "You move and you're dead."

"Don't shoot!" Bailey said as he slowly placed both of his hands on the steering wheel.

Keeping the pistol jammed against his side, Lyons dragged him out of the car and Blancanales patted him down.

"He only had this," Blancanales said, flashing an Airweight Smith & Wesson .38 Agent Special before pocketing it.

"Since you seem to like our motel room so much," Lyons said, nudging Bailey with the pistol, "let's take a closer look at it. Who knows? I might even offer you a drink."

Bailey started to walk across the street.

"We're on the way up with the package," Blancanales announced to let Schwarz know that they were coming.

"Copy," Schwarz replied. "I'm ready for him."

BOB BAILEY WAS GOOD. He didn't lose his cool when Lyons and Blancanales hustled him into the room, frisked him and slammed him into a chair. He didn't even try to struggle when Schwarz cuffed his wrists to the chair's arms. Until he found out what these guys wanted with him, he wouldn't panic. After all, he had an ace in the hole. He didn't think that they had the slightest idea who they were messing with. He was confident that when they found out, their attitude would change.

Blancanales flipped open the wallet he had taken from Bailey's pants pocket and saw his CIA identification card. "Ironman," he said, "this guy's from the Company."

Bailey kept himself from smiling. The Central Intelligence Agency usually had that effect on people, particularly guys like these thugs. The Company wasn't what it had been back in the good old days, but its name still made people think twice.

"Is he, now?" Lyons held his hand out to examine the ID card. "Okay Mr. CIA Agent Robert Bailey, how about you telling me why you're following us?"

"I'm not going to tell you anything," Bailey said. "And I advise you to turn me loose immediately. It's over for you clowns, and there's no point in your making it worse by adding kidnapping charges."

"Adding them to what?" Lyons snapped. "I want to know why you're following us."

"It's going to be the 'good cop, bad cop' routine, isn't it? You guys should know better than to try that one."

"I'm the only guy here who was ever a cop," Lyon

said, "so in this case, it's just going to be bad cop, real bad cop. I don't know if you've seen that one before, but it's not pretty."

"Let me put it to you this way, Mr. Bailey," Blancanales stated. "You seem to have been following us, which means that there has been a major breach in our security somewhere. And since we don't know what's going on, I'm sure you can understand that we're naturally anxious to find out. And you won the information lottery because you're the first guy we've had a chance to talk to about this.

"Under normal circumstances, we'd take a more cautious line dealing with someone from the CIA," Blancanales continued. "But due to certain unusual circumstances we're working with, we have to forgo the niceties. Therefore, we're not going to try to beat the information out of you or anything crude like that."

He shrugged. "To be honest with you, we really don't have the time. Also we can't afford to take you with us when we pull out of here. As you can see, our options are few, but yours are even fewer. You can either talk to us and we let you go, or we kill you, leave your body here and then try to find another informant a little farther down the road."

"But I'm a government official." Bailey was starting to get concerned. He wasn't used to dealing with people who talked so casually about killing a CIA agent. "You can't do that to me!"

Lyons leaned over the CIA man. "If you were prop-

erly briefed on us, pal, you'll know that we don't particularly care about a man's official connections. You
could be the goddamned director of the CIA, and your
options would be exactly the same. Under the circumstances we're dealing with here, you have no hostage
value to us, mister. Absolutely zip.''

"But," the agent spluttered, "when the other guys
on the surveillance team report that you killed me,
you'll have every cop and FBI agent in the country
after you. You can't afford that right now."

"That's a risk that I'm willing to take," Lyons said.
"Are you willing to risk that I'm lying to you when
I say that I don't care if you live or die?"

He glanced at his watch. "You have one minute to
make up your mind, Bob, and to make your peace with
whatever you believe in."

In this three-on-one scenario, Schwarz hadn't said
anything yet. Now he walked over in front of Bailey,
pulled his 9 mm Beretta pistol and quietly screwed a
sound suppressor onto the end of the barrel. Slipping
off the safety, he pulled back on the slide to chamber
a round, then stood with the pistol in his hand looking
at Lyons.

"Time's up," the ex–LAPD detective announced.
"What's it going to be, Bob?"

"But…"

Schwarz raised the pistol and centered the sights on
Bailey's forehead. "Are you done praying?" he asked.
"I hate to kill a guy while he's trying to get right with

Jesus. But you've got to hurry it up, man. We're kind of on a tight schedule here. I know you'll understand.''

Schwarz had a benign smile on his face as if he were waiting to help the man on with his coat instead of waiting to cancel his ticket on the karmic railroad. Had he been acting like a tough guy, it might not have worked, but there was something about the open smile that did it. It was downright unsettling.

"Okay, okay." Bailey turned to Lyons. "I'll tell you what I know, but I really don't know what's going on. Whatever it is, it's sure as hell not worth dying for."

Not moving the muzzle of his pistol, Schwarz looked over to Lyons, who nodded.

"I don't know everything," the agent said, his eyes following Schwarz's pistol as he lowered it, "but I'll tell you what I was briefed on."

"For a start," Lyons said, "I want you to answer a couple of questions. Like what in the hell is the Company doing operating against American citizens? That's been off-limits for a long time now."

"All I know is that Geoffrey Whitworth pulled several of us in from our field assignments and told us to locate you three guys and follow you wherever you went."

"And report our locations to him?" Blancanales asked.

"Yes."

"Who is this Whitworth guy?" Lyons asked.

"He's the director of communications."

None of the Able Team trio had the slightest idea why the CIA's director of communications would want to take them out, but they would wait until they were alone before they discussed it.

"And," Schwarz asked, "what were you told that made us 'persons of interest,' so to speak?"

Bailey looked confused for a moment. "You're cartel hit men on the domestic-terrorist list."

That was another shocker for Able Team. They were the last people in the world who could be accused of being cartel hit men, but they had to take what Bailey said at face value. Someone had fingered them, and they were going to have to work with it.

"How did you find us anyway?" Schwarz asked to change the subject.

"That's easy. You've been under constant surveillance ever since you crossed the border back into the United States."

The three Able Team commandos looked at one another with complete surprise. If that was the case, and again they had to assume that it was, they were in deeper trouble than they thought. And it brought up another question. If they were on a domestic-terrorist suspect list, why were they being allowed to run loose? All of the possible answers to that question raised even more questions.

Something was rotten, and it pointed to Stony Man being under siege.

"Speaking of surveillance," Blancanales said,

"where's your partner? On this kind of gig, you Company guys always work in pairs."

Bailey looked embarrassed. "Things were slow, so he took off to catch Mickey Gilly at the Goat Roper's Café."

"I didn't know that you guys went in for country music."

"He's from Nashville."

SCHWARZ SLIPPED a set of earphones over Bailey's head so they could discuss their predicament without his overhearing them. "What are we going do with him?" he asked, jerking a thumb in the direction of the agent. "We can't take him with us, and we can't leave him behind for his buddies to find."

"I know that he's supposed to be one of the good guys," Schwarz said when he saw Blancanales start to speak, "but it's our asses on the line now. If what he said about them being on us since Mexico is true, we're in deep shit. We have to disappear pronto."

"Let's leave it up to him," Blancanales said.

"Say what?"

"Let's give him the score and let him decide if it's worth dying for."

Lyons shrugged and walked over to take off Bailey's earphones. "Let me put it to you this way," he said. "Even though you're just following orders, you're in well over your head this time. One of my partners wants to cut our exposure by leaving you dead so you can't cause us any trouble. And the way he lays it out, it makes a lot of sense to me.

"So here's the way I see it. I can do as my partner wants, and that will buy us a little time. But I really don't want to do that. So, I'm going to explain something to you and hope that you're smart enough to see things my way."

Even though he said nothing, Bailey's relief was evident. There was a chance he would live.

Lyons continued as if he hadn't noticed. "This Geoffrey Whitworth who sent you after us is a rogue agent. I don't care who he is and what office he's sitting in, he's bad. And I know for a fact that this operation against us hasn't been cleared by the Oval Office. Even though you're following orders, you've stepped well over the line on this one. I'm going to get to the bottom of this and, CIA or not, I will kill anyone who keeps me from doing that. Before you tell me all the bad things that will happen to me for killing a Company man, let me tell you that no matter who I have to kill to get this sorted out, I will do it and I won't worry about the bodies I leave behind.

"Why, you ask yourself? It's real simple. We happen to work for the Man, the guy you know as the President of the United States. As the nation's Chief Executive, he has the power to pardon anything I do. And I would like to add that he has already pardoned me, many times. You wouldn't be the first or, unfortunately, the last American that I have had to kill in the line of duty."

The matter-of-fact way that Lyons spoke put a chill in Bailey. There had obviously been some kind of mistake, a big one. Only a man who was speaking the truth could talk so confidently about killing. Apparently he had stumbled onto some kind of clandestine presidential wet team.

"My advice to you," Lyons continued, "is to simply call in sick, take a few of those vacation days you have on the books and find a place to hide until this is all over. When it's over, I'll square things for you with the White House. You'll be able to continue your career right where you left off before you were called in to do something illegal, namely go into action against American citizens within the boundaries of the United States.

"If, however, you decide that I'm blowing wind and you try to get involved with this again, remember that I'll kill you on sight the next time I see you."

Bailey swallowed hard. "I understand."

"Good."

"To keep you from doing anything foolish," Schwarz said as he laid a small electronic box on the table next to Bailey, "I'm going to leave this little device with you. When I set the switch, it will respond to anything louder than a whisper by detonating a quarter pound of C-4 backed up by a handful of ball bearings, a mini-Claymore, as it were. If you try to call for help or thump on the wall, boom, you're history. I've set it for twelve hours, so if you wait it out, you'll be okay, it'll turn itself off."

Putting his finger to his lips, Schwarz flipped a switch and a red light came on next to the digital clock on the face of the device. Leaning over Bailey, he whispered, "Adios, Company boy. Remember, not a word."

Bailey tried not to even breathe too loudly as he stared at the red light on the box. It was going to be a long twelve hours.

"WHAT WAS IN THAT BOX you left back there with our boy?" Lyons asked Schwarz as he pulled the van out of the motel parking lot onto the highway. "We didn't have any demo packs like that, did we?"

Schwarz grinned. "It's just a digital clock with a red diode added to the case. If he waits for that light to go out, he's going to be waiting a long time."

Lyons laughed.

"If you two are done patting each other on the backs," Blancanales said, "we'd better think about dumping this ride or at least changing the plates. We have to try to shake those guys."

"Good point," Lyons said. "Where can we find a car lot open at this time of night?"

"Let's try a rental agency at the airport," Blancanales suggested. "This is a big enough place that they should still be open. We can pick up something for a one way to California, then dump it in the morning when we find something more suitable at a used-car lot."

CHAPTER SIXTEEN

Colombia

By early the next morning, Hawkins's fever had broken.

"How you feeling, T.J.?" Calvin James asked his patient and teammate. He had spent the night in the dispensary and was relieved to see him looking so much better. Apparently the priest's native poultice and a good night's sleep had worked wonders.

"I've felt a hell of a lot better in my day," Hawkins admitted, "but I think I'm going to be okay now. My leg's started to throb, and I know that's supposed to be a good sign. Just put me on my feet, point me in the right direction and I'll try to keep up with you guys."

"Oh, no, you don't," James cautioned. "You're staying right here until that thing's had more time to heal. I don't want you to relapse on me because I don't want to have to carry your heavy ass through the woods."

Hawkins looked around the open-sided hut that

served as the dispensary and was startled to see the village and the Indians. "Where are we, and who are those people? I don't even remember coming here."

He shook his head. "Man, I must've really been out of it."

"You were," James agreed. "This is some kind of jungle missionary camp for a small band of Indians run by a Catholic priest."

"Where'd he come from?"

"He hasn't said, but Rafael says that his Spanish has a faint American accent and he speaks English."

"If he's one of us, he's a long way from home."

"So are we, my man, so are we." Then James changed the subject. "You ready for something to eat?"

"Sure, what've you got?"

"Well, I've been watching the locals roasting some real big spiders and cracking them like crabs. Rafael says that they're pretty good that way."

"I may be sick, man," Hawkins said, sounding disgusted, "but I'm not that damned sick."

"I guess it's MREs for breakfast, then," James said as he reached for his backpack. "And it's either spaghetti and meatballs or chicken Alfredo."

"On second thought, maybe I will try a little of that roasted spider. Does it come with a side? Maybe a few grubs or monkey brains?"

James shook his head. "I'm going to tell David that you're ready to hit the road again."

"That's what I told you."

MACK BOLAN WAS WALKING slack for the two Indians who were on point. They had started tracking again at first light, and while the scouts were moving at a fast pace, their jungle-born senses weren't missing a thing. There were signs that a large force had moved through the area not long ago. But with the jungle as wet as it was, the tracks were difficult to read after even a few hours, so they couldn't tell how long ago it had been.

They were into their third hour when the pointman signaled danger. The scouts went to ground instantly, their weapons ready. After several long minutes, the point man signaled for them to move out again, cautiously.

When Bolan went forward, he saw the scout standing over a decapitated corpse. The man hadn't been dead very long, his face and exposed skin not yet eaten by the scavengers of the jungle. The body was wearing U.S.-issue woodlands-camouflage-pattern jungle fatigues like the attackers at Fort Apache. His weapon was missing, but he still had his field gear, again all U.S. issue, and his ammo pouches were full of 5.56 mm M-16 magazines.

To have come up against two guerrilla forces both equipped this way couldn't be a coincidence. This man had to be connected with the group that had attacked the DEA outpost, and that meant the attack had been aimed at him and Grimaldi.

Bolan noticed that the Indians were talking in their dialect and pointing to the body. "What are they saying, Carlos?" he asked the scout's leader.

"They say that this is the work of El Machetero."

"Who is this 'Machete'?"

"He is a very bad man, *señor*," the scout said. "He fights for whoever pays him and he likes to kill his enemies with a big knife."

A big, sharp knife, Bolan noted. Even through the gore, he could see that the corpse's head had been taken from his body by a single blow. The question was why the man had been killed. Since Bolan was certain that he had been part of the mercenary force that was chasing Phoenix Force, it made sense that he had been executed for some failure on his part.

And if that was true, it could mean that Phoenix Force had managed to break free of the forces that had been brought against them.

"We need to look around this area for signs of an ambush," Bolan told the scout. "And look for signs that my friends were able to fight their way through it. They will be heading east for the coast."

It took only a few minutes for the scouts to find the site where Phoenix Force had ambushed the mercenary blocking force and had broken out of the cordon. As had been the case with the decapitated man, the enemy bodies had been left unburied though their weapons had been taken.

Seeing large-caliber-rifle hits in upper bodies of several of the corpses, Bolan knew that he was looking at Gary Manning's handiwork. The Canadian was good with his sniper's rifle. Several of the dead, though, looked to have been shot sometime after the ambush. They all bore minor wounds that had been bandaged, and their killing wounds were all to the fronts of their bodies.

Considering the gunman who had been decapitated, it was entirely possible that this El Machetero had executed the survivors of his blocking force for having allowed Phoenix Force to get past them. If that was the case, he was acting like a mad dog, but that wasn't unusual for a mercenary leader. Bolan regretted not having a link to Stony Man because Kurtzman would probably be able to give him some background information on the man.

"*Señor,*" the chief scout called, "one of my men thinks that he has found which way your friends went."

"Where's that?"

"There is a track that looks like it is going up into the mountains. But it is heading to the coast like you said it would."

Hearing that, Bolan knew that McCarter could have tried to take that way out. It would be easier going if they kept to the valleys, but from the signs left by the enemy force, all the valleys were well covered.

"Let's follow it, Carlos."

"*Sí.*"

JUAN CHICINO WAS only in his mid-twenties, but he was a veteran fighting man. He had been fighting ever since his fourteenth birthday when the National Police swept through his village looking for Communist guerrillas. His father had protested when one of the policemen took an instant liking to the boy's older sister and had been shot for his pains. His sister had been raped, his mother roughed up and he had been severely beaten when he rushed to his mother's defense.

When the police left the ruins of what had been a prosperous mountain village, the guerrillas moved back in. When their leader found the boy digging a grave for his father, he walked up to him. "Do you want to be a man and have revenge for what they did to your family, or do you want to cry about it like a boy?"

Wiping the tears from his eyes, young Juan Chicino tried to make himself taller in front of the hatchet-faced guerrilla. "I am a man today," he said. "It is my fourteenth birthday."

The guerrilla laughed. "Being fourteen does not make you a man. But if you come with me, I will teach you how to be a man and how to get back at the dogs who did this to your family."

Chicino straightened to his full height. "As soon as I have buried my father, sir, I will come with you."

"Call me 'Comrade,'" the guerrilla said. "In my group, everyone is equal."

That sounded good to the young boy, and he followed his new equal when the band left the village.

Chicino spent most of the following year in a remote mountain camp learning to be a fighting man. Fueled by his desire for revenge on the men who had killed his father, he learned his new trade fast and soon started going with the guerrilla band on their raids. The first time he saw them take apart a village that was loyal to the government, he was shocked to the core. They were doing the same brutal things that the government troops had done to his family.

When he complained to his leader, he was told that in the struggle for the hearts and minds of the people, it was sometimes necessary to purge the reactionary elements for the greater good of the country. At the time, he had been too young to see the hypocrisy in the Marxist explanation, but he didn't stay that young very long. Another thing that made him grow up more quickly was the fact that whenever his guerrilla band stumbled onto a government unit, they ran instead of standing and fighting.

Finally, after being forced to run from a government unit yet again, he thought back and realized that the only time the guerrillas stood and fought was when they were ambushed and had no choice but to fight. He also realized that if the Communists wouldn't fight the government troops, he would never have a chance to get his revenge.

The mental image of the man who had shot his father and raped his sister had been seared into his mind, and it hadn't faded with time. It was as clearly imprinted as if it had been carved in stone. He came to the decision that his best chance of finding that man was to join the government forces. That night, he used the fieldcraft he had learned to slip away from the guerrillas.

Once he was safely away, he got rid of his weapon and military equipment. Two weeks later, he enlisted in the National Police under his father's name and went through military training for a second time. He was careful, though, not to show his trainers that he was as experienced with firearms as he was.

It took almost three years for Chicino to find the man who had destroyed his family. He was part of a security unit guarding a political rally in the capital when he saw the man he had been seeking for so long. The man was older than Chicino remembered him and he had gained a lot of weight, but there was no doubt in Chicino's mind that it was the right man. He was now a sergeant major of the Police Security Battalion stationed in the capital.

Since Chicino was just a private, it wasn't easy for him to get close to someone as important as a sergeant major. He learned where the sergeant major drank and which bordello he visited.

One Saturday night, Chicino put on his uniform and went to the small whorehouse in the poorer part of town. Going around the back, he entered the rear door and went directly to the room he had been told the sergeant major used for his visits. In the dim light, he saw the face he had remembered.

When the sergeant major began to sample the delights of the young woman he had chosen for the evening, Chicino stepped forward silently and, without speaking a word, shot him in the back of the head. The prostitute screamed hysterically as she extricated herself from the corpse and fled the room.

Chicino didn't feel as happy as he had thought he would. The pig was dead, but his father was still dead and his mother and sister still suffered. Stripping off his Security Police armband, he dropped it on the corpse.

On the way out, he added the sergeant major's .45 to his arsenal. Now that he had finally found his man, he was going back to the clean air of the jungle.

Now Chicino ran what could only be described as a freelance guerrilla force allied with no one. At times he fought the government's troops, sometimes he fought the armies of the drug lords or the few remaining Marxist groups. He fought anyone who ventured into the part of the jungle that he called his own. The men and women who made up his band were mostly Indians or ex-peasants who had been driven off their lands by one side or the other.

When he had first heard that the drug lords were moving troops into the region around the mountaintop lab, it didn't concern him. They often moved in troops to guard their labs when they were making cocaine. Now, though, the reports were starting to worry him. A small group of commandos had tried to attack the lab and had been beaten off. Normally that wouldn't have concerned him, either. This time, though, the well armed drug troops were pursuing this small band and driving them deeper into the jungle.

That still wouldn't have been a problem for his force except for one thing—El Machetero was reported to be the man leading the drug troops.

Before the famous mercenary had started calling himself El Machetero, he had been the Marxist guerrilla who had taken Juan Chicino from his village and taught him his trade. He could thank El Machetero for having done that, but he couldn't forget that the guerrilla had run from the government forces, thus denying Chicino his vengeance. Also El Machetero had ravaged innocent villages just as the government forces had done, and for far less reason.

Chicino's group was highly mobile. They lived like the Indians, but there was only so much jungle they could hide in. With El Machetero's army on the loose in his territory, there was too great a chance of their crossing paths. And if El Machetero found them, he would spare no one. For that reason alone, Chicino was prepared to go to war against El Machetero, but there was another, more personal reason why he wanted the mercenary's blood.

Though the man who had shattered his family was dead, to complete his vengeance, he would destroy El Machetero as he had destroyed the sergeant major. Doing that would soothe his soul and it would also protect the people in his little kingdom who wanted only to live their lives in peace and depended on him for protection.

CHAPTER SEVENTEEN

Stony Man Farm, Virginia

Hunt Wethers found Aaron Kurtzman at his workstation.

"I have an idea," Wethers said cautiously, "and I'd like to bounce it off you."

Kurtzman leaned back in his chair. "Shoot."

"There's one thing we haven't done yet, and I think that we ought to investigate it before we go much further."

Kurtzman spun his chair to face his colleague. "What might that be?"

"Do you remember that tech report that came through a little over a year ago about the CIA funding a black research project on a super-clipper chip?"

Kurtzman thought for a moment. "Vaguely." That kind of background, or filler, information came in all the time. It was gone over and then filed away. Most of it was never looked at again, but it was there in case it was ever needed.

"I think we ought to take a closer look at that project," Wethers said.

"How so?"

"Well, the program was designed to see if a multi-level clipper chip could be developed. One that could handle any kind of encrypted code regardless of the media."

Kurtzman dug into his encyclopedic memory, nudged a few brain cells and came up with a recollection. "But it was going to require a mainframe to drive it, correct?"

Wethers nodded. "That's right, but mainframes aren't as expensive as they used to be. You can get a pretty decent machine for much less than a million dollars today."

"So you're thinking that someone drove down to We-Be-Computers, put a mainframe in the back of their minivan, took it home and plugged a clipper chip into it so they could read our mail? Piece of cake, as McCarter would say, any high-school kid with a million bucks in his jeans could do that."

Wethers knew that Kurtzman was tired and under the gun, so he wasn't offended by the sarcasm.

"What if it wasn't a teenage hacker?"

"I know it wasn't a hacker, Hunt!"

"What if it was someone in the CIA?"

That gave Kurtzman pause. The Company said that they had cleaned their house of all of their rogue agents in the aftermath of the Iran-Contra Affair and the Ames scandal. But what if there was still a faction within the bureaucratic agency that wanted to see Stony Man take a fall? He didn't want to think that was the case, but he also knew that it wasn't outside the realm of possibly.

"Keep talking," he growled.

"I just ran through our file copies of the Company's budget forecast for the last fiscal year, and there was no funding for the super-clipper chip, not even in the black budget. And when I ran a search for anything else relating to that project, I came up with a complete scrub. There's absolutely nothing, including the original item, anywhere. The project simply doesn't exist anymore."

Kurtzman thought about that for a long moment. The CIA wasn't known for dropping funded items from their budget, no matter how unlikely they were to ever bear fruit. Since a government agency's power in Washington was directly related to the amount of money it could spend, it was unlikely that they would have deleted the funding from their budget.

"What I want to do," Wethers said, "is to go back and find out what happened to that clipper-chip project. Then I want to go over the original data we used to put our last two missions together. I want to track it all the way back to the original intel feeds that were used to create the documents that we relied on to plan the mission. I want to know what they said and exactly who said it."

"Do you really think that the CIA set us up on this?" Kurtzman asked.

"I really don't know what I think. And I'm trying not to form an opinion until I can sort out the facts at hand. But I do know that an advanced clipper chip went from being front-page news in the world of clandestine intelligence gathering to a complete blank, and I'd like to know why that happened. If, just if, this chip exists in someone's hands, it could explain how we ended up with someone reading our mail. Then, if I can prove that we were fed phony data to lure Phoenix and Able into the field, we'll know for sure what went wrong."

Suddenly Kurtzman felt invigorated. "Get on it," he ordered.

"I already have," Wethers replied. "And I've opened an outside channel to do it."

"Don't tell Hal."

Wethers smiled tiredly. "Don't worry."

Colombia

BOLAN'S SCOUTS were up at first light. Building a smokeless fire, the Indians boiled coffee to go with their breakfast rations. Knowing how far voices carried in the cool morning air, they spoke in muted undertones as they ate. Bolan studied his map while he drank his share of the coffee and ate a trail bar.

They had covered almost half of his search area the day before and should have most of the rest of it covered by the time Grimaldi returned. If they hadn't made contact with the missing men by then, he would have the chopper take them to another location and start the search again.

When their breakfast was over, the ashes of the fire were scattered and the six men moved out again. The high mountain jungle still held the coolness of morning, and the men moved quickly because the heat would soon be upon them. As before, though, the DEA scouts missed nothing.

The scouts had just spotted signs where a fairly large group of men had passed the day before when two men appeared in front of them as if they had sprung from the earth. They were dressed in what looked like cast-off fatigue pants and homespun shirts, but the AKs in their hands looked well maintained. The muzzles of the weapons weren't threatening, so Bolan didn't fire.

"Don't shoot!" the lead scout said, motioning for Bolan to lower his weapon. "I know these men. They live here in the mountains, and they do not bother anyone."

"Why the guns, then?"

"Here, *señor,* a man without a gun is a dead man."

From what Bolan had seen of this part of the world so far, he could only agree. By civilized standards, this was an out-of-the-way part of a remote region of the world. But for what should have been a green wasteland, there was a lot going on and far too many armed men.

"What are they doing here?" Bolan asked.

"That is what they want to know about us," the

scout replied. "They do not know who we are, and they fear that we will be trouble for them."

"Tell them that we aren't going to hurt their people," Bolan replied. "And then ask if they have seen the men we are looking for."

Bolan spoke a little Spanish, but the scout was speaking an Indian dialect, so he couldn't follow the conversation at all. When the scout turned back, his face was grim.

"He says that El Machetero has an army of men in the jungle and that they are chasing four white men like you and one black man. One of the men has been wounded, but they think that he is still alive."

In this part of the world, that description could only fit Phoenix Force. Rafael Encizo was Cuban, but to an Indian, he would be considered a white man.

"Does he know where these men are now?" Bolan asked.

"He says that they were seen going to the village of a priest they call Padre Gringo because he is a Yankee like you."

Finding an American missionary in the jungle was no surprise to Bolan, they showed up in the least-expected places. "Can they take us to this village?"

The scout nodded. "He says that he can lead us there, but that we will have to go through El Machetero's men to get to the village."

Bolan smiled slowly. "I think we can deal with that."

THAT MORNING, El Machetero didn't wait to find the Yankee commandos' final destination before he called for his helicopter to start ferrying his men back from the blocking positions in the east. In retrospect, he saw that he had jumped the gun by sending them out there, but he'd had to do something to satisfy Jordan. Now that he knew where the Yankees had really gone, he needed all of his forces on hand to make sure that they didn't slip away again.

After issuing his instructions, he drank a quick cup of coffee before taking up the faint trail again. As he had done the day before, he walked well out in front of his men and stood still for a long moment. When he could feel where the Yankees had gone, he started to run again.

When the faint track he was following led to the ridge line where McCarter and Encizo had spotted the village in the valley, the mercenary stopped cold. Now he knew where the Yankees had gone. He had almost forgotten about this miserable little village and the gringo priest who lived with the Indians. It had been a long time since he had last raided the village to gather women for his troops, and they should have a new crop ready for use.

He doubted that the Yankees had known about the priest and had purposely sought him out. More than likely, they had stumbled onto the village in their blind flight to break out of the net he had thrown around them. It made sense that they would try to hole up there. He was certain that one of the commandos was wounded. All of the signs pointed to it, and his gut told him that it was true. Since the priest was a jungle doctor, the Yankees would ask him to treat their wounded comrade.

Depending on how badly the man had been hit, they might stay there for a few days, but he couldn't count on that happening. Calling for his radioman to come up, he started planning his encirclement of the village. This time Phoenix Force wouldn't get away from him.

BOLAN AND HIS SCOUTS stayed on the heels of the two guides as they ran through in the jungle, without leaving a trace of their passage. He was no stranger to operating in the jungles of the world, but he had to admit that these men were as good as any he had ever seen in this kind of terrain and vegetation. But since they had been born here, he would have expected no less.

Within an hour, the two guides stopped and motioned for the scouts to take cover. As soon as they had gone to ground, one of the guides crawled back to the lead scout and whispered in his ear.

"He says that El Machetero's men are right ahead of us," the scout in turn whispered to Bolan.

"How far away is the village?"

"Maybe two kilometers or a little more."

"Good," Bolan said. "Tell them thanks and that we will go on alone from here."

"They also say that their leader, Juan Chicino, is in the area and that he is after El Machetero."

Bolan wasn't happy to hear that. What was supposed to have been a simple raid on a drug lab had turned into some kind of interjungle turf war. The last thing he wanted was to get caught between two warring private armies before he could get Phoenix Force extracted. He didn't really care what happened after Grimaldi showed up to fly them home, but until that time, he had to try to keep a lid on it if at all possible.

"Carlos, ask them if they can take a message to their leader for me. I'd like to ask him to hold off on attacking El Machetero until I can get my men out of here. We've stumbled into something that we don't understand, and it's not our fight. Explain to them that we came here to blow up a drug lab, not to fight a turf war."

"I will try."

After another whispered consultation, the scout came back. "He says that he will give Chicino your message, but he doesn't know what he will do. He and El Machetero have been enemies for a long time and he cannot allow him to raid into his territory."

"Tell them that I don't want to keep their leader from fighting El Machetero. I only want enough time to get my men out of here first. What happens after that doesn't matter to me. From what I have seen, if he kills El Machetero, it will be a good thing."

"I will try to explain."

After another conversation, the two guides slipped away like shadows and were gone in an instant.

BOLAN GAVE the two Indians only fifteen minutes to get clear of the area before he told the scouts to move out. The situation was getting a little too confused for his taste, and he wanted to link up with Phoenix Force as soon as possible. Grimaldi would be coming back with the chopper in a couple of hours, and he wanted to get out of there.

The first of the mercenaries they came across was chasing a monkey with a bayonet tied to the end of a pole. Apparently the gunman had dinner on his mind, but he was trying to keep his hunt quiet and had his M-16 slung across his back.

The monkey was so intent upon getting away from the human with the sharp stick that it didn't see the other humans hiding quietly in the jungle below the tree he had taken refuge in. The mercenary spotted his prey and was moving in for the kill when a scout rose from the brush in front of him, the machete in his hand poised to strike.

The gunman froze for an instant before bringing the makeshift hunting spear up across his body in an instinctive blocking position. The scout's razor-sharp knife cleaved through the pole before going on to slice deeply into the man's neck.

The mercenary clawed at the gash that was pouring blood into his lungs before collapsing without a sound. The scout dragged the body back and stashed it under a clump of brush.

Just then, the mercenary's hunting partner appeared,

his M-16 at the ready. Seeing the scouts, he snapped off a burst before diving back into cover.

Bolan triggered a short burst in return from his H&K. "Run for it!"

The jungle erupted in return fire. Thinking that they were under attack, the mercenaries were firing blindly, endangering their comrades. Dozens of slugs from the M-16s slashed the vegetation, cutting leaves and branches from the tree.

As Bolan quickly followed the scouts, he could hear their leaders yelling for their men to cease fire, and other men crashing through the jungle.

Three men ran through the brush toward Bolan, desperately seeking safety from the gunfire. Drawing his Beretta 93-R, he thumbed the selector switch to full-auto as he brought it up.

The first gunman took a 3-round burst to the left of the center of his chest, which tore out his heart. The second was bringing up his M-16 when the lead scout cut him down with a short burst. The third man turned to run, but he couldn't outrun the Executioner's bullets. Bolan caught him with a burst to the upper body.

"Go! Go! Go!" he shouted to the scouts as the six of them ran for safety.

CHAPTER EIGHTEEN

Washington, D.C.

"I still think that we should have gone to the Farm," Gadgets Schwarz muttered as he pulled the van into the parking lot of the post office in downtown Washington, D.C. The Able Team trio had driven in relays all the way from El Paso without rest except to stop for gas and a cold meal. "This is the last place we should be right now, man. Look around. This place is crawling with cops."

"It's always crawling with cops," Carl Lyons replied calmly. "It's just part of the urban scene in our nation's capital. If it wasn't for all the cops, this place would completely disappear within a week, every last brick, board and garbage bin."

"How about the drunks, dealers and addicts?" Rosario Blancanales asked. "Where would they go?"

Lyons shrugged. "They'll just move into Congress and no one will notice."

Though they were only a few blocks from Pennsylvania Avenue, the part of the nation's capital they were in looked like any East Coast, inner-city war zone. It looked like Beirut at the height of the civil war. The derelicts and drug addicts standing in front of boarded-up store windows, the graffiti, the trash in the gutters, the sense of urban neglect and despair were all-too-familiar to any American with a TV set.

Nonetheless, the hard-eyed D.C. cops in their cruisers were the last thing that Schwarz wanted to see right then.

"Just don't take too much time in there, Carl," Schwarz muttered as he eyed the razor wire around the post office.

Lyons sealed the manila envelope and reached for his door handle. "I won't."

It was a long five minutes before Lyons came out again. "Now," he said as got back into the van, "let's find a place to sleep."

"Then what?"

"Then we're going to pay a visit to the CIA."

"You've got to be joking." Schwarz couldn't believe Lyons had said that. Things were going from bad to worse big time.

The big ex-cop didn't smile. "No. The way I figure it is that if the Company's after us, the best way we can find out what this is all about is to go talk to them about it."

"Carl, we dodge cops and Company men all the way across the entire United States and now you want us to turn ourselves in? You're out of your freaking mind!"

"I didn't say that we were going to turn ourselves in to the bastards. I said that I wanted to talk to them."

"That doesn't sound a hell of a lot better to me," Schwarz muttered. "Langley's really the last place in the world we should be right now."

"It might actually be the best place for us to be," Blancanales argued. "After all, if the Company expects us to be on the run, they aren't going to be looking for us on their home turf."

"I guess," Schwarz conceded grudgingly. "But it makes me nervous. If we get caught in there, we'll never see the light of day again."

"More than likely, we'd just commit suicide or something more convenient like that," Blancanales stated. "We're absolutely the last guys in the country who will ever see the inside of a courtroom."

"Thanks for reminding me," Schwarz said. "I've been trying to practice positive thinking, hoping that this will all go away."

"Forget it," Lyons told him. "If we want something positive to happen, we're going have to make it happen ourselves."

THE MEN OF Able Team picked a motel outside of the Beltway in a middle-class residential area. Telling the desk clerk that they needed a room away from the street noise, they ended up in the rear of the building where they could park their van out of the sight of cruising cop cars.

"We need to ditch our ride again," Schwarz said

after they had carried the last of their bags upstairs to the room. "We've been driving it since we left El Paso."

"I'll go with you," Blancanales offered.

Lyons dug into his pocket and came out with what had begun as a large roll of hundred-dollar bills and handed it to Blancanales.

"Don't spend any more of this than you absolutely have to," he cautioned. "We're running out."

"I'll do what I can."

"You want us to get another van," Schwarz asked, "or do we want to try a sedan for a while?"

"Let's stick with the vans, but make sure you get one with another V-8."

"Right, boss," Schwarz said. He wisely refrained from adding that there was no V-8 in the world that was going to drive them out of trouble if they stepped in it inside CIA headquarters.

Stony Man Farm, Virginia

HUNT WETHERS CALLED UP the last document on his list and quickly scanned it. As he had expected, the information he was looking for wasn't there. His entire search through a long list of government sources had yielded absolutely nothing, but that was what he had expected to find—nothing. There were those times when a complete lack of information spoke loudly. And this was one of those times.

The most interesting thing he had found hadn't

come from a government publication, but from a small-town newspaper published in Midlands, Texas. Two articles in particular told him everything he wanted to know. The first was a report about a break-in that had occurred in a small cyber-tech firm on the outskirts of the town. One man had been killed in the break-in, a Rodney Gillmore, the company's owner and chief designer. The article speculated that he had been working late, had surprised the burglars while they were looting the factory and had been gunned down for his pains.

The second item in the paper that caught his eye was the obituary of the late Rodney Gillmore. The article reported about Gillmore's meteoric career, starting in the local high-school computer club and ending up with his starting his own company in his hometown. There was mention made of the work he had done for various aerospace companies and the government.

Running Gillmore's name through a computer publication data bank, Wethers came up with an article in an obscure journal devoted to the more esoteric uses of computer mathematics. Some of the articles were about programs that were used to try to decipher Mayan hieroglyphs and other ancient languages. Other programs were designed to solve the mysteries of the universe through mathematics.

Gillmore's article had to do with using macroformulas to create multidimensional encryption systems. Since the reverse of that process would allow a person to break encrypted messages, Wethers knew that he had finally found the smoking gun. The article didn't mention creating clipper chips, but that was only a technical exercise after someone had the macros.

Wethers made a couple of notes and headed for Aaron Kurtzman's workstation. "I've got it," he announced. "I know what happened and who did it."

"Shoot."

"There was a guy named Rodney Gillmore, kind of a computer prodigy, who ran a small cyber-tech firm in Midlands, Texas...."

"Was?"

Wethers nodded. "He died in a break-in at the company about six months ago. Shot three times in the head with a small-caliber pistol. The local police figured that he surprised the burglars."

Both of them knew that a triple tap to the head with a silenced .22- or .25-caliber gun was almost a registered trademark of the CIA wet teams, their hit men.

"Anyway," Wethers continued, "it appears that he came up with a series of macroprograms that allowed him to do multilevel encryption. He was so proud of his work that he published an article on it."

"And you think that his programming was used to make this super-clipper chip you were talking about?"

"Well, his firm was contracted to the Company before he died."

"And after his death?"

"The contract was paid off to his estate, and that was the end of it."

"It looks good," Kurtzman admitted. "But we need more than conjecture. We need to find the CIA's fingerprints on something before we can go with it. But get me hard copies of what you have, and we'll take it to Hal. He's the one who has to make the final decision."

As tempting as it was, the usually cool, calm, collected Weathers didn't give in to the sudden urge to strangle Kurtzman where he sat. While he was completely convinced that he had found the tie-in, he knew that the Bear was right. They had to find more than a circumstantial link before they took on the Company. To borrow a phrase, he had to find the smoking clipper chip.

Colombia

THE SOUNDS OF GUNFIRE brought all five of the Phoenix Force commandos running for the tree line on the north side of the village, their weapons at the ready. The fighting was at least a thousand yards or more away, but it sounded as though it was coming closer.

David McCarter quickly assessed the situation. "Rafe, you and Gary go deep and try to find out what's going on in there. We'll fan out here and cover you."

"We're on it."

Manning and Encizo melted into the jungle, moving in bounds to each other as they headed toward the sounds of battle. They had gone only two hundred yards into the trees when they spotted two of Bolan's DEA scouts. They were drawing down on the Indians in the tiger-stripe uniforms when they spotted Bolan.

"Jesus, Striker," Encizo said, pulling his weapon off target, "we almost blew you away."

"Is that village close by?"

"About half a klick west." Encizo didn't bother to ask how Bolan knew about the village. The way the situation was unfolding, it had to be a long story.

"You'd better get us out of here, then," Bolan said. "We might have picked up some trackers back there."

"How did you find us here?" McCarter shook his head in complete amazement when he saw Bolan. "We're not even sure where we are. We ran completely off the map."

Bolan pointed to the DEA Indian scouts with him. "These guys are real good at what they do. We picked up your trail when you broke out after that ambush, and we were tracking you when we picked up a couple of local guides who told us you were here."

"What was that firefight we heard back there?"

"The woods are full of people looking for you. They're closing in on this place, so we're going to have to get out of here as soon as Grimaldi shows up."

"What about the guy who's been on our ass?" Encizo asked. "How're we going to deal with him?"

"El Machetero?" Bolan said. "He'll just have to

wait until another day. We need to get out of here so we can find out what has happened at the Farm. We might be needed back there.''

"How do you know about him?" McCarter asked.

"He left an example of his handiwork on the trail where you broke through his blocking force, and the scouts told me all about him. He's pretty well-known around here.''

"That's what our host, Father John, told us," McCarter commented. "He's come through here before and he helped himself to several of the locals, both men and women. These people know him well.''

"Our bailing out of here is going to cause a problem, Striker,'' Encizo said, frowning.

"How's that?"

"These people." The Cuban gestured to the villagers. "When El Machetero comes here looking for us and we're not here, he's likely to tear these people up pretty badly. Like David said, he's been through here before to kidnap young men and women and they never come back. We can't just bug out and leave these people to face him alone. He'll be pissed off in a big way if we're not here.''

"Even with the scouts I brought," Bolan stated, "there's not enough of us to defeat this guy. According to the scout's estimates, there are at least fifty or sixty of them, and you already know that they're well armed.''

"That's a fact," James muttered. "They almost

chopped us up at the lab site. If they hadn't blown the ambush early, we wouldn't be here. As it was, T.J. got hit, and his wound got infected to the point that he couldn't go on. The priest took him in and treated him. He didn't have to do that, and we owe him for it.''

"Okay," Bolan said. "Let's talk to this priest about relocating his people somewhere out of the line of fire, then. When I can get Grimaldi in here, we can load this entire place out in just an hour or two. We should be able to airlift everything worth taking in just a couple of trips, three at the most. We can find a nice out-of-the-way hilltop and drop them there, out of the line of fire.''

THE PRIEST LISTENED to Bolan's proposition to relocate his people with a blank face.

"I appreciate your concern for us," he said in his rusty English, "but that will not be possible. This mountain is sacred to these people because of the Thunderstone, and they will not leave it. The last time that El Machetero's men came through here, I begged them to leave, but they would not consider it.''

"What is this Thunderstone thing you mentioned?" Manning asked.

"I think it is a large meteorite," the priest explained. "But the Indians think that it was sent by the ancient gods to mark the place on earth where they have to live. They never go more than three days' journey away from their sacred rock. Their ancestors have lived here for over a thousand years, and they simply will not leave.''

"Not even to save their lives?''

The priest shrugged. ''They say that they will not have a life if they do not live where their ancient gods told them to live.''

"But," James said, ''I thought that you were making good Catholics out of these guys?''

"Yes," the priest said, ''they worship the Savior, but that does not mean that they do not also follow the gods of their ancestors. That has always been the way of the people in this part of the world.''

Bolan looked around the cluster of huts before turning to McCarter. ''If they're going to stay here," he said, ''we'd better start seeing what we can do to fortify this place. In case your people don't know it, there's a small army moving in to surround this village, and they're going to have to fight if they want to live.''

"That is also not their way," the priest argued. ''They do not fight. They will scatter into the jungle and will hide until El Machetero leaves.''

"They might not be able to do that this time," Bolan said. ''The mercenaries have already surrounded the valley. I'm not sure that they will be able to escape.''

"I'd better put the lads to seeing if we can do something to better our positions here, then,'' McCarter growled. "There's bugger all for defenses around here."

"Get on that," Bolan said. "And I'll try to have my scouts talk these guys into leaving. Maybe the villagers will listen to them."

CHAPTER NINETEEN

Jack Grimaldi cruised at eight thousand feet above the part of the jungle Bolan had chosen to search for traces of Phoenix Force. He had spent the past twenty-four hours on the ground with Dave Nesbit and the DEA men at Fort Apache. Nesbit had the situation there under control and was rebuilding his base camp as quickly as he could. To give the DEA a hand, the pilot had hauled a couple of loads for them. One had been sandbags and fortification materials for the camp, and the other load was twenty men transferred in as reinforcements.

Now the twenty-four hours were over, and Grimaldi was back in the air looking for Bolan and the DEA scouts. At the altitude he was flying, he should be able to talk to him no matter where he was in the search area.

"Striker, Striker, this is Flyboy, over."

He waited sixty seconds to give Bolan time to get to his radio. "Striker, this is Flyboy. How copy, over?"

"Flyboy, this is Striker," Bolan's voice came in over Grimaldi's headset. "Where are you, over?"

"I'm in the middle of the search area at eight thousand feet, over."

"Go into an orbit, we need to talk."

As Grimaldi put the big chopper into a wide orbit, Bolan told him that he had made contact with Phoenix Force, but that they would be staying on the ground for at least another day.

"You've gone completely loco, right?" Grimaldi asked. "You've caught some kind of jungle fever, and you're out of your mind. Now that we finally found the guys, we've got to get our asses out of here."

"I haven't lost my mind. It's just that we've got a situation down here."

Bolan quickly briefed him on El Machetero and the village Phoenix Force had taken refuge in. "Even though the locals know what they're up against," he said, "they aren't willing to let us evacuate them. And when we pull out, the opposition is likely to take it out on them. We're going to stay here until we can convince this El Machetero to go away and leave these people alone."

"You're talking about starting a small war, aren't you?"

"It might come to that," Bolan admitted. "And that's why I need you to make a quick trip to Panama for us."

Grimaldi sighed. "What do you need?"

Bolan quickly outlined what he had in mind.

"You're crazy, Striker, completely crazy."

"But you can do it, right?"

"If the Army will help me, yeah," the pilot reluctantly admitted.

"Use the Green Ramparts authority and you shouldn't have any problem," Bolan replied. "But get back here as soon as you can."

"Roger that." Grimaldi banked the chopper away to the northeast. Panama City was only a couple of hours away.

EL MACHETERO FROWNED as he tried to understand the report from his unit along the northern part of the encirclement. Four or five men had apparently fought their way into the village. He didn't think that there were any firearms in the village and, even if there were, he would have expected armed men to try to break out. The only thing that made any sense to him was that there was another group of Yankees in the jungle. Maybe some of the DEA troops had been flown in to look for the missing Phoenix Force.

Another handful of men, no matter who they were or how well armed they were, wouldn't have any real effect on the outcome of this operation. As soon as the last of his men got into place, the village would be turned into a killing ground. The only people he would spare were the younger Indian women. His men had been in the jungle for a long time now and needed the relaxation the women could provide.

Picking up his radio microphone, the mercenary

leader called the pilot of his helicopter. The shuttling of his men into position was taking much longer than he liked. The pilot kept making excuses about why he couldn't carry as many of them on each flight up to the mountains as he had on the original flights down to the plains.

The mercenary leader didn't understand the pilot's excuses about air density, air temperature and lift, and was tired of hearing about them. As far as he was concerned, the pilot wasn't doing his job and, as soon as this was over, he would pay the price. El Machetero hadn't gotten where he was by letting people who worked for him fail to do their jobs.

Stony Man Farm, Virginia

WHEN BARBARA PRICE walked into the first-floor, corner office of the main house that had been set up for Hal Brognola, she had a smile on her face for a change. It had been so long since he had seen that particular expression that he was alarmed. "What's wrong now?"

"You're not going to believe what I just received from U.S. Mail," she said, holding out the distinctive red, white and blue cardboard envelope of the post office's priority service. "We just got a letter from Carl."

"Where are they?" he asked.

"Washington, D.C."

"Why didn't they come here?"

"He says that they have some business to take care of with the CIA first."

Brognola came halfway out of his chair. "What!"

"You remember Hunt Wethers's theory that someone in the Company has been using a super-clipper chip to break our security? Well, Lyons confirms that the CIA is involved in this whole thing."

"Not the CIA." Brognola shook his head. "They wouldn't be doing this to us. We're supposed to be on the same side."

"I don't know if it's an authorized operation," she replied. "But Carl has proof that someone in the Company's been busting our chops. He says that they popped a CIA surveillance team that had been dogging them halfway across the country. He plans on going down to Langley to see what's going on."

"I've got to get to the President with this immediately," Brognola said, standing.

"I don't know if you want to do that," she cautioned. "Carl thinks that we've been set up as a 'domestic terrorist' organization. If that's the case, you would be in danger the minute you stepped off the grounds. When it comes to domestic terrorists, they're shooting first and asking questions later these days."

That gave him pause. Since the Oklahoma City bombing, domestic terrorism had been high on the short list of hot-button topics with the nation's law-enforcement agencies. If someone in the CIA had placed the Stony Man personnel on the domestic-terrorist Wanted list, they would be in extreme danger.

"You said that they are going to take their investigation to the CIA? If they're right about this, that's going to put them in danger, too."

"I agree. But Carl thinks that they can get a lead on the man they think is behind this."

"Who's that?"

She looked down at the letter. "According to their informant, it's some guy named Geoffrey Whitworth. He's supposed to be the director of communications."

Brognola frowned. "Why would he want to take action against us?"

"I don't know, but I've got Aaron and his crew digging into this guy as deeply as we can. Of course, if he is the one behind this, he'll soon find out that we're onto him and it might make him ratchet up the pressure on us."

"Let him go ahead," Brognola growled. "We can deal with the bastard. It's about time that we went on the offensive on this. I'm tired of being a damned target."

Price smiled. That was more like the Hal Brognola she knew and loved. Like the rest of them, he hadn't taken well to being a helpless observer reacting to events instead of being a proactive player. If Able Team could put them back in the game, they would all feel better.

"By any chance," he asked hopefully, "did they set up a way for us to get in touch with them?"

"They got a P.O. box number in Washington."

Brognola shook his head. "This is a hell of a note.

We're supposed to be the nation's most technologically advanced agency and we've been reduced to using the damned mail to keep in contact with our field teams.''

"Technology does have its limitations."

"Tell me about it."

Washington, D.C.

"IT CAN'T BE this easy," Schwarz muttered as he pulled the rented four-door sedan into the single lane that led to the security checkpoint at the Langley, Virginia, headquarters of the Central Intelligence Agency. "There's no way that they're going to buy this."

"Just drive, will you?" Lyons muttered.

"I'm driving, I'm driving."

Lyons had to admit that his plan to get into Langley was a bit lame at best. And he wasn't sure what good it was going to do them. But he felt that he had to do something. Agitating a powerful enemy could go both ways. But if it spooked this Whitworth guy enough, he might make a mistake they could exploit to their advantage.

Even if it didn't cause Whitworth to panic, it sure as hell would let him know that they were onto him. But that carried a risk, as well. Even though they were using the DEA IDs and personae they had used for the aborted raid in Mexico, he knew that all visitors to Langley were videotaped on surveillance cameras. But with their Fed clothes and sunglasses, there would be little to tell them apart from any of the other cookie-cutter Feds who moved in and out of the facility.

Schwarz was sweating profusely when they parked the car and walked into the front door of the CIA headquarters. Ever since the main-gate assassination of a CIA agent a few years earlier, security was tight to the extreme. After showing their IDs, they had to walk through a body scanner before the hard-eyed security men let them into the main lobby.

The message center was plainly marked, and they walked to it and handed over their envelope. When it was signed in, they simply walked back to the parking lot and got into their car.

Lyons grinned at Schwarz. "I told you it would be a piece of cake."

WHILE LYONS AND SCHWARZ were making their foray into the CIA fortress, Rosario Blancanales had been doing his thing. Armed with nothing more than a U.S. government phone book, he had started digging to see what he could come up with on Geoffrey Whitworth, director of communications at the CIA.

One of his first calls was to the Langley motor pool. "This is Silverstone from protocol," he said when the dispatcher came on the line. "What car to you have assigned to Director Whitworth?"

"Just a second," the dispatcher said. "He's been assigned a Buick, why?"

"Well," Blancanales replied, sounding embarrassed, "he has a meeting coming up and he needs to show 'face,' if you know what I mean. Can you get him a Lincoln for a couple of days?''

''No problem. I'll give him 634,'' the dispatcher said, giving the last three numbers of the government license plate. ''It's a '94 with a full VIP pack.''

''Thanks a lot.'' Blancanales made a note. ''And do you have the phone number for that?''

''It's like all the rest of them,'' the dispatcher said in the tone of voice underlings used to tell the brass what they should already know. ''It's 555-9, and the last three from the plate.''

''I appreciate it.''

Another call to the tech-support company that maintained the government's phone network didn't go as smoothly. But in the end, he got the frequency that the CIA mobile phones worked off. A third call to the CIA's cellular-phone provider got him that number, as well. Now they had a way to eavesdrop on Whitworth when he was outside his office. In the grand scheme of things, it wasn't much. As an experienced spy, the CIA man would be cautious about what he said on the phone. But it was a start.

When he started to try to find out where the director lived, however, Blancanales struck out. Apparently Whitworth lived in one of the anonymous executive mansions that the CIA provided for their top brass. This would be a more difficult nut to crack, so he would put Schwarz on it when he got back. Gadgets had a way with addresses.

CHAPTER TWENTY

"How'd the drop go, Gadgets?" Blancanales asked Schwarz when he and Lyons got back to the motel room.

"Ask Carl," Schwarz grimaced. "I've got to go change my shorts."

"That good, huh?"

"It was a piece of cake," Lyons said. "Gadgets let his imagination run away with him. We just walked in like any other Fed flunkies, handed the package over to the message center and strolled back out."

"Just like that?"

Lyons grinned. "Just like that."

"Now what?"

"That depends on what you came up with while we were gone."

Blancanales quickly briefed him on what he had been able to learn about Whitworth through his phone calls. "That's a pretty good start," Lyons said. "Now I want you to go downstairs and talk to the guy at the office for a while."

"What do you want me to say to him?"

"Anything you like, but make sure that he will remember you. And while you're gone, I'll put Gadgets to work."

Blancanales reached for his coat. When Lyons was on a roll like this, all he could do was to go with it. "Whatever you say, boss."

"Where's he going?" Schwarz asked when he stepped back into the room.

"I sent him down to make sure that the desk clerk will be able to recognize him when someone shows him a mug shot."

"That means that you're expecting visitors, right?"

"That's why we sent Whitworth the invitation."

Schwarz sighed. "I guess I'd better get busy then."

"I was just going to suggest that."

As they always did, Able Team had taken a second-floor motel room. As a defensive tactic, a second-floor room had its pluses and minuses. On the plus side, no one could come in at them from a ground-floor rear window. As the minus, it gave them only one exit and that was the same way that any attacker would be coming at them. But since they wanted their enemy to come to them, that wasn't a problem.

A HALF HOUR LATER, "James Jordan" stared at the envelope that had just been delivered to his office in the CIA headquarters. It was a standard government-issue "shotgun" envelope used for interdepartmental communications. It was addressed to him by his real name and title, Geoffrey Whitworth, director of communications. Inside the envelope was a single sheet of paper with a crudely drawn ace of spades, the death card, and the words "Able Team" printed below it in block letters.

Punching in the phone number of the message center in the lobby, he asked who had delivered the envelope. "It was signed in by two DEA agents, sir," the clerk said. "A Dan Jackson and a Ralph Scruggs."

"Thank you," Whitworth said as he wrote down the two names.

Whipping through the pages of the federal government phone book, he found the number of the personnel department of the Drug Enforcement Administration and dialed the number.

"This is Whitworth, director of communications at Langley," he said when a clerk came on the line. "What can you tell me about two of your DEA agents, a Dan Jackson and a Ralph Scruggs?"

"Just a minute, sir," the personnel clerk said.

Whitworth stared at the paper as he waited for the clerk to come back on the line. "Mr. Whitworth, I'm afraid that Jackson's and Scruggs's files are flagged."

"What do you mean?"

"They're taking part in a classified operation code named Green Ramparts, and I can't release any information about them without the action officer's approval."

"Who's in charge of that operation?"

"I'm not sure, sir." The clerk sounded puzzled. "The action officer is listed as a Hal Brognola, but he's a Justice Department liaison officer, so there must be some mistake. If you'd like, sir, I can call the liaison office for you and find out what the story is.''

"Don't bother with it," Whitworth replied casually. "Thanks a lot. You've been helpful."

"No sweat, sir," the clerk said cheerfully. "We both work for the same government."

The hell they did, Whitworth thought as he hung up the phone. There were two governments in the country, and he was trying to get rid of the second one. He had to admit, though, that his operation hadn't gone exactly the way he had planned it. He also knew that no matter how carefully thought out, no plan ever did. But Phoenix Force was almost in the bag, and Able Team had just made a serious mistake.

They should never have taunted him, particularly not on his own turf. Now he knew that they were in the area. They had also shown him that they knew who he was, and that was a serious tactical mistake, as well. In a way, he was a bit disappointed that it had gone down this way. Even though he was going to destroy Able Team, he had expected them to be better opponents. But like the rest of the Stony Man operation, they had turned out to be lightweights.

He didn't even have to wonder about how they had gotten his name. The man who had turned up missing from the surveillance team in El Paso had to have talked. His car had been found on the street, and there had been signs in their motel room that Agent Bailey had been captured. Able Team had to have taken him with them when they pulled out. Either that or they had simply killed him and dumped the body somewhere. No matter what his fate, though, Bailey was obviously the one who had talked, and now Whitworth had to deal with it.

He briefly considered putting out a national alert on the three, but he decided not to. Having every cop in the nation looking for them would smoke them out quickly enough, but it would also raise questions, questions that he didn't want to have to answer.

The surveillance team in California that had brought in the highway patrol when they were trying to cover the cabin in Sonoma had made a big mistake. It had caused Able Team to rabbit, and Whitworth didn't want that to happen again.

The men of Able Team weren't the only people in Washington, D.C., who could look for information on their enemies, and Whitworth's resources were considerably more extensive than anything Able Team could do on its own. Since they were cut off from the cybernetic resources of Stony Man Farm, they were just three men on their own while he had all the resources of the Central Intelligence Agency to call upon.

One phone call had put a small army of agents to work scouring the city and its suburbs looking for the two men who had signed into the CIA building as Jackson and Scruggs. He knew that it was a long shot that they would have used those same two names to check into a motel or hotel, but it was worth looking into.

The license-plate number of the car they had driven had been logged in at the main gate, and he could track it down, too. He knew that it would turn out to be a rental, but there was a chance that the rental agreement would have information about them that could be followed up.

It had been very foolish for Able Team to have challenged him in his own city. Washington was a Company town, and there was very little about it that wasn't known. For years, CIA trainees had practiced their investigative techniques and tradecraft on the streets of the city. There was hardly a cracked sidewalk or a manhole cover within a fifty-mile radius of the capital that wasn't listed in the Company's database. And that information included a detailed list of every hotel, motel and boardinghouse room in the area.

Since the CIA was prohibited from operating on American soil, this was a secret database that not even the FBI had access to. But the information was in the hands of the people he had looking for Able Team, and they would use it to run them down.

And when Able Team had been located, he couldn't use the Company men working for him to make the hit. While the agents were all loyal to him, there was too great a chance that one of them would ask the wrong question. He had anticipated this problem, how-

ever, and that was why he had borrowed four cartel
gunmen to handle this part of the operation.

The only questions they would ask would be where
the targets were and how he wanted them killed. Plus,
since the men of Able Team were better than your
average gangster when it came to defending themselves, if one of the Colombians were to be left behind
with a bullet in him, the hit would go down as another
D.C. drug shooting, case closed.

Picking up his phone, Whitworth punched in a cellular phone number that connected him to the CIA
agent who was running the surveillance teams. At the
end of the conversation, he took the envelope and the
piece of paper and ran them both through the shredder
at the end of his desk.

NOW THAT HE HAD GONE active against Able Team,
Whitworth decided that it was time to move on Hal
Brognola, as well.

The Justice Department liaison officer had disappeared into the black hole of Stony Man Farm several
days earlier and hadn't come out. Whitworth had expected the man to run there when things went sour,
but it had always been his practice, according to the
blacksuit who had at one time been in Whitworth's
pocket, to surface after a few hours, or a day or two
at the most, and fly back to Washington.

Brognola had broken the pattern this time and apparently was still at the Farm. This was both good and
bad. It was good because it left the President hanging,

and the Man didn't like to be left in the dark. Anything that made the Chief Executive unhappy with Stony Man's performance fit into Whitworth's long-range plans. The downside was it meant that he couldn't take Brognola out as he had intended, thereby further isolating Stony Man.

He had planned Brognola's demise very carefully so that it would appear to be a typical urban incident and wouldn't become the subject of more than the most cursory police investigation. He had two of the cartel's gunmen covering the little neighborhood Korean market that Brognola often stopped at to pick up last-minute necessities. An E-mail message from his wife would get him to stop by the store for a head of lettuce, a loaf of bread or a block of cheese.

The cartel shooters would simply catch him shopping and blow him away along with the shopkeepers and anyone else who happened to be in the store. Brognola would become just another crime statistic among thousands, and no particular political importance would be attached to his death.

But with Brognola hiding behind the muscle of the Stony Man teams, Whitworth was going to have to change his tactics. It was a hell of a note when the nation had to depend on men like him, and that was only one more reason why Stony Man had to go. The Company had made its mistakes in the past, but at least the CIA employed *men*.

Picking up his phone again, he dialed a Washington number. After a brief conversation, he smiled. Another carefully prepared packet of misinformation was on its way to the ATF, and they would take care of Brognola for him.

NOW THAT WHITWORTH had the solution to the problems of Able Team and Brognola in the works, he tried to get in contact with El Machetero for an update on the Phoenix Force situation. He was never comfortable running an operation through second parties, particularly one as sensitive as this was. In the old days, he would have led El Machetero's mercenaries himself. He loved being on the ground and in command. But now that he was the director of communications, there was no way that he could get out of Langley for more than a couple of days.

If the mercenary did screw up by letting Phoenix Force get away from him again, they were sure to go back to Stony Man. Their presence would complicate the grand finale he had planned for the Farm, but it wouldn't change the outcome. Hal Brognola and his outlaws would go down in a blaze of gunfire; the trigger-happy ATF guys would be more than happy to see to that. There was that old saying that if you went looking for trouble, you were sure to find it.

In fact, if that part of the operation went the way he had planned it, the ATF's secret air force would finally make the top of the six-o'clock news, and that should put an end to that organization, too. The sight of armed ATF Bronco gunships swooping down on the Stony Man Farm, their guns and rocket pods blazing, would be the same kind of top-of-the-hour story that their incredible debacle at Waco had been. And when it was later revealed that they had shot up a government operation, there would be hell to pay.

Best of all, Whitworth knew that Stony Man Farm was well defended. Taking out the Farm wasn't going to be as easy as the Waco massacre had been. The ATF wouldn't be going up against women and children this time, and their blacksuited agents would finally find out what it meant to be in a real firefight. Knowing the ATF as he did, they wouldn't like it.

It had been so simple back in the good old days when the CIA and the FBI alone had been America's muscle. Now the ATF, the DEA, the INS and the Park Service were all fielding their own little private armies with snipers, SWAT teams and armed aircraft. Nearly everyone in the U.S. government except the GS-3 mail clerks was carrying a gun and playing Rambo.

He had a couple of senators and congressmen ready to introduce separate bills that would disarm everyone in the federal government except for the CIA, the FBI and the border police. The end result, however, wouldn't be fewer armed Feds. There would be the same number of armed officers, but under this plan they would all belong to the CIA, the FBI or the border police, making those three organizations even more powerful than they had ever been before.

Then, and only then, would Whitworth make his bid to be named the new director of a revitalized CIA. The same computer hacker team that had shut down

Stony Man for him had also been able to dig up enough dirt on the current director to convince him to retire for "personal reasons."

Glancing at his watch, he decided to go down to the computer room and look in on the people he had keeping track of the Stony Man communications. So far, the Farm had kept itself shut down, afraid of letting the unknown listener in on their conversations. That had been a smart move on their part, as it made his job more difficult, but it also isolated them. Their isolation was about to end, though, the ATF would see to that.

CHAPTER TWENTY-ONE

Over the Gulf of Mexico

Jack Grimaldi kept the big Sikorsky Sea Stallion below two thousand feet as he made the approach to the Army airfield at Fort Clayton in Panama City. His IFF had been squawking all the way in to show the air-traffic-control radar that he was a legitimate government aircraft, not a bandit. Having to dodge air-to-air missiles fired from the F-16 Falcons defending the canal wasn't on his agenda.

"Mayday, Mayday," he radioed to the air-traffic controllers in the tower. "This is Delta Echo Alpha Six Niner Five. I am inbound vector three-four-eight, twenty-five miles out. I am declaring an in-flight emergency and request immediate landing clearance. Over."

He was in a hurry, and declaring an in-flight emergency would ensure that he wouldn't have to waste time waiting to take his turn to land. Waiting was for people who had nothing better to do, and he had a lot on his plate right now. Bolan and Phoenix Force needed him back on station ASAP.

"DEA Six Niner Five," the tower answered. "This is Clayton Tower. Please state the nature of your emergency. Over."

"This is Six Niner Five. I have turbine surge, and the EG needle is pegged in the red. Over."

Turbine surge and the exhaust-gas temperature in the red was one of those problems that could quickly spell disaster. It was also very difficult to track down after you landed and looked at the engines. Simply changing out the fuel filters would make it go away, and no one would be the wiser.

"This is Clayton Tower. Roger. You are cleared to land on Helipad Zero Three. Turn to two-seven-three and begin descent now."

"Six Niner Five, roger."

With his declared emergency, Grimaldi didn't do anything spectacular. He just brought the twin-rotor machine in for a quick, safe landing.

DEA aircraft weren't uncommon visitors to the Army airfield. Since it was the only U.S. base between the United States and the cartel-controlled areas of Latin America, the drug agency based many of their aircraft there. Grimaldi was met by two MPs when he climbed down out of the chopper, but it wasn't a problem. He flipped open his wallet, flashed the DEA identification card that was a part of their original mission cover and he was welcomed.

After arranging to have his chopper serviced and

refueled, he set out to talk to the base commander to ask a big favor.

The Army colonel in charge of the airfield didn't have much contact with the DEA personnel who shared his facility, and was a bit curious when Grimaldi came calling.

"I'm part of the Green Ramparts operation, Colonel," the pilot explained as he showed his ID. "And you can really help us out if you will."

"How's that?"

"If you can see your way clear," the pilot said, "I really need to borrow some firepower from one of your armed helicopters. I've got some people on the ground in a situation where I need to be able to put out a little fire before I can get them out."

"These are Americans you're talking about, right?" the colonel inquired.

As a general rule, he didn't mind lending a hand whenever he could to the various governmental agencies who were working in Latin America. But past history had made him cautious about getting involved with operations that were sponsored by any of the local governments. More than one military career had been cut short over that.

"Yes, sir. They're as American as Mother's apple pie," Grimaldi replied, stretching the truth to the breaking point. "Every last one of them."

The colonel punched a button on his desk intercom. "Tell Chief Warrant Officer Blackstone that I'm sending a DEA Fed down to see him. He's to help him with anything the man needs just as long as it doesn't compromise our operational readiness.''

"I really appreciate this, Colonel." Grimaldi stuck his hand out.

The colonel shook his hand. "Anything to help you guys get the bastards."

Grimaldi still didn't know which particular set of bastards he was going to get. But with a little fire-power on board, he'd sure as hell get someone. "Believe me, sir, I'll do my best."

CHIEF WARRANT OFFICER Blackstone was an old hand at turning harmless, everyday helicopters into fire-spitting weapons of war. He'd started as a door gunner late in the Vietnam War and had continued practicing his trade through every brushfire conflict since then, including the Gulf War. Now there were dozens of ready-to-go armament systems specifically designed to be attached to helicopters. Even so, turning a Sea Stallion into a gunship was a new one, even for him.

"Let me see if I have this straight, mister," he said, eyeballing Grimaldi severely after hearing his request. "You want to arm this ship so you can fight it by yourself from the left-hand seat?"

"That's right, Chief, and call me 'Jack.' This 'mister' stuff makes me feel my age."

"Okay, Jack," the armament expert said. "I knew you DEA types have been running a bit shorthanded lately, but can't you guys even afford a copilot? You're going to be busier than a one-legged man in an ass-kicking contest trying to fly and fight that thing at the same time."

"I know, Chief, and that's why I need something simple. I was thinking of a single 7.62 mm minigun pod rigged to fire forward, and maybe a couple of 2.75-inch rocket pods, the eighteen-round ones."

"You've done this before."

Grimaldi smiled with quiet confidence. "As a matter of fact, Chief, I have."

Blackstone knew better than to take his questioning any further than that. In his experience, a lot of ex-Army gunship jockeys had signed on with the DEA because the drug agency offered them more live-fire time than the peacetime Army. Whoever this guy really was, he had obviously flown gunships at one time or the other.

"Okay," he said. "You know the drill, then. I'll mount a gunsight out of an Apache in front of the left seat and wire it to your cyclic."

"That's the way I like it." Grimaldi smiled. "And I'll be glad to show your boys exactly where to put it."

"Where's your ship?"

"It's being refueled."

"AND ONE OTHER THING?" Grimaldi asked Blackstone as soon as the weapons techs were busy bolting on the rocket pods.

"Name it."

"You wouldn't happen to have a couple of FAEs I could borrow, would you?"

As odd as arming a Sea Stallion was, this request was really off-the-wall. "And what do you need a Fuel Air Explosive bomb for, may I ask?"

Grimaldi shrugged. "I may need to clear a PZ before I can make my pickup."

Fuel Air Explosives had been developed during the Vietnam War exactly for that purpose. Ten-thousand-pound tanks of propane gas had been kicked out of C-130s flying low over the jungle and allowed to float down to earth on parachutes. A set distance above the jungle, an explosive charge would detonate, breaking open the tank and allowing the gas to settle to the ground. A flash charge would then detonate and the propane, by then mixed well with oxygen, would explode.

The results were spectacular. A "Daisy Cutter," as the FAE bombs were called, could blow a hole hundreds of yards wide in the densest triple-canopy jungle right down to bedrock.

"I'll need the altimeters set for 250 feet above ground level," the pilot explained. "And I'd like to have them hung on LAPES rigs."

"That's going to be cutting it a little close, isn't it?" the warrant officer asked.

LAPES, or Low Altitude, Parachute Extraction System, had been developed to deliver pallets of supplies when a plane couldn't safely land to off-load. The transport lowered its rear ramp and flew close to the runway without actually touching its wheels down. When the parachutes were popped, the supplies were jerked out of the rear of the plane and slammed right onto the runway. Grimaldi would be using the LAPES rigs to pull the FAE bombs out of the chopper at a higher altitude.

"You get a nice small LZ that way," Grimaldi replied.

The chief also knew that you also got a twenty-foot-deep crater in the ground the size of a city block at the same time. But if his DEA flying cowboy wanted to blast some drug lord's mountain hangout into oblivion, that was okay with him.

"You do know that you want to be at least two miles away from that thing when it goes off because of the shock wave, don't you?"

"Been there, Chief. Done that."

The warrant officer smiled. "It's your funeral, Jack. But if I were you, I'd drop from at least fifteen hundred feet above ground level and have that chopper of yours tached out at a 110 percent. Any less than that, and you're not going to be far enough away when that Daisy Cutter goes off. The shock wave can be a real mother."

"Thanks for the tip, Chief."

The two FAE bombs were rigged and loaded into the rear of the chopper right as the minigun and rocket pods were checked for the last time. The minigun had been mounted under the port-side door, and the Army ordnance techs had bolted a 50,000-round ammunition-feed system down to the floor plates. That sounded like a lot of firepower, but with the minigun blazing at full speed, 18,000 rounds per minute, even that amount of ammunition would run out in a few short minutes.

But if Grimaldi was light on the trigger, it should be enough to take care of whatever Phoenix Force had to deal with. If it wasn't, he always had the FAE bombs.

With a last wave of thanks to the ordnance men who had worked so hard to give him some teeth, Grimaldi strapped himself back into the helicopter. After cranking up and taxiing out to the runway, he used the Green Ramparts authority again and got instant clearance from the tower to take off. Minutes later, he had both turbines tached out as he flew southeast to Colombia. He didn't want to keep Bolan and Phoenix Force waiting.

Colombia

FATHER FULLERTON WAS in his dispensary making sure that his surgical instruments and bandages were ready for the wounded he knew would come if fighting broke out. The African-American commando had offered to help him care for any wounded if he had the time. But the priest feared that the worst would happen, and he wasn't prepared, nor was he supplied, to deal with battle casualties.

He had come to see that the commandos were good

men, and they were fighting the good fight against the destroyers. Nonetheless, he wished that they had never stumbled into the village. He wished them no harm, but they were men of violence and they had brought violence with them like a biblical plague that would sweep through his people, who didn't know war.

At least he had been able to get the village's children to a place of relative safety. They had all been sent up to the Thunderstone to take cover behind the ancient stone slabs that ringed it like a fence. The stones were as tall as a man and thick enough to stop a bullet, so they would be safe for the time being. What would happen to them if, or more likely when, El Machetero's men broke into the village was something that the priest didn't want to think about.

He knew that he badly wanted the commandos to win this fight and to kill El Machetero. In fact, even though he was well aware that it was a sin for him to pray for another's death, he had prayed that the mercenary would die.

Bursts of gunfire ringing out from the forest drew the priest's attention. Looking to the east, he saw the commandos and their Indian scout allies race for their fighting positions. The thing he had tried so hard to prevent was upon him.

Giving up a quick prayer for the safety of his people, he took cover in his dispensary.

EL MACHETERO HAD WAITED long enough, and the time had come to finally put an end to the Yankees.

All of his men were now in place around the village, and it was also time that they started to earn their pay. He had seen the defenses the Yankees had dug, and while they covered the best avenues of approach, they weren't impressive. A determined assault should take them with no difficulty. And he had no doubts that the men would be determined to get this over with as soon as possible. He had promised them the women of the village after it was captured.

"Go!" he transmitted over the radio.

Since the mercenaries didn't have any heavy weapons with them, the attack wasn't announced with the traditional mortar or artillery barrage. One minute all was calm, and the next, automatic-weapons fire from the tree line slashed across the open ground. The villagers raced for cover. An RPG rocket arched over the compound and detonated in front of one of the huts.

CHAPTER TWENTY-TWO

McCarter and Encizo shared a fighting position right in the middle of the mercenaries' main attack route. Their hastily dug fighting hole had an earthen berm in front, but little protection on the sides. Nonetheless, the two veterans got down to work. They were shooting in tandem, and their well-aimed single shots started taking a toll on the opposition.

Bolan and James had teamed up and they, too, poured single-shot fire into the tree line, saving the full-auto for the assault that was soon to come. Over the storm of gunfire, they could hear the mercenaries shouting to their men to charge.

With his leg still not a hundred percent, Hawkins had been given the job of watching the back door and providing what assistance he could from the center of the village. Finding cover around the edge of one of the huts, he started sending long-range fire into the tree line. He wasn't making every round count like Manning was with his Remington, but he wasn't too far behind.

Gary Manning had gotten permission from the Indians to position himself at the edge of the old stone enclosure around their sacred Thunderstone with his Remington 700 sniper's rifle. The range to the tree line was roughly four hundred yards, well within range. The only thing limiting his usefulness was the amount of 7.62 mm ammunition he had for the rifle, a little under forty rounds. But at that range, he should have no trouble making every round count.

Snuggling the butt of the rifle into his shoulder, he brought the scope to his eye. The first target that presented itself was a gunman in the U.S.-issue camouflage fatigues Manning had come to expect as the uniform of their tormentors. When the man's chest was centered in the scope's sight reticle, he squeezed off a round. The gunman spun from the impact and crumpled to the ground. That was one.

Normally Manning would have had a spotter working with him to point out the targets, but since they were so shorthanded, he was spotting for himself. Sweeping the edge of the tree line again, he spotted his next victim and dropped him, as well. That was two.

Suddenly there was a shout as two dozen men charged out of the woods. Manning got too busy to count his kills.

JUAN CHICINO HAD MOVED his fighters into position behind the ring of steel El Machetero had thrown around Father Fullerton's little village. It was going to be just like what had happened in his home village so many years earlier. The mercenary was going to kill the Yankees and then he would massacre the villagers. The Indians who lived there were much the way Chicino's people had been, and they wanted only to be left alone so they could live their simple lives in peace.

When he heard the firing begin, he ordered his men to attack the mercenaries from behind. There were only twenty-three guerrillas, but they could do a lot to even the odds if they could fight their way into the village and join up with the Americans. Even if they couldn't, every mercenary they could kill was one less who stood between him and his settling the score with his old guerrilla leader.

IN THE POSITIONS around the village, the Phoenix Force Warriors and the DEA scouts had their hands full. Even though the enemy was attacking across open ground, they simply couldn't kill them fast enough. In the initial rush, one of the scouts had been hit, and when his comrade in the next hole went to help him, he had been hit, as well, opening a gap in their thin perimeter.

The mercenaries spotted the gap and with a shout they headed for it, their weapons blazing. With so few guns on their side, the defenders didn't have any depth and they were in danger of being flanked if they didn't pull back to a tighter perimeter.

"Gary, T.J.," McCarter called urgently over the

com link. "We've got to fall back. Can you give us a little covering fire?"

"Roger," the sniper replied, training his scope in that direction and zeroing in on the gunman leading the charge. "The first one's coming up."

Although he had already used half of his ammunition, Manning burned through what he had left trying to break the assault. Saving the ammunition wouldn't do him any good if they got inside the village.

From his cover, Hawkins also started burning through his magazines.

IN THE LEFT-HAND SEAT of the Sea Stallion, Jack Grimaldi was flying to the rescue as fast as the roaring twin turbines could carry him. As he approached the village, he keyed his mike. "Striker, this is Flyboy, over," he radioed to Bolan on the DEA frequency,

"Striker, go," was Bolan's curt reply.

In the background, Grimaldi heard a storm of small-arms fire. Once more, he had arrived too late for the start of the party.

"I'm five miles out," the pilot answered. "Do you have a target for me? Over."

"You can shoot damned near anywhere around here and hit somebody," Bolan replied. "But come in from the north and work the east side of the clearing first. That will do us the most good right now."

"Roger, I'll call again before I make my run. Out."

EL MACHETERO HEARD the helicopter coming long before he saw it. Since he hadn't called for his own machine, this had to be an enemy ship. No one else would be flying in that part of the remote jungle. It further convinced him that the men who had fought their way into the village were some kind of rescue team that was looking for Phoenix Force, and they had called in the chopper.

Taking his field glasses from his pack, he scanned the sky for the aircraft and spotted it approaching the village. He knew that the big helicopter usually carried troops or cargo, but there couldn't be enough men in there to make any difference to the outcome of the battle. Even the Indians who had joined the Yankees weren't enough to make any difference. His men had forced them back into the confines of the village, and it was just a matter of time before they were overrun and wiped out.

Suddenly the chopper dived on his positions, and El Machetero saw the bulges of the rocket and mini-gun pods under its nose. The big aircraft had been rigged up as a gunship!

"Take cover!" he yelled, and the cry was taken up by the mercenaries. The problem was that there was little cover beyond that offered by the trees and underbrush.

"STRIKER, THIS IS Flyboy," Grimaldi radioed as he lined up for his attack run. "Get ready, 'cause here it comes."

"Roger, Flyboy," Bolan answered. "Go to it.

We're all close in, so anything outside the ville itself is a good target.''

"Roger, rolling in now."

Grimaldi peered through the jury-rigged gun sight bolted to the instrument panel in front of him. It wasn't the best installation he had ever seen, but it would serve his purposes well enough this day.

He had decided to attack with rockets first to break up the enemy concentrations, then work them over with the minigun on the second pass. Over the centuries, the Indians had kept the jungle around their village thinned out enough that he could catch glimpses of movement from the air. Lining up with the first of his targets, he pulled the trigger on his cyclic stick, and 2.75-inch rockets leaped from the pod in pairs. Trailing dirty white smoke, they screamed toward the jungle.

For this job, he'd had the armorers at Panama City fit the rockets with antipersonnel warheads. Similar to the Beehive rounds of the Vietnam War, these warheads detonated in the air, spraying deadly fléchettes in a cone in front of them. They worked best on troops out in the open, but he was confident that enough of the fléchettes would get through the jungle canopy to do some damage.

Nudging the cyclic control and the rudder pedals, Grimaldi kept the heavy aircraft on a steady path through the sky as he continued to fire the rockets. The puffs of dark gray smoke from the detonating warheads showed him that he was on target. Each puff marked the place where dozens of small, hardened steel darts were seeking a home in living flesh. Most of them ended their brief careers in the trees or the red earth of the jungle floor, but enough of them were finding glory in human flesh to justify their existence.

To guarantee that he could deliver his rockets accurately, Grimaldi was low enough to be within rifle-fire range. He had both turbines screaming at a 110 percent power, but the heavy chopper just wasn't as fast as a real gunship. Also it presented better than twice the target area of the smaller machines.

The worst thing was that his minigun armament wasn't turret mounted as it would have been on a real gunship. His gun pod was fixed to fire straight forward, and he couldn't swing it around to cover his flanks as he flew past the enemy positions. He also didn't have door gunners to fire to the side to keep the gunmen's heads down.

His pucker factor was high because he knew that there was no way that he was going to escape taking hits today. He just hoped that they didn't hit anything too important until he had delivered all of his ordnance on target. If he had to walk home after that, it was no big deal. He'd done that several times before.

ON THE GROUND, Phoenix Force and its allies watched the big helicopter approach on its gun run. The Indians had come out of hiding when they heard the sound of the aircraft's rotors. Before, they had only seen such flying machines in the distance, and never had they seen one that was spitting flame like the flying serpents of their ancient legends. This time, though, the flying monster was defending them from their enemies. Surely the gods had sent this machine to fight for their sacred Thunderstone.

McCarter saw the mercenaries head back for the cover of the trees and fired a couple of short bursts to hurry them along. Dropping back behind his berm, he dropped the magazine from his H&K and slapped a fresh one into place to get ready for the next attack.

GRIMALDI SAW the small lights winking at him from the jungle below and knew that they were the muzzle-flashes of AK-47s. The only good part of that was that the intermediate 7.62 mm ammunition the assault rifle fired wasn't the world's best antiaircraft round. But more than one Huey had gone down in Vietnam after being shot up with an AK-47.

Even though his ears were covered by the earphones in his helmet, he heard the sharp metallic thunks of full-metal-jacketed slugs punching their way through the thin aluminum skin of his aircraft.

He lifted his finger off the firing trigger and stomped down on the rudder pedal to throw the chopper into a skid. It threw his aim off, but it also took him out of the line of enemy fire for a moment.

By dumping his collective control and chopping his throttles, the rotors instantly lost lift and the helicopter abruptly fell from the sky. This was an old gunship move, but the chopper wasn't some hot-rod Cobra.

With the weight of the minigun ammunition and the two FAE bombs he was carrying in the back, the aircraft fell like a stone.

Slamming the throttles back on, he carefully fed in pitch on the collective to keep the rotors from stalling and trashing the transfer case. The renewed bite of the blades drew power like a cold start. The tachs showed that the turbines were on the verge of a flameout, and he was still falling. Gently feeding in more pitch and balancing it against his turbine rpm, Grimaldi played the laws of aerodynamics, rotary-wing version, like the master pilot that he was.

The ship's belly scraped the treetops before the rotors were spinning fast enough to generate enough lift to pull the heavy chopper back into the sky. Now that they were in sync with the turbines, the pilot twisted the throttle back up against the stop and went back to killing the mercenaries in the jungle.

JUAN CHICINO AND his men had fought their way almost to the western edge of the village when the helicopter started its first gun run. Most of their kills had been silent, as his men were skilled with knives and garrotes. But with the storm of small-arms fire echoing through the forest, the mercenaries had hardly noticed the odd shot or two from behind them. Now, with the helicopter forcing the mercenaries to keep their heads down, he motioned for his men to break through and run for the village.

"Father Juan!" Chicino shouted in Spanish as he

approached the perimeter. "We have come to help you!"

The priest heard his shout and, when he recognized Chicino, he realized that his prayers had been answered. He hadn't known that this roving band had even been in the vicinity. One of the reasons that Father Fullerton's village had escaped much of the predation that so many of the other small villages in the mountains had suffered was that Chicino's people roamed the jungle around them and kept most of the intruders away.

"Hurry, Juan," the priest shouted. "Help the Yankees. There are only a few of them."

"HEADS UP!" McCarter snapped out over the com link as he spun to face the new threat. "Behind us!"

"They're friendlies," Bolan immediately sent back. "The priest is with them."

McCarter didn't have time to sort them out now, but if they were on their side, they were welcome. With two of Bolan's scouts down, they needed all the help they could get. "Try to get them to reinforce the northern side of the perimeter."

Bolan ran over to the man who seemed to be in charge of the ragtag band. "Have you come to help?" he asked in Spanish.

When the man nodded, Bolan pointed to the perimeter defenses they had abandoned earlier. "Put your men over there."

"*Sí, señor.*"

Even with Grimaldi doing his best with his make-shift gunship, this wasn't over yet. They were going to have to do a lot more killing before they convinced El Machetero to give it up.

CHAPTER TWENTY-THREE

At the end of his firing run, Grimaldi climbed high enough to get above the range of small-arms fire.

"Striker," he radioed down to Bolan, "this is Fly-boy. Are you ready for another one?"

"Bring it on down," Bolan replied. "This time, though, you'd better get a grip on that thing. If you put it in the trees, we won't be able to come out and get you. Over."

"The same thought occurred to me. Where do you want me to put it this time?" Grimaldi asked.

"Did you see our fighting positions on the northern edge of the clearing?"

"Roger," Grimaldi replied. It was a hell of a note when a few shallow foxholes scraped into the red earth had to pass for fighting positions.

"Put it about a hundred yards in front of that."

"Coming at ya, and I'll be using the minigun this time."

Kicking down on the rudder pedals, Grimaldi snapped the tail around and pointed his nose toward the jungle. When he had the target area in his sight reticle, his finger lightly stroked the firing trigger for the minigun.

Over the roar of the turbines and the carrier-wave hiss of the radio in his earphones, he heard the heavy ripping-canvas sound of the minigun spitting flame. The electrically driven weapon fired so fast that it didn't even sound like a machine gun.

Each of the short bursts, no more than three seconds in duration, sent hundreds of 7.62 mm slugs chewing into the jungle. Grimaldi kicked the rudder pedals from side to side as he triggered the minigun, zigzagging the fire to cut a broad swath. As had been the case with the fléchettes he had fired earlier, most of the slugs ended up drilling into the trees or the dirt. But with thousands and thousands of rounds falling, the jungle was being chewed to bits as if it were being worked over by a giant buzz saw. Chunks of leaves, small branches and splinters of wood fell like rain.

This time there was hardly any return fire from the mercenaries. It took more than a brave man to stand up in the face of a snarling minigun. It took someone who simply didn't understand what was going on all around him. The jungle was being torn apart, and any man who got caught up in the storm of lead rain was going to get shredded, too.

ONCE HE WAS SAFE again above the range of ground fire, Grimaldi took the time to tighten the fingers of both of his flying gloves. Now that he had fired all of his 2.75-inch rockets and most of his minigun ammunition, it was time to get serious with the enemy. And to successfully pull off the little maneuver he was going to try next, he didn't need his hand slipping at the wrong moment.

"Striker," he radioed, "I'm almost out of ammo. All I have left is a few thousand rounds of minigun. From up here, it looks like they've pulled back several hundred yards, but they're still in position to block you if you try to withdraw. How does it look from down there? Over."

"We can't see too far into the wood line from down here," Bolan answered. "But I don't think that they're going to give it up. They'll just wait for you to leave and then come back at us."

"Roger," Grimaldi answered. "That's the way I see it, and if all of you can find some real good cover down there, I have a big surprise for them. I have a couple of Daisy Cutters sitting on the rear ramp."

Bolan knew the FAE bombs and the destruction they caused. He also knew that they were usually dropped from faster aircraft that had a better chance of getting away from their blast effect. "Are you sure about doing that, Jack? You've got a slow bird this time."

"I got it covered," the pilot replied, sounding confident. "I'm ready to deliver them if you need them."

Bolan made the decision instantly. "Give me five minutes to get everyone under cover," he replied.

"Roger. Call me when you're ready."

GRIMALDI WENT into a wide orbit over the village to give the men on the ground time enough to get behind something that could withstand the blast that was coming. The Indians would lose most of their huts, which would never stand up to the shock wave. But they were easy to rebuild and the villagers would be alive to do it, which they wouldn't be if the mercenaries had their way.

While he loitered in the sky, Grimaldi went over the procedure for his third act. Dropping an FAE bomb from an aircraft was usually considered a team event. But since he was the pilot, copilot, bombardier and kicker all rolled up in one, he was going to be a busy lad for the next few minutes.

A column of smoke rising from a burning hut gave him the direction and strength of the ground winds. Since he would be dropping the bomb from a fairly low altitude, he didn't need to worry about the winds higher up. The FAE bomb's altimeter had been set for 250 feet above ground level, and he decided to allow himself only three thousand feet above that and hope that would be high enough to keep him out of the worst of the shock wave. Since he didn't have a bomb sight, any higher than that and he couldn't guarantee hitting the target.

"Flyboy, this is Striker," Bolan radioed. "We're set down here. But don't miss the target with that damned thing."

Grimaldi laughed. "I'll try hard not to."

"You'd better try real hard. We don't have the best cover in the world down here."

"Roger, copy."

Taking the wind and his speed into consideration, he headed out over his target. "I'm rolling in on my bomb run," Grimaldi warned Bolan.

"Bombs away!" Grimaldi radioed as he pulled sharply on the nylon cord that was tied to the D-ring on the LAPES rig of the port-side FAE bomb.

Pulling the D-ring released the spring-loaded pilot chute and shot it out into the chopper's slipstream. When the chute billowed open, it pulled the three bigger cargo canopies out of their packs. A split second later, the cargo chutes were fully open and their combined drag jerked the FAE canister past the friction locks and out of the rear of the chopper.

The instant Grimaldi felt that the FAE had been pulled out of the rear ramp, he dropped the nose of his ship slightly and ran his rpms up to the limit. With the weight reduced, the chopper immediately picked up speed and was flying at a little over two hundred miles per hour. When this mission was over, both of the aircraft's turbines would need replacing. But Uncle Sam could afford it, and it would be money well spent.

Behind him, the large gray FAE canister floated to the jungle on its trio of forty-eight-foot cargo parachutes. When the altimeter indicated that the jungle floor was 250 feet below, it tripped the detonator to the propane tank's bursting charge. The shaped charge detonated, cutting through the steel-walled tank. Released of the pressure that had kept the propane in a liquid form, it flashed into a dense gas.

Though it was a colorless gas, the propane descended on the jungle like a thick, dome-shaped fog because it was denser than the surrounding air. But unlike fog, it descended in a mass instead of dissipating. It did, however, mix with oxygen on the way down, creating an explosive cloud some 150 yards across.

When the bottom of the dome-shaped cloud touched the ground, a second flash charge detonated to set off a nonnuclear explosive whose power was awesome beyond belief.

A searing light as bright as the sun flashed into being in the jungle, followed by a roiling ball of orange-red flame. From a distance, the fireball would have appeared to be a flattened dome.

Immediately following the flash, a deafening thunderclap echoed off the hills surrounding the valley, announcing the blast.

The shock wave tore through the jungle at supersonic speed, the force so great that it uprooted trees that had withstood tropical storms for centuries. Six-foot-thick trunks snapped like matchsticks as the blast scoured the jungle down to bedrock.

The mercenaries who had been at ground zero of the blast were simply vaporized; nothing of them would ever be found. Those who were farther away were crushed to death in an instant as their chests collapsed from the pressure of the shock wave. Their flattened corpses were then ground to bits along with the chunks of trees and brush.

Those who were far enough away to be out of the immediate ring of destruction simply had their eardrums popped, and they bled from their eyes, nose and ears.

The shock wave also blasted into the sky, driving the air before it like a supersonic hammer blow. Grimaldi felt as though he was riding a runaway bucking horse when the wave front hit him. He had turned the nose of his ship away from the blast, and it drove the tail of his chopper up at a dangerous angle. As he fought to bring the aircraft under control, he glanced down at the airspeed indicator and saw that he had picked up an extra sixty miles per hour.

Since the rotors were already spinning beyond their maximum design speed, he chopped his throttle to keep from overrevving the turbines and trashing the transfer cases. This was no time for him to end with his nose down in the dirt.

Once Grimaldi had regained complete control of his helicopter, he ran an instrument check to see if the turbines or rotors had suffered any damage from the shock wave. Everything looked to be in the green, but he climbed up into an orbit over the village to make sure he could still fly.

One of the characteristics of FAE bombs was that they sent a small mushroom-shaped cloud into the sky. This time, though, since the earth that had been caught up in the blast was so moist, the cloud quickly dissipated. When the smoke and dust settled, Grimaldi saw that a three-hundred-yard crater had been blasted out of the red earth where the trees and brush had been. The hole wasn't all that deep, but it had been scoured completely bare of foliage. Ringing the crater was a twenty-foot-tall wall of tangled tree trunks and branches forming an impenetrable barrier.

Nothing inside that perimeter could have survived, and not much for five hundred yards around it would have remained undamaged.

The mercenary threat was over.

EL MACHETERO WAS fortunate not to have been at ground zero. He had been close enough to it, however, that the concussion had picked him up and thrown him against a tree as if he was a rag doll. Again his luck was strong because he didn't break any bones.

When he staggered to his feet, he stared in shock at the mushroom-shaped cloud that rose high over the top of the jungle. Not knowing that the FAE's characteristic cloud wasn't the sign of a nuclear blast, he panicked. If the Yankees were using nuclear weapons against him, all was lost and Jordan had betrayed him.

The men who had been at his command post with him were also stunned and in shock. Those who had survived without major injuries dropped their weapons and started running blindly. Others with broken arms and legs started to crawl away as fast as they could.

In an instant, El Machetero had lost his army, and there was nothing left for him to do but run, as well.

BOLAN WATCHED the smoke column rise from the place that marked the spot where Grimaldi had dropped his Daisy Cutter. He knew what he would find if he went to the blast area. Any of the gunmen left alive would be bleeding from their eyes, ears and nose from the blast. They would be half-blind and unable to hear. They would no longer be a threat, and even those who had been on the other side of the perimeter away from the blast effects would be in no mood to carry on the battle.

Once more, airpower had decided the outcome of a ground battle.

The villagers were completely stunned and had no idea what had caused the unbelievable noise they had just heard and the storm that had followed it. In all of their experience, they had never seen or heard anything like the tremendous explosion that had rocked the hills. Even in their tribal lore, the only thing like it had been the arrival of their Thunderstone so many generations earlier. According to the stories that had been handed down, it had also arrived with a blast that had torn the jungle away.

If the gods had announced the arrival of the sacred rock with a ground-shaking blast, maybe they had sent this explosion, too. No other explanation fit their limited view of the world.

"Are we going to go out there and do a BDA?" McCarter asked as he brushed mud and bits of shredded vegetation from his uniform.

"I'll let Jack do the bomb-damage assessment for

us,'' Bolan replied. ''But we're going out there to see if we can find this El Machetero.''

''Do you think he survived?'' McCarter asked as his eyes swept the tangled remains of the jungle. He, too, knew the damage an FAE bomb could do both to living flesh and to the forest.

''I don't know,'' Bolan admitted. ''But if he did, and if he's in any condition to talk, we need to interrogate him. He wasn't waiting for you guys by accident, and we need to know who he was working for when he tried to kill you.''

''You've got a point there.''

''We going in there after El Machetero?'' James asked when he and the others walked up.

''Yeah,'' Bolan replied. ''But T.J., I want you to stay here with the priest and the wounded scouts in case any of them stumble this way.''

''I owe the bastard,'' Hawkins reminded him. ''I want him taken down.''

''We all do,'' McCarter said. ''And we'll bring him back if he's still alive.''

Hawkins wasn't the only one who wanted to make sure that El Machetero went down. Juan Chicino had an even bigger stake in seeing the guerrilla dead at his feet. He turned to Encizo and said, ''My men will help you find El Machetero. We have hunted for him for a long time.''

''I need him alive,'' Bolan warned.

''He has to die for what he has done,'' Chicino said, his dark eyes locked on Bolan's face. Though he tried to stare the gringo down, he had to look away after a few seconds.

"I'll give him to you after we have learned what we need to know," Bolan promised him.

"Okay," Chicino answered in English. Whoever this gringo was, he wasn't a man to be crossed.

CHAPTER TWENTY-FOUR

It took El Machetero half an hour to get away from
the tangled wreckage the bomb had created. Once he
was in the clear, he ran through the forest like an animal being pursued. And like an animal, he was blind
to anything but his personal survival. In all of his years
as a jungle fighter, he had never suffered a defeat like
this.

He had always been able to slip away from ambushes by superior forces and steer clear of fights he
knew that he couldn't win. His reputation as a successful guerrilla fighter had been built by carefully
picking his battles. But no man could win against the
kind of overwhelming force the Yankees had unleashed on him.

As he ran, he steadily cursed the man he knew as
James Jordan. In his mind, the Yankee had knowingly
set him up to be killed. Only a tactical nuclear weapon
could have caused that much damage, and he knew
that the use of such weapons had to be approved at
the highest level of the American government. He
didn't stop to ask himself why the Americans would

want to use such a weapon to kill him. He was a legend in his own mind, and his ego didn't allow for such rational thinking even on a good day, and this was the worst day of his life.

As he desperately fled deeper into the jungle, all the man could think was that Jordan had lied to him, and that thought drove him on. When he reached safety, he would find a way to get his revenge on the treacherous gringo. Even if he had to go to Washington, the man would die, and El Machetero vowed that he would take a very long time doing it.

BOLAN'S DEA SCOUTS quickly found where El Machetero had orchestrated the attack on the village. His radios, a map and the remains of a meal showed the site to be his jungle CP. One man lay dead, speared through the chest by a splintered branch driven into him at bullet speed. Another man, though both of his legs were broken, was still alive.

After the scouts splinted his legs and gave him a drink of water, the wounded mercenary was more than willing to tell the scouts where his ex-leader had gone. The famous El Machetero had fled like a rabbit without even trying to help him, so he owed him no loyalty.

"'The Coward,'" the wounded man growled, "is more like it. He took one look at what you did to us and he ran." He pointed to the southwest. "You should have no trouble following him. He was crashing through the brush like a bull in heat."

Heading in the direction they had been given, the scouts soon picked up the trail of one man traveling alone. Like the wounded mercenary had said, this man was running blindly, so they took up his trail.

BY THE END of the third mile of his run, El Machetero was exhausted. Running in panic through everything in his path instead of carefully picking his way through the dense vegetation had sapped his strength. He staggered to a halt, gasping for breath, and went down to his knees. He was reaching for the canteen hung from his belt when he felt a sharp, sudden pain in the middle of his right hand.

Looking down, he stared in horror at the blackened tip of a native blowgun dart sticking out from the palm of his hand. Already the cold numbness of the poison was spreading to his fingers. His only chance to live was to cut off his hand to keep the poison from spreading up his arm and to his chest. When it reached his chest, it would paralyze his muscles and he would die of suffocation.

With a cry of rage, he reached his left hand over his shoulder for the long knife slung behind his back. Holding his right wrist against the trunk of the tree, he awkwardly drew the machete back as far as he could in his left hand. Giving a strangled cry, he swung the blade with all his strength.

The meaty sound of the blade chopping through his wrist sounded loud in his ears. The blade felt ice cold for an instant before the nerves of his severed wrist could react to having been severed.

Then he screamed again as raw pain washed over his arm.

Falling to his knees, he jammed the spurting stump against his leg as he reached his left hand down to his boot to strip the lace from it. Though the poison was gone, he would bleed to death if he couldn't bind the wound. When the boot lace was free, he quickly bound the stump and the bleeding slowed to a slow drip. Reaching into his side pocket, he pulled out a small flare and ignited it. As an old jungle warrior, he knew the cleansing power of flame.

He whimpered against the pain as he passed the flame of the flare over the raw stump. The stench of burning flesh, his burning flesh, filled his lungs and he retched. Choking it back, he gritted his teeth and finished cauterizing the stump. At the end of the ordeal, he fell back against the tree and fought to catch his breath.

Through his blurred vision, he saw the shapes of green men rise from the jungle and approach him. He reached his left hand for the pistol on his belt, but when one of the Indians raised his blowgun in warning, he froze. From the pain in his arm, he could tell that he had rid himself of the poison with the amputation. Had he not been successful, there would be no pain, only a feeling of creeping numbness. But one more poison dart, particularly one to the chest, would finish him.

EL MACHETERO'S SCREAMS had guided Phoenix Force to his location. They approached cautiously, halting only when they saw a dozen near naked, green-painted Indians who stood in a loose circle around the wounded mercenary. When they saw that El Machetero was no threat, they turned their attention to the Indians.

"Who are these guys?" McCarter asked.

The Indians looked like they had stepped out of a TV special on Stone Age tribes in the twentieth century. These were small, dark men wearing little more than loincloths and a few feathers. Their bare skin had been painted with some kind of green paste that blended in perfectly with the background colors of the jungle. Some of them carried bows longer than they were tall, with feathered arrows almost as long. Others were armed with blowguns designed to shoot poisoned darts. The weapons were primitive, but they were effective in the jungle. The Indians had been defending their homelands with them for centuries.

When Juan Chicino saw that El Machetero had somehow lost his right hand, he rushed over to meet the Indians. After speaking with them for several minutes, he turned back to Encizo and Bolan.

"What's the story on those lads?" McCarter asked. The muzzle of his rifle was down, but his hand was on the pistol grip ready to bring it into play.

Chicino seemed a little preoccupied as Encizo put the question in Spanish. "I have never seen those people before,'' Chicano answered. ''But they say that they have come to defend the Thunderstone.''

''How did they hear that it was endangered?''

''I don't know.''

The lead scout then walked over to the bowmen and started to talk. Much of his communication was carried on through hand gestures, but he seemed to be getting through.

''Take a look at this,'' James said as he kneeled beside the wounded man. ''I think he cut off his own hand.''

The blanched hand lay palm up beside the bloody machete. The dark point of the poison dart showed plainly in the middle of the curled fingers.

When one of the scouts saw the severed hand, he motioned for James to leave it alone. The poison was still active and would stay that way until the rain dissolved it.

''What are they going to do now?'' McCarter asked when the scout came back.

''They say that they are finished with El Machetero. They are going to go into the jungle, find the rest of the soldiers and drive them off.''

''Tell them to be careful,'' Bolan cautioned. ''Guns can shoot a lot farther than those bows of theirs.''

The scout grinned. ''They know all about guns,'' he said. ''They've been killing men with guns since the Spaniards came long ago.''

Bolan knew that to be more than bravado. Indian bows had proved to be more than a match for the matchlocks of the Spanish conquistadors. "You've got a point there."

As silently as they had come, the Indians disappeared back into the jungle.

"Let's cut a couple of poles," Bolan said, "and make a litter to get him back to the village. I want to have the priest take a look at his arm before we transport him."

FATHER FULLERTON HAD DONE all he could do with his limited resources to clean up the stump of El Machetero's right arm. The intense heat of the flare he had used to cauterize the wound had left a serious burn. But if it didn't get infected, it should heal cleanly.

"Will he live?" Bolan asked the priest.

The man shrugged. "He is still in shock now, but he should recover. His hand, of course..."

He had prayed for this man's death, but had instead ended up saving his life. Looking at the feared El Machetero now, he didn't see the devil incarnate. He just saw a wounded man with a stump where his right hand should have been. Once more, he had been given a lesson in God's will. This time, though, the Almighty had used a band of commandos to impose his will.

"We'll be flying him out of here soon," Bolan said, "and I'll see that he gets any more treatment he needs. Also, I'll see what I can do to get your clinic some medical supplies. I have contacts who support medical missionaries, and I'll see what I can do to get you regular deliveries.''

"That would be very helpful," the priest said gratefully.

"I figure we owe it to you for what happened here. It's the least we can do for all your help."

While the priest had been tending his unwanted patient, Juan Chicino's men had returned to the village and reported that the surviving mercenaries were still on the run, trying to escape to the west. Chicino himself had stayed with the wounded El Machetero, not willing to take his eyes off of him for a second. He might have lost his right hand, but as long as he still had his left, he couldn't be trusted.

"What are you going to do with him?" Chicino asked when James and Manning came to take the litter to the chopper. "You said that I could have him after you talked to him."

"I'm not done talking to him yet," Bolan said, "and I want to get him to a place where he can get medical treatment. He's no good to me dead."

"Then I am coming with you."

"That's okay with me," Bolan replied. "Our first stop will be Fort Apache so I can take the scouts back and get him looked at."

DAVE NESBIT WAS relieved to see Bolan step off Grimaldi's chopper. He hadn't had any communication with the mystery man since he had "borrowed" his scouts and disappeared into the jungle. The men who filed off the aircraft after him had to be the commando team he had gone to find. They didn't quite look like a DEA field team; they looked more like the Anglo mercenaries who went from job to job in the region fighting for anyone who would pay them. But considering the secrecy of Green Ramparts, who knew what kind of men they had working for them? Maybe they had signed up hired guns for their classified operations.

"I see that you recovered your team, Mr. Belasko," he greeted Bolan.

"Thanks in large part to your scouts. But I'm afraid that I got two of them shot up a bit. Neither one of them is hurt too badly, though. Give them a week or so off, and they'll be fine."

"If I give everyone who gets shot around here a week off," Nesbit said, grinning, "I won't have anyone left. I just give them a bonus payment when they're well enough to go back to duty, and they use it to get drunk."

Bolan laughed. "Well why don't you let me finance a small celebration for all five of them and pass the rest of it to their families? I owe them."

"Will do," Nesbit said, but his attention was drawn to the stretcher being taken out of the back of the chopper. Belasko hadn't mentioned any other casualties. The man lying on the stretcher looked very familiar, but Nesbit was having trouble placing him.

"Have you ever heard of a man called El Machetero?'' Bolan asked when he saw the frown on the DEA man's face.

"I sure as hell have." Nesbit was stunned. "Is that him?" El Machetero was a major bogeyman in this part of Latin America, responsible for hundreds of deaths in half a dozen countries. No one had been able to bring him to justice.

"That's him."

"What happened to his hand?"

"He took an Indian blowgun dart in the hand, so he cut it off to keep the poison from spreading."

Nesbit shuddered. He well knew how effective the Indians' nerve poison was. Though it was derived from the secretions of a tiny tree frog, it was considered to be one the most deadly of all of the natural toxins.

"Jesus! I wouldn't wish that on anyone."

"At least he's alive," Bolan replied. "This operation isn't over yet, and he's the key to wrapping it up."

"Is there anything I can do to help?"

"I need your medic to pump him full of antibiotics and give him a bag of Ringer's solution if you have it. I need to be able to talk to him as soon as possible."

Nesbit turned to the men with the litter. "Follow me."

WHEN BOLAN AND ENCIZO went to the outpost's medic bunker, they found El Machetero having his wound seen to a second time while being given antibiotics in a glucose IV drip. He was still pale from shock and loss of blood, but he was alert, so they started to interrogate him. Like the wounded man he had left behind at his CP in the woods, the mercenary was more than willing to talk about his having been betrayed by the man he knew as James Jordan. He also knew that in Washington his contact's name was Geoffrey Whitworth and that he was the director of communications of the CIA.

As Encizo translated what the mercenary said, Bolan took notes. The story wasn't a new one to him. The CIA had made pacts with various devils in their fight against the Communist guerrillas in Latin America. He was surprised, however, at how extensive Whitworth's contacts were. His network of corruption extended throughout Central America and touched the legitimate governments, as well as the drug lords and the revolutionary factions.

El Machetero wasn't too clear on why Whitworth had wanted him to kill the men of Phoenix Force, but as the story unfolded, there was no doubt that he had. There was no chance of getting to Whitworth as long as he was in his impregnable CIA office, and getting him out of the country wasn't going to be easy. But Bolan had the perfect bait to draw him into a kill zone in Colombia—El Machetero himself.

Now that he knew about the ''James Jordan'' persona Whitworth had used for his Latin American operations, it should be easy to reel him in. Geoffrey Whitworth's name was barely known outside of the halls of Langley, and no one would know him as James Jordan. But a message sent to his nom de guerre would get his immediate attention. The hard part had been getting Jordan's American E-mail address out of El Machetero. Now that Bolan had it, though, he knew exactly how to use it.

In his rambling story of his association with Whitworth, El Machetero had mentioned that the CIA renegade maintained a safehouse in the Pacific coast town of Cartagena, Colombia. It would be easy enough for them to fly there and send him an E-mail message that should get him out of Langley. There was something about an electronic message that caused it to be taken at face value, particularly when it was sent from the right place.

Even though El Machetero's recitation showed that Jordan was a cautious man, he would see that the message had originated in Cartagena and would tend to believe it was authentic. Human nature dictated that.

CHAPTER TWENTY-FIVE

Washington, D.C.

Geoffrey Whitworth didn't have to wait long for the return call from his surveillance teams canvasing the city. Able Team had been tracked to a motel in the suburbs, room 219. Along with the report came faxed photos of the motel grounds, shots of the outside of the room and a section of a city map showing the access routes.

After studying the package, he punched in a fax number and sent the information to the leader of the wet team he had borrowed from the cartel. That was the biggest benefit of operating in cyberspace—it provided him with the perfect cutout. He had never met these men and wouldn't know them if he saw them, nor would they know him.

He followed up the faxes with an E-mail message indicating when and how he wanted the job done. They were to take a kilo of coke, drug scales, plastic bags and the rest of the window dressing of a drug dealer with them to plant in the room. Making the scene look like a gang hit would ensure that the police didn't look into the incident too closely. Most of the homicides in the Washington area were connected to the drug trade in one way or another.

As soon as he received his confirmation from the Colombians that they knew what to do and where to do it, he went down to the gym in the basement of the building for his scheduled workout. He generally exercised three times a week, and it wouldn't do for him to break his routine. The director of communications for the CIA was known to be a methodical man and a stickler for detail. Plus, a good workout was an effective way to relieve the stress.

A LITTLE AFTER ten o'clock that night, the Colombian known as Rizo sat in the front passenger seat of the four-door sedan that had brought him and his three gunmen to a cheap motel in the D.C. suburbs. His driver was in the motel's office talking to the desk clerk.

The car was parked away from the brightly lit office with the lights off to be as inconspicuous as possible. In California, a cruising cop car would check them out as a suspicious vehicle. But in the D.C. area, as long as they weren't dragging a dead body or a naked woman into the car, no one really cared.

The driver returned and slid in behind the wheel. "The clerk said that they're in 219, just like we were told," he said in Spanish.

"Did he identify them?"

The driver nodded. "Two of them."

"Did you silence the clerk?"

"Of course." The driver sounded almost offended. "And I took all of the money so it will look like a robbery."

"Good. Now, pull up right next to the stairs so we don't have to run to get to the car when this is over."

Once they were parked again, Rizo stepped out and looked up at the open walkway in front of the second-floor rooms. He didn't like doing second-floor jobs, as the only way in to the target room was through the door. But this wasn't a job he could refuse. He and his three men had been sent to D.C. with orders to do anything that this Mr. Jordan told them to do. As was the cartel custom, before Rizo had left Colombia, he had been warned about the consequences of failure.

After silently checking their weapons, the four men climbed the stairs, their rubber-soled shoes making no noise on the concrete steps. As they approached room 219, none of the four gunmen saw the small video cameras Schwarz had installed in the ceiling of the covered walkway to look down on both sides of the passage in front of the room. They also didn't see the microphone attached to the corner of the room's big window facing the walkway.

"COMPANY'S COMING," Schwarz hissed. "At least four of them."

He didn't have to say which way they were coming from because there was only one avenue of approach to the motel room—right through the front door. There was also the picture window in the same wall that looked out over the parking lot, but the inclination would be for them to come through the door.

Blancanales reached out and flipped the TV remote control to the comedy channel and turned up the volume. The hit men would hear happy sounds coming from the room and assume that the occupants were completely unaware of what was coming at them.

Schwarz grabbed his weapon and flicked it off safety. His CAR-15 had been fitted with a 100-round snail drum magazine. But at 600 rounds per minute, that was only ten seconds' worth of 5.56 mm ammo. If ten seconds wasn't enough, they were in deeper trouble than they thought. Fastening his Kevlar bulletproof vest at the neck, he took his position behind the heavy wooden desk.

Lyons flicked the safety off of his SPAS-12 assault shotgun and took cover around the edge of the bathroom door. The interior walls in the room were drywall and didn't offer much protection, so his Kevlar bulletproof vest would have to soak up any strays that came his way.

Blancanales had the point, as it were. He was positioned behind the bed directly in the line of fire from the doorway. He had the mattresses from both of the beds bunched up in front of him to soak up rounds and had his vest zipped all the way up.

Schwarz readied a flash-bang grenade with the fuse

set for one second and held it in his left hand ready to toss.

RIZO AND TWO of the gunmen took their places to the left of the door while the fourth man readied his heavy police-style door opener. When Rizo nodded, one blow from the twenty-pound ram snapped the door open as if it had a bungee cord attached to it.

"Grenade!" Schwarz yelled, and the trio shielded their eyes from the sudden flash of too bright light.

The flash-bang stunned the attackers, but they fired blindly through the open door.

The roar of Lyons's SPAS-12 was deafening in the small room, but its bite was far worse than its bark. The first blast of Magnum buckshot ripped through the foam-core door and tore into the gunman hiding behind it. He staggered out and got a long burst of 5.56 mm lead from Schwarz's subgun.

Blancanales's H&K took care of the man with the door ram. He didn't even have enough time to bring his weapon into play before his chest was torn open with a burst of 9 mm slugs. Return fire chewed up the mattresses in front of Blancanales, but the double thickness was enough to soak up the lead and none of it got through.

A blast from Lyons's assault shotgun took care of the third gunman, the double-aught buckshot almost eviscerating his torso.

Rizo tried to turn to run, but Schwarz's blazing

CAR-15 caught him in midstride and almost cut him in two.

It was over before Schwarz even had a chance to use up more than half his magazine. One of the attackers had made it all the way into the room, one was lying halfway through the door and the other two were littering the walkway outside.

"I GUESS WHITWORTH got our message," Schwarz said as he rolled the body on the floor over with one boot. Like the other three corpses, this recently deceased appeared to be Hispanic and he was dressed just differently enough to mark him as a newcomer to the United States, not a native or a long-time immigrant.

"These clowns sure aren't CIA," Blancanales announced. "They look more like cartel or Mob thugs to me."

"My bet is cartel." Lyons pointed. "Look at their clothes. No self-respecting wiseguy would be caught dead wearing green pants."

"Whoever the hell they were," Schwarz said, reaching for the laptop he had stashed out of harm's way under the bed, "we need to evacuate the premises before the cops show up. I don't think our get-out-of-jail-free cards will work for us this time."

"Let's do it."

Bailing out quickly was something they could do in their dreams, given all the practice they'd had. Schwarz was the last one to reach the van because he'd had to take down his surveillance gear. It wouldn't do for the local cops to find his toys.

They were pulling onto the street when they saw the first cop car round the corner, lights flashing and siren wailing. "These guys have a pretty good response time," Lyons said approvingly.

"They should," Schwarz said, being careful to keep his speed well within the limit. "They sure get enough practice at it."

"Now where?" Blancanales asked as he watched the cop car pull into the motel behind them.

"Let's find another motel in the area. Then I'll need a pay phone to give our man Whitworth a call."

"Are you out of your freaking mind?" Schwarz asked. "In case you took a blow to the head and are suffering from a short-term memory loss, that bastard just sent his side boys to kill us."

"That's my point," Lyons said calmly. "I want to let him know where to go to pick up his boys. He might want to send them home for decent burial."

"Jesus wept, Carl."

"My thought exactly," Lyons said. "I'm sure that even though our visitors were cartel hit men, deep inside they were good Catholics and would appreciate receiving the last rites of the church."

Schwarz just shook his head.

"And somewhere along the way, we need to find a post office that's open at this time of night. I know there's a couple of late-hour branches in this town. We need to send the Farm another priority letter. I need to tell Barbara that we've confirmed Whitworth as our man, and if we mail it tonight, they'll get it in the morning.''

GEOFFREY WHITWORTH was awakened from a sound sleep by the ringing of the phone on the nightstand. "Whitworth," he said as he picked up.

"There's been a shoot-out at a D.C. motel," a voice he didn't recognize said. "I thought you might be interested in knowing that."

Whitworth sat bolt upright in bed. "Who is this?"

The line went dead.

Putting the phone back down, he turned to the security-system control panel installed by the head of his bed. Everything was in the green. It took a second for him to realize from the readout on his answering machine that the call had been forwarded from the mobile unit in his car instead of having been placed directly to his classified home number. After duty hours, when he wasn't in his car, his mobile phone went on standby and his calls were automatically forwarded to his unlisted number.

That could only mean that Able Team had somehow been able to ferret out his mobile phone number.

Reaching for the phone again, he quickly placed a call to the cellular phone of the CIA agent who was heading the team that had tracked Able Team to the motel. "This is Whitworth," he said. "I just got a call about a shoot-out at the motel. I want you to look into it and get back to me ASAP."

"Yes, sir."

Even though he had made the call, Whitworth knew

what his surveillance team was going to find at the motel. They were going to find a half a dozen D.C. cop cars, ambulances, the medics and the medical examiner. The objects of their attention would be the bodies of the four Colombians he had sent to take out Able Team.

Whitworth then did something alien to his nature. He came to the conclusion that he had made a mistake. There was no doubt that he had seriously underestimated Able Team, and he was beginning to think that he might have made a mistake with Phoenix Force, as well. His hatred for the Stony Man operation had blinded him to the reality of the situation, and now that Able Team was onto him, he needed to reevaluate his options.

So far, he had been able to run the operation from his office at Langley without having to get personally involved. As the director of communications, it had been easy for him to enlist the aid of several computer techs to use the clipper chip to intercept Stony Man's communications and to plant the false data that had sent Phoenix Force to the jungles of Colombia and Able Team to northern Mexico.

He had spent enough time in the field, however, to know that there were those times when the leader had to lead in person. That time had come now. He would join his surveillance teams and make sure that they got back in contact with Able Team. This time he'd call them into the ATF as terrorists and get an Emergency Response Team sent in after them.

He crossed the room to his closet and started to dress. This time he put on the kind of clothing he had

worn in Latin America, not the tailored suit he wore
to his office at Langley. Boots, Chino pants, a blue
work shirt and a safari jacket. A pair of sunglasses
went into his jacket pocket, and the slim-line holster
with the government-issue 9 mm Beretta went on the
right side of his belt, with the magazine carrier on the
left.

Dressed like that, Whitworth looked nothing like the
faceless Washington bureaucrat who walked the halls
of the CIA building at Langley. In the loose clothing,
his gym-trim form took on a bulkier appearance.

He was checking the ammunition in his spare magazines when he heard the chiming of his computer
terminal telling him that he had a priority message
waiting for him. Crossing the room, he activated his
E-mail and saw that the message was from Cartagena,
Colombia, and called it up.

Reading the message drove everything else from his
mind. The last thing he needed was a message from
El Machetero, particularly a message that the mercenary was trying to blackmail him. He thought that the
man would have had better sense than to try something
that stupid. At least, though, he had finally eliminated
Phoenix Force for him. All of them, that was, except
for the one who had been captured alive and was being
using as El Machetero's bargaining chip. The mercenary said that he wanted a million dollars or he would
tell his prisoner how his comrades had been betrayed
before releasing him.

Whitworth's earlier misgivings about trying to run
the operation from a distance were proving to be true
in spades. It was too late for him to change any of that

now, but it wasn't too late for him to take a quick trip to Colombia to take care of El Machetero himself. This was one assignment that he couldn't afford to farm out, not even to his associates in the cartel. His relationship with them was based on mutual strength. If the drug lords knew that the man they knew as James Jordan was weak enough to be blackmailed, they'd be all over him like stink on shit.

Able Team was still loose somewhere in Washington, but they didn't present a real danger to him at this time. At the most they were an irritant he could afford to ignore for the moment.

El Machetero, however, wouldn't wait.

The Friday night red-eye for Cartagena, Colombia, left from Dulles International Airport in two hours, so he could make it with time to spare. Calling the CIA Langley com center, he told the duty officer that he would be away from home for the weekend and to contact him on his mobile unit if anything urgent came up. The fact that his mobile phone wouldn't quite reach to Colombia didn't concern him. No one ever called the CIA's director of communications on the weekends anyway. He had a staff to take care of any emergencies that came up.

When he was ready, he called a cab to take him to the airport. It wouldn't do for his car to spend the weekend in the parking lot. Someone might notice it.

CHAPTER TWENTY-SIX

Stony Man Farm, Virginia

Barbara Price found Hal Brognola in his makeshift office. "Carl Lyons just confirmed that Geoffrey Whitworth is our man," she announced.

"The director of communications in the CIA?" Brognola asked, his voice cold.

"It's set in stone," she answered confidently. "There's no doubt about it anymore. Carl baited him by making a visit to Langley, and Whitworth tried to take them out with a cartel hit team last night."

"Were any of our guys hurt?"

"No, but they left four bodies behind in their motel room and then called and told Whitworth about doing it."

"Get Katz to the War Room. We need to talk."

"You want the rest of the team?"

"Not until I decide what we're going to do about this bastard."

By the time Hal Brognola reached the War Room, he was raging mad. The idea that a high-ranking official of the CIA was trying to kill him and his teams was beyond outrageous. That was the kind of behavior he expected from the Mafia or the cartel drug lords, not from a sister government agency. This was taking interdepartmental in-fighting to new heights, and it had to be stopped.

"We can always send Carl, Rosario and Gadgets after him," Yakov Katzenelenbogen suggested after hearing Price's report on Able Team's activities of the previous evening.

"No," Brognola replied. "If we do it that way, we're no damned better than he is. We have to expose this guy and bring him to justice."

"Why do you say that?" Katz asked. "This guy isn't any better than a hundred other scum we've put down without going through the legal formalities. This guy has seriously moved against us, and he needs to go down hard. Remember, this thing isn't over yet. We're still cut off from the outside world, and Phoenix and Striker are still doing God only knows what in Colombia."

"Sorry, Katz," Price said. "But I agree with Hal. Regardless of what Whitworth has done, the CIA is a sister agency. If we put this guy into the glare of the media's eye, the Company will suffer, and they won't forget who caused it. Things will never be the same, and our guys will always be looking over their shoulders."

"I didn't think of that," Katz said. "But you have a point. In order to do the things that we're supposed to do, we need the fullest cooperation of the CIA from time to time. Pissing them off is only going to hurt us in the long run.''

When he saw the look on Brognola's face, he continued. ''I know that this has offended you personally, but if you want to bring this guy to justice, why not just give it to the Company and let them clean their own house?''

''No, we can't risk doing it that way, either. We don't know how deep into the Company structure this thing goes. If it's more than just Whitworth and a couple of his cronies, we'd just be signing our own death warrants if we did that.''

''Which we'll be doing anyway, Hal, if any of this is made public,'' Price argued. ''You know what the media and Congress will do to the Company if they get wind of this. The CIA is the agency they love to hate, and there'll be a feeding frenzy. And in the frenzy, there's too great a chance of Stony Man being revealed and destroyed.''

''Okay, okay,'' Brognola conceded. ''We'll handle it ourselves. But how?''

''Like I said, with Able Team in place in Washington, we can just have them take care of it.''

''Not good enough,'' Price said. ''If Carl's report on the CIA surveillance team is accurate, he'll know that they're running loose and he'll be on guard. Considering the kind of protection he can call upon, we'd be risking them being taken out instead and we can't afford to lose them.''

"We need to get him out of the country, then," Brognola said. "Can you come up with something that will draw him out of Langley?

"Offhand, I don't know what that would be," Katz admitted. "But I'll get together with Aaron and we'll work on it."

WHEN BARBARA PRICE answered her phone, it was the security chief. "Barbara," he said seriously, "I've got a problem out here."

She started to snap back that they all had problems, but she heard the genuine concern in his voice and didn't indulge herself at his expense. "What's that?"

"There's a power company crew down by the main gate and they're working on the line leading into the compound."

That snapped her awake. "Did you ask them what they were doing?"

"Yes, I did," he replied. "They said that they have a work order to cut our power."

This could be the move they had been waiting for. With their electricity cut, they would have to rely on their backup generators to provide power for the web of electronic security that was their first line of defense.

"Put everyone on full alert instantly and crank up the generators. And," she said, her voice hard, "stop those people. I don't care how have to you do it."

"Yes, ma'am."

She punched the button on her intercom connecting

her to Brognola's office. "Hal, I need you in the War Room again ASAP."

"What is it?"

"I think it's happening. The power company is cutting our power."

"On the way."

KISSINGER WAS ON TOP of the game. He had been monitoring the security chief's cellular phone call and headed for the generator room the instant he heard his warning. Electrical power supply was the weakest link of any modern defense, but the Farm had a bank of military diesel generators that had been installed for just such an emergency. They could provide enough power to keep them up and running until the fuel ran out.

"Barb," he radioed, "I've got the generators running and I recommend that we keep them on-line until this is over. Even if we stop them here, it's too easy for them to cut our power somewhere down the line where we can't prevent them from doing it."

"Good point," she answered. "Keep them on-line."

"Roger."

After making sure that the power was flowing properly, Kissinger left the generator shed and went back to his post at the compound's defense control center. If an attack commenced, he wanted to get into the action, too.

WHEN KISSINGER CHECKED the Phalanx air-defense system's control panel, he found that he had another problem with it. The IFF module he had recently replaced in the number-two gun mount had crashed again when he had switched over to generator power. This time, though, it had taken the master IFF recognition module with it.

"I'm at the Phalanx console," he called in to Price. "And the IFF on the number two 20 mm is nonoperational again, and this time it took the main IFF module with it. I want to take the system off-line for a while to try to figure out why the IFFs keep crapping out on us."

"Go ahead," she replied, "but keep me informed."

"Will do."

Fortunately Kissinger was sitting at the Phalanx master console when the number-three gun came alive and started to track a target. The IFF screen came alive, as well, as the system tried to identify the aircraft, but failed. From the code, though, he saw that it was tracking an aircraft that was squawking the ATF's IFF sequence.

He lunged for the master override and shut the system down an instant before the guns started to fire.

After making sure that the guns were safe, he called Price again and reported what had happened. She immediately brought Brognola on the line for a conference call.

"What in the hell is the ATF doing flying over us

anyway?" he said. "We're listed on all of the federal and civilian charts as being restricted airspace."

"The thing that bothers me," Kissinger said, "is why the IFF system didn't accept the plane's squawk that it was a friendly. We were only a second away from blowing the damned thing out of the sky, and you know what would have happened next. Those boys are flying armed Broncos now and they're trigger-happy to the max. They'd have been all over us, guns blazing."

Price and Brognola both reached the same conclusion at the same time. "That's it," he said. "That's what this is all about."

"Are you thinking what I'm thinking?" she asked him.

"You first."

"We're being set up again, just like with the phony mission that sent Phoenix and Able into ambushes. This time, though, we're being set up to be taken out by a federal agency. If we had shot at that ATF airplane, we'd have a war on our hands by nightfall. In fact I'll bet that there's an ATF task force somewhere close by right now waiting for the word to roll in here and take us down."

"You won't get my money on that one, lady," Brognola growled. "That's a sucker's bet."

"So," Kissinger asked, "what are we going to do? If they send their gunships in on us, can I shoot back?"

Brognola took a deep breath. "If we are attacked,

we will return fire. We will not initiate contact, but we will not let anyone step foot inside our perimeter."

As a firearms designer and weapons smith, Kissinger hadn't had the field time of the Phoenix Force or Able Team warriors, but he knew his weapons. If it came down to defending the Farm, he would more than get his licks in.

"I'll make sure that doesn't happen."

HAL BROGNOLA WAS fighting mad, and he didn't care who knew it. Sitting around waiting to become a target hadn't sat well with him. To find out that yet another federal agency was threatening him was too much to take.

"Barb, open an outside line and call my chopper. I have to get back to Washington and I have to do it now. I can see the President and get this stopped in an hour."

"I don't know about that," Price told him. "That may be exactly what Whitworth wants you to do. Remember, we still don't have any hard evidence that he's actually behind this. All we have is circumstantial evidence, and while that's good enough for me, we don't want the President thinking that we have gotten into some kind of clandestine-world turf war with the CIA.

"Plus," she added, "we can't protect you when you're in D.C. It's too easy to die in that town."

Brognola knew that she was right—there had been other attempts on his life—but he still wanted to take the fight to the enemy, proved yet or not. And Katz's earlier suggestion to use Able Team sounded pretty good to him right now. "I think it might be time that we open our outside lines and talk to Carl, Pol and Gadgets. I know that Whitworth's listening in, but we can talk to them in the clear and get our message through."

"What do you want me to tell them to do?"

"I want to find out what in hell the ATF is doing."

"That should be easy enough," Price replied. "If Carl could invade the CIA headquarters, he should be able to do the same thing to the ATF."

Washington, D.C.

EVEN THOUGH SCHWARZ knew that the Farm was off-line, out of habit he had kept his laptop on standby. When he saw that he had an E-mail message waiting, he frowned but clicked on it. When he saw that it was "in the clear," he called Lyons over.

"That's more like it," Lyons said after reading it. "Now we have something useful to do."

"But what about Whitworth?"

"Let the bastard stew in his own juices for a while. It'll do him good."

LYONS TOOK Blancanales with him this time when he walked into the Washington, D.C., headquarters of the Bureau of Alcohol, Tobacco and Firearms. To keep

Schwarz from biting his nails down to the second knuckle, he had been left in the car.

The two men's Justice Department IDs worked as well here as their DEA IDs had worked at Langley. But that was no surprise, because the credentials weren't bogus. Hal Brognola made sure that the government documents he provided for the action teams were completely legitimate and could pass any scrutiny. Their ID cards didn't, however, list their supposed GS rank, only a code letter. Such IDs were the mark of special agents who answered only to the highest officials.

"Can you direct us to the operations center?" Lyons asked the man at the main reception desk in the lobby.

"That's a restricted area," the man said, locking eyes with him. "Do you have ATF clearance?"

Lyons flashed his Justice Department ID again and smiled. "When you call to clear us, make sure to use the code word Green Ramparts."

The man flipped through a list of current code words, saw the two words and instantly changed his attitude as he reached for the phone.

"It's on the fourth floor, sir. Take the elevator on the left, and I'll have someone meet you."

"Thanks."

When the elevator opened on the fourth floor, Lyons and Blancanales saw that they had a reception committee. Three polished Washington suits were waiting to greet them. Once more Lyons flashed his ID and mentioned the magic words, Green Ramparts. Again the reaction was instantaneous.

"Please follow me, sir," the senior suit said.

The ATF ops center was behind two armed guards and a key-lock door. When Lyons and Blancanales were passed through to the inner sanctum, another ATF official met them. Another flash of the ID had the man spouting "Yes, sirs," and "No, sirs."

A series of aerial photos of the Farm that had been pinned to one wall immediately caught his eye. Walking closer, he saw that circles of red marker pointed out gun emplacements and surveillance equipment around the Farm's perimeter. Had he not known where he was, Lyons would have thought that he was in Kissinger's defense center looking at their own diagrams of the Stony Man defenses.

"Very impressive," he said. "This is the information that came from the CIA, right?"

The official looked stunned. "Why, yes," he said. "But the information about where that information came from is supposed to be classified."

Lyons looked at him with a superior smirk, playing the D.C. one-upmanship that was so much a part of everything that was done in the nation's capital. "I know," he said. "I'm the one who classified it."

"Of course, sir."

"Now," Lyons said, turning away. "I want to look at the attack plan."

CHAPTER TWENTY-SEVEN

It was an hour and a half before Lyons and Blancanales returned to the parking lot. Schwarz could tell from the look on Lyons's face that the news wasn't anything he wanted to hear.

"What's going on?"

"Wait until we're on the road."

Schwarz signed them out of the parking lot and turned onto the street. Lyons let him drive for two blocks before he spoke. "The Farm's being set up just like we were. This time, though, Whitworth's going to use the ATF to bring them down."

"Oh, shit," Schwarz said softly. "Those guys will go in shooting first and asking questions afterward. And if our guys are attacked, you know what our defense plans are. It'll be a bloodbath."

"I know it. And I think that's what he's counting on."

"Why do you think he's trying to wipe us all out? It just doesn't make sense."

"Yes, it does," Blancanales said, "in an odd way. If Whitworth wants to go back to the good old days of the Cold War, when the CIA was more important to national defense than the military. When you look at the Company today, it really doesn't have a job except for gathering information and running a few foreign spies to keep everyone honest. Most of its wet teams have been disbanded, and we take care of the bulk of Uncle Sam's heavy work now. If we weren't here, though, the President would have to go back to the old system, then the CIA would have plenty to do."

"But that's crazy," Schwarz said. "The Farm works with the Company all the time. We only get called in when the job's too sensitive to risk having the media getting wind of it."

"That's exactly the point," Lyons said. "In the old days, the CIA didn't have the media on its ass all the time. Executive orders from the President gave the same protection back then that we enjoy now. It would be easy enough for him to do that again and get them out of the public eye."

"What are we going to do about this ATF operation, Carl?" Schwarz asked.

Lyons smiled, but it wasn't a pretty thing to see. "We're going to go to war with the ATF."

"But they're Feds, too. We can't be killing those guys. They're on our side."

"Not this time, they aren't," Lyons snapped. "But we won't kill any of them unless we absolutely have to. There's more than one way to fight a war."

"But can't we get it called off? Can't Hal fly up here and talk to the President?"

"Not this time. According to what we saw, the ATF has the Farm surrounded. They're armed with Stinger missiles and have orders to fire at any aircraft attempting to take off from the Farm. Any vehicle leaving the place is also to be fired upon if it doesn't stop the instant the driver's told to. He's trapped in there like the rest of them."

"What in hell does the ATF think is going on down there, anyway?"

"Whitworth used bogus CIA information to convince them that the Farm is the headquarters of a domestic-terrorist ring with connections to the cartel."

"How did he come up with information like that, and why did they believe it?"

"The same way that he came up with the information we got that went into the mission that sent us down to Mexico to get our asses shot off. Computers don't lie. He created the intel feed and put it in the computers."

"But someone had to have approved the operation, right? Someone like the President."

"That's the kicker on this one. They have a go-ahead from the Oval Office."

"And it came to them over a computer, right."

Lyons nodded.

"That figures."

"But," Lyons stated, "there's a time-honored way

to counter enemy misinformation—action. We're going to bail out of here and join the guys at the Farm."

"And leave Whitworth alone here to cause us even more trouble?"

"For now, yes," Lyons said. "But on the way to the Farm, we're going to make a couple of stops and give our regards to the boys of the ATF."

Virginia

SCHWARZ PULLED the van behind the Tastee-Freez Snack Shack across the highway from the small civilian airfield on the outskirts of Wilmings, Virginia, and killed the lights. They had approached the snack stand from the rear so as not to attract attention at that late hour. Wilmings was a small farm town, and there wasn't a lot of traffic on the roads after midnight.

The three commandos were wearing blacksuits when they stepped out of the van. Even though combat cosmetics darkened their faces and hands, they wore dark balaclavas in case they were spotted.

After crossing the road, they split up as they approached the airfield that had been commandeered as a base for the ATF aircraft that had been targeted against Stony Man Farm. Blancanales headed for the hangar while Schwarz and Lyons headed for the chain-link fence.

The six matt black ATF O-10D Broncos they had come for were lined up beside the hangar as if they were being displayed at an air show. According to the press releases that had been released when word of the machines leaked out, the military-surplus Broncos were to be used by the ATF for aerial surveillance only, not ground attack. But since the machines were D models, they had the capability of carrying ordnance left over from their days of military service as night-intruder gunships in Vietnam and the Gulf War.

Normally the ATF didn't fly their Broncos with the weapons mounted. It tended to make people nervous and ask too many questions about the machines. Even in the dim light, the ordnance hardpoints under the wings and the machine-gun pylons jutting from the fuselage were visible. That the planes had been fitted with their weapons wasn't a good sign. Particularly not when it was matched up with the plans Lyons had been shown back in Washington.

"Those bastards really are getting ready to go after the Farm!" Schwarz was highly offended when he saw the weapons mounts.

"That's why we're here to stop them," Lyons reminded him. "When we get done here tonight, these things won't be going anywhere for a couple of days."

"A couple of weeks is more like it." Schwarz grinned. "The stuff I'm using dissolves, but it takes time."

"I have a guard at eleven o'clock at the corner of the hangar," Blancanales reported as he scanned the area with his night-vision goggles.

"Only one guard?" Lyons asked. "They're confident bastards."

"That's all I have so far."

"Keep looking. I want to make sure that we have them cold before we go in."

"The fence is cold," Schwarz reported when the needle on his current detector didn't move. "And I don't see any surveillance devices."

"Like I said, they don't lack confidence..." Lyons's voice was almost like the purr of a big, mean cat.

"I have the other one," Blancanales reported again. "He's reading a skin magazine in the van."

"You take him, and I'll handle the one by the hangar."

"I'm on him."

LEAVING SCHWARZ to start cutting a hole in the fence, Lyons worked his way around to the back of the hangar. When he came up behind his man, the ATF guard didn't seem to be taking his duties too seriously. After all, who in his right mind was going to mess around with the ATF?

Lyons wrapped his arm around the guard's neck and jammed the barrel of his .357 Magnum Colt Python against the side of his jaw. "Yell and you die," he said.

The man froze. "Okay, mister," he whispered.

"Up against the wall," Lyons snapped. "You know the drill."

The ATF man assumed the position while Lyons patted him down and found the hideaway gun on his right ankle. "Okay," the former LAPD detective said quietly as he drilled the muzzle of his Python in the hollow behind the guard's ear, "slowly move your hands behind your back. I'm going to cuff you."

As soon as the man was cuffed, Lyons backed away from him. "On the ground and lay facedown."

The guard awkwardly knelt, then Lyons helped him lie flat. "Feet together," he ordered.

Slipping the heavy-duty riot restraint over the man's boots, he snugged it around his ankles. A double wrap of duct tape went over that so the guard couldn't try to snag the plastic tie against something in hopes of breaking it. "Now roll over onto your back."

Taking a piece of surgical gauze from his side pocket, Lyons wadded it up into a ball. "Open wide."

"Please, mister," the man said quietly, "don't gag me. I won't be able to breathe. I won't try to shout, I promise."

"This is gauze," Lyons explained, "and it'll let you breathe, but you won't be able to yell. It's either that or duct tape."

"Okay."

"Since you're going to spend the night here, do you want to be on your back or your belly?" Lyons asked.

"On my back please," the man said politely.

When the man submitted to the gag, Lyons holstered his Colt. "You stay there like a nice boy, and your buddies will get you in the morning. If I have to come back here, you won't like it. Understand?"

The man nodded.

"Pol?" Lyons called over the com link.

"I've got mine," Blancanales answered.

"How's it going, Gadgets?" Lyons called.

"I'm finishing up the second one now," Schwarz answered. "It's difficult to get the powder in all four fuel tanks. But I think that another fifteen minutes and I'll be done."

"Take your time and do it right. Nobody's going to bother us tonight."

The problem Schwarz was having was the method they had chosen to sabotage the ATF Broncos. Rather than damage the valuable aircraft, he had come up with an idea that would take them out of action for several days, but wouldn't destroy them.

One of their stops on the way to Wilmings had been to an EPA warehouse. There, they had picked up several pounds of a powdered seaweed extract that was used to clean up chemical spills. The powder reacted with petroleum products to form a gel. When mixed with the JP-4 jet fuel in the aircrafts' tanks, it turned the fuel into jelly, and there was no way the turbines would run on the mixture.

Over time, the gel would break down into a liquid again and the tanks could be pumped dry, but that would take several days. It was true that the ATF had more Broncos in their inventory. But they had been dispersed to other parts of the country, and it would take a while before they could be flown in and have the weapons mounted.

Climbing up onto the broad wing of the last Bronco,

Schwarz removed the fuel cap of the first of the air-craft's four fill points. Taking the one-pound bag of the seaweed extract from his pocket, he poured it into the filler neck. Using a stick, he reached into the tank and stirred the mixture before moving on to the next filler cap.

Ten minutes later, he was done and jumped down to the ground. "I'm clear, Ironman," he called to Lyons.

"We'll meet you by the hole in the fence."

IT WAS THREE O'CLOCK in the morning when Able Team turned onto the dirt road leading to the ATF's command post on the hill only a few miles from Stony Man Farm. For this phase of the operation, Lyons and Blancanales were back in their Fed suits and had their Justice Department IDs ready. After dropping off Schwarz a quarter of a mile away, they drove up to the checkpoint a hundred yards from the collection of vans that was serving as the command post for the operation.

"We're from the Green Ramparts command-and-control team in Washington," Lyons announced as he flashed his ID to the two men standing by the ATF van parked off of the road, "and we're here to see how your operation is progressing. Who's the agent in charge here?"

"Tonight that's Agent Jensen, sir. Dick Jensen."

"Can you point him out?"

"If you'll park your van over there with the other vehicles, sir, I'll take you to him."

Agent Jensen had been alerted by the other guard and was waiting by the open door of the big trailer van that was his command center. He was just the night-duty officer and hadn't been expecting a surprise visit from the D.C. brass. Only two men were monitoring the radios. After the proper introductions had been made, Blancanales confused the three men with a barrage of questions, while Lyons pretended to study the situation map mounted on the wall.

As he looked around for a good place to drop the highway flare in his pocket, he saw something that changed his plan. In accordance with the federal regulations for destruction of classified material, a thermite grenade had been mounted in a glass front container on the wall by the locked file cabinets. For starting a rip-roaring fire, nothing was better than a thermite grenade.

Using his body to hide his actions from view, Lyons opened the door of the thermite grenade's container, unclipped it and placed it on the floor. After the pin was pulled and the safety handle loosened, the grenade ignited with a whoosh and a burst of flame when the top blew off.

"There's a fire!" Lyons shouted.

Jensen and his two radio operators jumped to deal with it, but they couldn't find a fire extinguisher. By now, the thermite had burned through the thin wall of the file cabinet and had ignited the paper inside, as well as the plywood walls of the van. When pouring the contents of the coffeepot on it didn't help, the ATF men were forced out by the smoke.

When Jensen sent his men to find a fire extinguisher, Lyons and Blancanales backed away. In all of the commotion, no one noticed the black-clad figure slipping from shadow to shadow toward the trailer that was serving as the antenna stand.

Reaching into his side pocket, Schwarz brought out a prepared quarter-pound C-4 charge and peeled the protective layer off of the adhesive coating on the back. Slapping the explosive against the side of the antenna, he flipped the switch on the radio-controlled detonator. Slipping around to the other side, he placed another explosive package against the control boxes and activated its detonator.

Looking around for another target, he spotted the generators providing the power for the big commo van and the lights. He had just reached the first generator when an ATF man ran up to him.

"Buddy, is there a fire extinguisher by that generator?" he called out.

"No," Schwarz called back. "I'll check the other one."

When the man ran on, Schwarz walked over to the backup generator and rigged it for demo, as well. He was on a roll and might as well make the best of it while everyone was preoccupied with other things.

He was down to his last demo charge and spotted a perfect place to put it. The pair of plastic portable washrooms sitting at the edge of the compound was too good a target for Schwarz to pass up. Lifting the door in back that was used to service the waste container inside, he stuck the charge against the side of the container. When that one went off and spread the contents, even the ATF would have to break camp and find some other place to put their CP.

His pockets empty, Schwarz moved back in the darkness until he was well clear of the CP area but still able to observe his targets.

Blancanales and Lyons kept clear of the ATF men who were fighting a losing battle with the fire that was consuming the commo van and calmly walked back to where they had parked their van. "Do it," Lyons muttered over the com link.

The first explosion sent half the radio antennas crashing to the ground; the second blast finished the job. Before the stunned ATF men could react, Schwarz triggered the charges he had fixed to the generators, and the compound went dark.

Lyons simply started the van and started back down the dirt road for the highway. When he saw the red glow of Schwarz's penlight a hundred yards down the road, he stopped.

"Wait a minute," Schwarz said as he opened the side door. "I have one more charge."

"Where'd you put it?"

"In the john. They're going to love it."

"Go for it."

The explosion was a bit muffled this time as the

quarter-pound block of C-4 tore though the plastic walls of the facility. When the blast echoed away, the breeze sent them a faint whiff of the results of Schwarz's handiwork.

"Let's get out of here before we have to change clothes."

"No argument here."

CHAPTER TWENTY-EIGHT

Stony Man Farm, Virginia

"Barbara," the security chief called on his radio, "I have a van approaching the main gate, and they're flashing the Able Team recognition code. Do you want me to let them come in?"

Even though she was only halfway through her first cup of coffee of the day after a long night, that news brought the mission controller bolt upright. "Bring them up to the house immediately."

"Yes, ma'am."

Price, Brognola and Katzenelenbogen were all waiting on the front porch when the muddy van pulled to a halt and the three men stepped out.

"You boys look a bit worse for wear," Katz said wistfully. Even though he was happy with his new role as the in-house tactical adviser for Stony Man operations, he hadn't forgotten what it was like to be in the field, and he missed the rush.

"You ought to see the other guys," Schwarz said, grinning. "We left some very pissed-off ATF guys

trying to find their asses with both hands and the pro-
verbial radar set. And from what I saw of them, they'll
still be looking this time next week.''

"What happened?"

"How about a cup of the Bear's brew first?" Carl
Lyons said. "We've been up all night trying to get
here. There's a cordon all the way around this place,
and we had to work our way through it carefully."

"I can do better than that stuff," Price offered. "I'll
have a real breakfast sent down to the War Room."

"Sounds good to me," Schwarz said. "As long as
there's a big pot of coffee included on the menu and
a couple dozen doughnuts."

"I think we can at least manage that for our con-
quering heroes."

IN BETWEEN SIPS of coffee and bites of his freshly
made doughnut, Lyons quickly briefed the Stony Man
team on what they had managed to accomplish the
previous evening.

"So," he concluded, "we bought you a little time,
maybe two or three days. With their aircraft grounded
and their command post burned to the ground, it's going to take them a while to get their act together
again."

Katz had a broad smile on his face. "I can't believe
that you were able to burn their commo van right out
from under them."

Schwarz shrugged. "I can't believe that they didn't
have a fire extinguisher handy somewhere or other. All

we intended to do was to take them off-line long enough to disrupt their command-and-control capability and hold up the operation until we could join up with you. But when the van burned up completely and I was able to blow their long-range radio antennas and their generators, we really did a job on them."

"And no one was hurt?" Brognola asked. Even though the ATF was after their blood, they were still Feds.

"A couple of guys got singed in the fire," Blancanales assured him. "And one of them sprained an ankle bailing out of the van, but nothing serious."

Brognola glanced at his watch. "It's time that I got back to Washington and put an end to this before it gets any more serious."

"I hope that you're not planning on flying," Lyons said casually.

"What do you mean?" the big Fed frowned. "I always fly. You know that."

"What I mean is that the ATF boys have orders to fire on any aircraft trying to take off from here. Your chopper will be able to land, but when it tries to take off, it'll be blasted from the sky."

"You're joking!"

"Stingers aren't very funny, and those guys have a couple dozen of them out there ringing this place."

"Who in the hell gave them rules of engagement like that? That's against every law on the books. They can't just shoot a plane down whenever they want to."

Lyons kept a straight face. "You told them to do it

that way when you gave them their marching orders to take this place down.''

"I did no such thing, Carl," Brognola snapped. "And I didn't have a damned thing to do with anything that's been going on out there."

"I know you didn't, Hal," Lyons explained. "But the ATF doesn't know that. The information that put them in gear came from your office code-marked Green Ramparts. And you also gave them the Oval Office's stamp of approval for the special rules of engagement on their op plan."

Brognola shook his head, wondering how things could have gotten so far off track. "I just don't see how this could have happened."

"It's the wonder of the computer age, Hal," Lyons said. "When a message comes up on the screen with the right sender's address, you take it at face value without questioning it. That's how Whitworth suckered you into sending Phoenix Force to Colombia and me and the guys down to Mexico. He just did it to the ATF this time, and he did it over your electronic signature."

"I'm going to have that bastard's head on a plate for this," Brognola growled.

"You're going to have to wait your turn," Lyons informed him. "McCarter and I have first dibs on him, and we'll have to flip a coin for the honor of taking care of him."

"Don't we have to get the ATF called off first?" Price brought them back to the topic at hand. "If what

Carl says is true, as soon as they can get organized again, we're still going to be invaded."

"Believe me," Brognola stated, "that's going to be the first item on my agenda as soon as I get out of here. And as soon as things are back to normal, I'm going to hand the director of the ATF his head, as well."

"Don't be too hard on them," Katz said. "They got sucked in the same way we did."

"That's no damned excuse," Brognola said. "After Waco, they should have known better than to try to do something this outrageous."

"That can all wait," Price said. "We need to get busy trying to extricate ourselves from this mess. And—" she looked Brognola straight in the eye "—you aren't going anywhere, Hal. It's simply too dangerous, and you won't be any use to us if you get killed."

"But—" Brognola began.

"If I have to, Hal, I'll have Carl lock you in a room somewhere. The only way we can get ourselves out of this is the same way we got in it."

"What do you mean?" Katz asked.

"Whitworth used a computer to set this whole thing up, so we're going to have to get back into cyberspace to get us out of it."

"Okay," Brognola reluctantly agreed. "Put the Bear's crew back on-line."

"And while you're doing that," Lyons said, "I'd like to get with Kissinger and the chief to see what we can do to beef up our defenses just in case you can't find a cybernetic solution to the problem.''

Without even looking over to see what Brognola thought, Price ordered Able Team into action again. ''Do it.''

NOW THAT THERE WAS something they could actually do, the Stony Man team jumped into action. The first thing Price wanted to do was to get Able Team off Whitworth's radar screen. But to do that they didn't use computer communications. Instead, they again used the regular mail system. An international priority mail package would be sent to a contact on Grand Cayman Island who ran a charter air service. He was instructed to report to the local CIA man on the island that he had flown Lyons, Schwarz and Blancanales to a remote airfield in Honduras.

''I thought that I'd seen the last of 'snail mail,''' Kurtzman grumbled as he put the instructions into the colorful U.S. priority-mail package.

''When was the last time that you actually mailed a letter?'' Price asked him.

''I honestly don't know. But who uses the post office anymore when they can send information by fax or E-mail and have it get there instantly?''

''But, as we have seen,'' Katzenelenbogen countered, ''you can get in real trouble when you do all of your communicating in cyberspace. It's too easy for the bad guys to read your mail.''

''And speaking of reading our mail,'' Price said,

"we need to get started on the misinformation campaign."

Even though Brognola had authorized them to go back on-line to do what had to be done, it wasn't going to be easy. Knowing that their codes had been broken and, for all intents and purposes, they would be speaking in the "clear," they had to be very careful about what they put into cyberspace.

Even though it was Saturday, Kurtzman knew that both the CIA and the ATF had full computer-room staffs at work in their headquarters. They would route messages onto the addressees, and they would be waiting on their desks Monday morning.

WHILE THE COMPUTER STAFF was setting up traps in cyberspace, Lyons, Schwarz and Blancanales met with Kissinger and the security chief to plan the Farm's defense against the ATF. Stony Man had several versions of a comprehensive defense plan designed to deal with an all-out assault by terrorists or foreign operatives. It had happened before, and if it happened again, they were prepared to kill.

This time, though, they wouldn't be facing cartel gunmen, a KGB hit team or Libyan terrorists. They would be going up against federal agents. They felt that they could hold their own against even the best the ATF could put up against them, but it would be a hollow victory. Saving their lives at the cost of killing several dozen federal agents wouldn't play well on the six-o'clock news. But the alternative wasn't attractive, either. None of them wanted to go to a grave, targeted by people fighting on the same side of the law.

"We need to figure out a way to keep those guys from ever setting foot inside our perimeter," Lyons said. "If they can't get to us, we won't have to shoot them."

"That means taking the war to them," Schwarz replied. "And if I remember correctly, somebody famous once said, 'the best defense is a strong offense.'"

"I think that was one of George Patton's better lines," Kissinger said.

"Whoever it was, we need to go on the offensive and do it quickly while they're still staggering around trying to recover from our visit last night."

"Let me come with you guys," Kissinger said eagerly. "There's not a hell of a lot left for me to do around here. Since this thing started, I've looked over everything here at least twice. I won't have anything useful to do until the air strikes start."

"If it comes down to that," Schwarz said dryly, "we're all going to be busier than we'd like to be."

Lyons realized that Schwarz had a point. Plus there was a good chance that the ATF didn't have a mug shot of the weapons smith on file, and that could work in their favor. A guy with an open face wearing blue jeans and a work shirt could easily pass for a local.

"Where's their closest roadblock?" Lyons asked.

THE FARM'S EVERYDAY vehicles looked no different than what one would expect to find on any of the working farms in the valley. All farm vehicles showed a certain amount of external battering and neglect, and that was the case with the ten-year-old GMC pickup Kissinger drove.

He slowed as he approached the dark blue van with the yellow ATF emblazoned on the side. Even though the three men in black SWAT suits with H&K subguns slung over their shoulders didn't seem ready to flag him down, he pulled to a stop anyway.

"Howdy, fellas," he called through the open window. "What're ya'll doing here? You broke down or something?"

One of the agents detached himself from the other two and walked over to Kissinger's truck. "You'd better move on, sir. This is a federal operation."

"Are you chasing some criminal?" Kissinger wasn't a Southerner, but his imitation of a northern Virginia accent was pretty good.

"Just move on, sir."

Kissinger smiled and said, "If you'll look around, son, you'll see that you're in deep shit."

When the agent looked away, he saw Lyons and Blancanales standing behind his two comrades with shotguns in their hands. He was still undecided when Schwarz rose from the back of the truck with his CAR-15 trained on him. "Hang it up, guy. It's too nice a day to die."

When the last ATF agent was cuffed and shackled, Lyons and Schwarz joined the three captives in the bed of the pickup for the short ride back to the Farm. Blancanales followed them in their blue ATF van.

KISSINGER DROVE around to the back of the house to the equipment sheds. Hal Brognola and half a dozen of the Farm's blacksuits were waiting for them, and they weren't smiling.

The ATF men were stunned to see their reception, particularly when Brognola showed them his Justice Department ID card.

"You men have been set up worse than your comrades at Waco," Brognola informed them. "You have been ordered to move against a top secret government installation, and heads are going to roll for this screwup. As a Justice Department officer, I'm placing you under arrest, and you will remain here until this is sorted out."

"What are you arresting us for, sir?" one of the agents said. "We were only following orders."

"I'm aware of that," Brognola said. "But for your information, following illegal orders isn't a defense. And as far as what you're being held for, you are in violation of the civil-rights laws."

"But we were the ones who were kidnapped!"

"On my orders," Brognola informed him. "And I advise you to remember your own rights and shut up. Unless, of course," he added, "any of you would like to tell me what in the hell is going on. Such information would be considered favorably when I consider what charges to write you up on."

"Look, sir," the third man said, "I don't know what's going on here, but I'll be glad to tell you everything I do know. There's obviously been some kind of screwup, and I'll be damned if I'm going to take the fall for it."

Brognola smiled. "Come with me, and I'll get you a cup of coffee and a doughnut while we talk. I'm sure we can get this sorted out, and then I'll let you men go."

The other two agents looked at each other for a brief moment. "We'd like to come, too, sir."

CHAPTER TWENTY-NINE

Cartagena, Colombia

From the minute that the Yankees had loaded El Machetero into the helicopter for the flight to Cartagena, Juan Chicino refused to leave the mercenary's side even long enough for him to relieve himself. He wasn't happy about leaving his jungle and flying to the big city. But he had been promised that he could have El Machetero when the Yankees had finished using him as bait for the mysterious man named Jordan. He still didn't completely understand why the big gringo was doing this, but he had seen enough of the commando's work to know that he had a way of making things happen. So far, though, all he had done was talk to the mercenary.

Late that afternoon, Bolan and Encizo walked into the room where Chicino was guarding his prize. "The message was sent to Washington," Bolan told him. "And Señor Jordan received it. Now we will go back to the mountains and wait for him to come to us."

"You are certain that he will come all the way

down here, *señor?*" Chicino asked. "That is a long trip for an important man to make."

"He'll come," Bolan reassured him. "The way I worded the message, he can't afford to stay away. Not if he wants to stay out of prison."

"But I do not understand, *señor.* If this Señor Jordan is a high-ranking American official as you say, why has he been working with a man like El Machetero?" He spit on the floor. "He is a murderer, little more than a mad dog."

"We have mad dogs in our government, too, and Jordan is one of them. But he has had to be careful about what he did himself. He found that El Machetero was useful when he needed dirty work to be done."

"I am glad that I live in the jungle where it is clean," Chicino said. "And do not have to get involved in the politics of the cities."

"There are times," Encizo said, "when I wish that I could go to the mountains with you, my friend. I envy your life, but someone has to make sure that the bad guys don't take over everything."

"We're packed up," McCarter said as he entered the room. "And we're ready to roll whenever you are."

A day in Cartagena had done a lot to restore the Phoenix Force commandos. They were showered and shaved, and had clean uniforms waiting for them to put on when they reached their destination later that day. Even Hawkins was getting along better with his leg. A doctor had been called in to check El Machetero's arm again, and he had said that the stump was healing as well as could be expected. When he said that it would need a skin graft some time in the future, no one mentioned that El Machetero probably wouldn't be around long enough to need it.

Bolan glanced at his watch. "We'd better get moving, then, if we want to beat the curfew at the army checkpoints between here and the airport."

"WELCOME TO the ass end of this part of the world," Hawkins said as he watched the sun going down over the semideserted village. "I still don't see why we couldn't have taken care of this Whitworth guy in Cartagena."

Grimaldi had flown them and the Toyota four-wheel-drive vehicle they had picked up in Cartagena to a road junction ten miles out of the village. After dropping them off, he had flown back to Fort Apache to await the outcome of the operation. As Phoenix Force had driven into the village, its few remaining inhabitants had taken to the hills, leaving it completely to them. They hadn't intended to drive the locals away. But maybe it was better this way, because they would be in the middle of a firefight if things didn't go smoothly. If Whitworth had brought the ransom money, they could pay the villagers well for their night spent in the open.

The only building worthy of the name in the entire village was the one they picked to set up in. It had adobe walls and a rusted sheet-metal roof and, in better days, it had apparently been a tavern. The heavy wooden tables and bar against one wall were still there, but with so few customers left in the village, it had been abandoned for some time.

"Whitworth would have instantly smelled a rat if we had tried to suck him into the city," McCarter explained. "He knows that El Machetero doesn't like big cities. He's always operated in the woods, and he only goes to town when he has to meet up with his cartel connections."

Since he still wasn't operating at one hundred percent, Hawkins had volunteered to play El Machetero's prisoner in Bolan's plan. To create the image, his field uniform hadn't been laundered and he was wearing bloody, filthy clothing. A field bandage had been dirtied and bloodied, as well, and had been tied back around his wounded leg. He wasn't wearing any of his field equipment, but he had a 9 mm Beretta tucked into the back of his belt.

El Machetero, however, had been cleaned up. It wouldn't do for him to look as though he had been dragged through the mud. He had even been given a weapon, one of the M-16s that Jordan had supplied to El Machetero's forces. His pistol holster, however, was empty.

"I took the firing pin out of his M-16 myself," James said when he saw Hawkins eyeballing the weapon. "So you don't have to worry about it."

"If he aims it at me, though, he's dead."

"I explained that to him," Encizo said.

"Just so there's no hard feelings if I blow him away."

Juan Chicino had been given a set of the woodlands-pattern camouflage fatigues that El Machetero's mercenaries had been wearing, and a battered maroon beret. He was carrying his old AK, but Jordan wouldn't notice a detail like that.

"What if we can't take him alive?" Hawkins asked.

"No problem." McCarter shrugged. "It'll save the taxpayers the cost of a trial. One way or the other, though, the man is going down. As you Yanks would say, he's polluted the environment long enough."

AFTER FEEDING himself left-handed, El Machetero submitted to having his remaining hand cuffed to the table leg. Since Bolan had no way of knowing when Whitworth would show up, Chicino, Hawkins and the mercenary would spend the night in the main room while Bolan and McCarter would take turns on patrol.

"Why are you doing this, Chico?" the mercenary asked as soon as they were alone. "Did I not rescue you from that village and teach you a trade? I don't understand."

"My name is Juan," Chicino replied. "I haven't been a 'Chico' for years. Not since I saw you burn down your first village. As to why I am going to kill you, it's simple. You lied to me. When you told me that you were fighting for the people who could not defend themselves, I believed you and left my home to follow you."

"But I am not the one who raided your village—you know that."

"The government troops killed my father and raped my sister, that is true. But in all the time I was with you, you never did anything to defend anyone. You only attacked those who were not strong enough to fight you. Every time the government troops came, you ran like a coward, and that is why I left you that night. I joined your band so I could find the man who had killed my father. But when I saw what you were really like, I knew you would never lead me to him. After I left that night, I went to the nearest town and joined the government's army."

"Did you find your man?" El Machetero asked with a sneer.

"Yes," Chicino said calmly. "I found him and I killed him. Now I have found you, too, and as soon as the American is done with you, I will kill you, too."

"And this will bring your father back to life?"

"My father is bones in his grave," Chicino said. "And nothing I can do can change that. But with you dead, as well, some family will not have to go through what I did."

"But, Juan—"

"But nothing," Chicino snapped. "If it was not for the big American, you would be dead now, so enjoy what is left of your miserable life."

Hawkins didn't speak enough Spanish to follow the exchange between the two men, but he could see that the mercenary hadn't had the better of it. Chicino was still a kid, but men grew up fast around here.

"How about you two getting some sleep," he said in English while he pantomimed sleeping.

"Okay, gringo," Chicino replied.

WHEN GEOFFREY WHITWORTH stepped off of the airplane in Cartagena the next day, he was completely back in his James Jordan persona. He had never been known by his real name in Colombia, and every trace of the Harvard-educated Washington bureaucrat was gone. He was in his operational mind-set now, and even his walk had changed to match his field persona.

A short cab ride took him to the small villa on the coastal side of the city that had been the safehouse for his Latin American operations. The villa was being maintained now by his cartel contacts and was kept ready for his infrequent visits.

The first thing he did was to go into his office on the second floor and disarm the booby traps that protected his wall safe from uninvited visitors. When the charges had been disabled, he spun the combination to open the safe. Inside was an impressive stack of Colombian currency, several thousand dollars' worth, and a holstered .45 Colt Commander pistol. The currency went into the side pockets of his cargo pants, and the pistol was clipped to his belt.

Once armed, he went to the garage and checked the Toyota Land Cruiser he kept stored there. The four-wheel-drive vehicle's tank was full of gas, and both spare gas cans strapped on the back were full, as well. He had a long trip ahead of him, and he didn't want to have to worry about trying to find gas in the mountains.

He opened a hidden compartment in the back wall of the garage and took out half a dozen brand-new AK-47s, the real thing, not the semiauto look-alikes. For each assault rifle, he took a fully loaded chest pack of 30-round magazines. Two thousand-round crates of 7.62 mm ammunition came next, and a box of U.S. Army M-26 hand grenades. He regretted not having stashed away a couple of RPG rocket launchers, but his stash should be enough firepower for what he had in mind.

If El Machetero expected him to drive into his hands all by himself, he was crazier than he was already acting. Whitworth was an old hand, and he hadn't done anything that stupid since he had been a green kid on his first assignment in Laos. When he made the trip to the village, he would have enough backup to see that things went his way and he wouldn't have to go through the mercenary to find men to help him this time.

Although the CIA man was allied with the Cali cartel, that didn't mean that he was without contacts with the other, smaller up-and-coming drug gangs. There were half a dozen smaller cocaine operations that never got their names in the American papers who would be more than willing to do a favor for the famous Señor Jordan. They, too, needed the kind of protection he could provide for their smuggling operations.

They all knew the brutal realities of the business they were in. As long as the Americans couldn't get enough of their product, every time one of the big boys went down, it left an opening that one of them could step into. That was how the Cali operation had become as big as it was today. When much of the Medellín leadership had all been taken down, the Cali group had taken its place on the top of the hit list.

It would always be that way, but each up-and-coming drug gang thought it would be different with them, and Whitworth didn't bother to tell them otherwise.

After throwing a tarp over his cargo in the back of his Land Cruiser, he opened the garage door and backed the vehicle out into the driveway. The Guzman family compound was a three-hour drive into the mountains to the east of Cartagena, but he should be able to make it there before nightfall. A quick meal with the brothers while they discussed business, and picking out his bodyguards would probably take another two or three hours. But by driving straight through the night, he should be able to reach the village El Machetero had chosen for the meet right before dawn.

He would then finish his business with the treacherous mercenary in time to get back to Cartagena early enough to have a late dinner before he had to catch the plane back to Washington.

By the time he returned to his Langley office, the ATF task force should have finished reducing the base in the Shenandoah to a smoking hole in the ground.

Stony Man Farm, Virginia

THE THREE CAPTURED ATF men had been relieved of their weapons, SWAT gear and uniforms, and were dressed in farmhand clothing. With an armed blacksuit escort, they were led to an empty storage room that would serve as their holding cell until this situation had been resolved one way or the other.

Blancanales and two of the Farm's blacksuits dressed in the discarded ATF gear for the next phase of the operation. Their snatch had gone off so well that they decided to see how big of a collection of ATF men they could amass. If nothing else, they were insurance against a mass assault.

With Lyons, Schwarz and Kissinger in the back of the captured van, Blancanales and the blacksuits went looking for another roadblock. This time they posed as a relief crew with the same results. Three more ATF agents made a quick trip back to the Stony Man Farm in the back of their own van while Able Team went looking for more victims.

By early evening, they had collected well over a dozen ATF men and four of their vehicles. Wherever the ATF had established their new command post, someone would be trying to figure out why a dozen of his men had suddenly vanished.

Colombia

WHEN GEOFFREY WHITWORTH left the Guzman family compound outside of Cartagena, it was close to midnight. He had been forced to stay there longer than he had planned, but the time had been well spent. He had come away with more going for him than he had hoped. The Guzman brothers had not only loaned him half a dozen of their retainers to pack the weapons he had brought, but they had insisted on coming along themselves and brought another four men as their bodyguards. They, too, knew of El Machetero and didn't trust him.

In return for the favor, Whitworth had promised the brothers that he would set them up with a protected cocaine drop as he had done for the other drug lords in the past. They didn't know that he would also sell them out to the Colombian authorities as soon as it was expedient for him to do so.

One of his first actions after taking over the reins of the CIA would be to make a dramatic move against the cocaine trade to show that the Company was back at the top of its game. As a quickly growing player in the drug trade, the Guzman brothers' operation would make a good first target. The fact that he would be setting up his old business partners didn't bother him one bit. As both James Jordan and Geoffrey Whitworth, his first and only loyalty was to himself.

Plus, to prepare for his ascension to the director's chair, he would reinvent his past. He didn't need to have loose ends like Jordan's association with guerrillas and drug lords hanging around to be picked up by some investigative reporter armed with the Freedom of Information Act.

In fact this would be the last time that he would ever use his James Jordan persona. When this mission was over, he would purge Jordan's existence from all of the Company's records, both hard copy and cybernetic. So much had already been destroyed from the old Iran-Contra days that no one would notice a few more pages missing.

CHAPTER THIRTY

Stony Man Farm, Virginia

Aaron Kurtzman and his computer-room staff were still working on their misinformation campaign when Hunt Wethers called out from his workstation. "Aaron, I've got something funny here from an E-mail service in Vancouver, B.C."

"What's that?"

"Well, it's titled a 'Strikergram' and it's in some kind of code. Is that what I think it is?"

"Damned straight!" Kurtzman's face broke out in a wide grin. "Send it over to me."

When the message flashed up on his screen, Kurtzman laughed. The code was simple, an old field code Bolan had used years before in Vietnam. But it was a code that was easy to remember and almost impossible to crack unless you knew what it was based on. Bolan had relied on the code on more than one occasion.

"Get Barbara and Hal in here ASAP," he said as he started putting the text back into English. "We're back in contact with Phoenix."

"You've got a message from Mack?" Price asked as she and Brognola rushed in a few minutes later.

"I sure do," he said, pointing to the screen.

Brognola and Price both read the message over his shoulder. Bolan was confirming what they already knew about Whitworth, but adding the new information about his "James Jordan" activities. With that piece of the puzzle in place, the whole thing made sense now. As a bonus, Bolan's plan to draw the renegade CIA man out of the country gave then the opening they needed to end the siege of the Farm.

"I think it's time for us to put an end to this," Price said.

"Past time," Brognola agreed. "Get Lyons and his crew in the communications room."

"OKAY," BROGNOLA SAID to open the meeting he had called in the communications room. "We've just learned that Striker has drawn Whitworth down to Colombia, and he's going to take care of him there."

"How did he manage to do that?" Lyons asked.

"I don't have the details right now, and it doesn't really matter. What is important is that with Whitworth out of the country, he can't feed the ATF any more of his bullshit. And since we're holding enough of them hostage to keep the rest of them from assaulting this place, it's time to wrap this up."

He turned to Schwarz. "Have you found their command-and-control radio frequencies yet?"

With all of the radios that had been captured, it had

been child's play for Schwarz to check the frequencies for traffic and crack what few radio codes they were using. "We can talk to every man jack of them practically by name," he replied. "When it comes to radio security, these guys are completely clueless. I've been monitoring their traffic for a couple of hours now, and I can damned near give you their duty roster."

"What's their commander's call sign?"

"Bold Thunder," Schwarz said with a smirk. "But, for as much as he likes to BS on the radio, it should be Big Hot Air. He's a nervous Nellie and has to keep checking on everything."

"Let me talk to him," Brognola said. "I think I can give him something to really be nervous about."

Schwarz flipped the radio to the ATF command frequency and handed over the microphone.

"Bold Thunder, Bold Thunder, this is Green Ramparts Alpha. Over."

It took a moment for the call to be answered. "Green Ramparts Alpha, this is Bold Thunder Com, over."

"That's his radio operator," Schwarz explained.

"Get Bold Thunder on the horn ASAP," Brognola snapped.

"Copy, Green Ramparts."

It took several minutes for the ATF commander to get to the radio. "Green Ramparts Alpha, this is Bold Thunder."

"This is Hal Brognola of the Justice Department. I understand that you have damned near all of the ATF lined up to start a small war in the Shenandoah Valley, and I'd like to know what in the hell you think you're doing. And be advised that I'm calling from your intended target area, so you better make sure that every one of your men knows who they'll be shooting at if they come in here. Unless they've changed the laws in the last couple of days, killing a federal official is still a capital offense. Plus, you might like to know that I have a dozen or so of your men here with me. If you'll check around, you'll find that they're missing.''

There was a long pause before the ATF agent came back on the radio. ''I think we need to talk, sir.''

''You're damned right we do, mister. Meet me at the main gate as soon as you can get here.''

''Yes, sir.''

Colombia

DAWN WAS BREAKING over the high mountain valley when Geoffrey Whitworth's two vehicles reached the turn in the dirt road that led into the valley and the little village where El Machetero had said he would be waiting with his Phoenix Force prisoner. Checking his map, Whitworth saw that there was a wooded hill overlooking the village and a field on the other side.

After consulting with the Guzmans, the elder brother took his four bodyguards and headed out through the woods to check out the high ground overlooking the village. The other brother took four of the gunmen Whitworth had armed and headed down into the valley below the cluster of small houses to sweep the other side.

CALVIN JAMES and Gary Manning had the high security watch on the little village. There was only one dirt road into the area, so there was not much to keep an eye on. While they didn't expect that Whitworth would simply drive in and quietly allow himself to be captured, they also didn't think that he would want many outsiders in on this particular piece of business.

Scanning the approach through the sniper's scope of his Remington 700, Manning spotted a man in dark clothing trying to keep out of sight as he made his way toward them.

"I've got a man coming in high," he called down to McCarter in the village. "He's keeping under cover, and I don't think that he's a local."

"Is he armed?" McCarter asked.

"Affirmative," Manning answered. "He's packing an H&K."

"Do it to him," McCarter ordered.

Reacquiring his target, Manning put the crosshairs of his scope on the center of his chest and squeezed the trigger. The Remington spit, and the man went down. Instantly there was a blaze of automatic-weapons fire slashing through the trees around him.

"We've got at least three or four more up here," Manning reported as James took the intruders under long-range fire to make them go to ground.

"Take them out."

WHITWORTH WAS at the edge of the village when he heard the firing from the hill. Instantly he realized that El Machetero was trying to double-cross him. Apparently he wasn't willing to be content with the payment he was supposed to be bringing for the Phoenix Force commando's ransom. The mercenary wanted to try for an even bigger payment by capturing him. But two could play that game.

Taking the walkie-talkie from his pocket, he told the younger Guzman, Ernesto, that he was sending his last two men down to him. It was imperative that they keep El Machetero's troops busy. When the drug lord acknowledged his orders, he flicked the selector switch of his AK to full-auto, and slipped behind the first hut.

"WE'VE GOT another group coming at us from the east," Encizo reported as he raised his over-and-under M-16/M-203 and sighted for the grenade launcher's range. "And I'm going to need some help with them."

"Roger," Bolan sent. "David's on the way."

The Executioner turned to Hawkins. "Get your hands behind your back," he told him, "but keep that Beretta ready. I think he's on the way. I'll be in the kitchen so I can watch the door."

"Chicino, you watch the back," Bolan ordered. "And remember, I want him alive."

"Sí, señor."

WITH THE FIREFIGHT keeping Phoenix Force busy, Whitworth was able to make his way from hut to hut unseen. The village was a miserable place, barely fit for pigs, much less humans. And from the look of things, the mercenary had already taken care of any locals who might have lived here after he moved in, but that was typical of him. The man was a good mercenary leader, but he was a butcher and now he had proved to be greedy, as well.

When the CIA man saw smoke trailing from the chimney of the biggest building in town, he knew that was where El Machetero would be waiting to hear the outcome of the ambush. The gunfire was dying down. Maybe the Guzmans weren't as good as they had said they were. But that didn't matter. They had diverted the mercenaries long enough for Whitworth to get to their leader.

Sliding along the adobe wall of the building until he reached the open door, Whitworth looked around the edge and saw El Machetero sitting at a table. An American in a bloodstained, muddy uniform was sitting against the wall with his hands tied behind him—the Phoenix Force bargaining chip. The only other man in the room was a guard, apparently one of the mercenary's more trusted troops.

Whitworth stepped into the room and was bringing up his AK when he felt the muzzle of a pistol jammed against his back. "Drop it," a voice said behind him.

The Phoenix Force "prisoner's" hands suddenly

appeared from behind his back, holding a 9 mm Beretta.

"Señor Jordan," El Machetero said in English as Bolan relieved him of his AK. "Welcome to Colombia."

"Shut up, you fool!" Whitworth snapped, his mind whirling to find a way out of this trap.

"Your name isn't James Jordan," Bolan said as he stepped to the side. "It's Geoffrey Whitworth, and you're the director of communications for the CIA."

Whitworth was stunned. "How do you know that?"

Bolan smiled. "Let's just say that you've been keeping too high of a profile lately. As a spy, you're supposed to know better than to do things like that."

"Who are you, anyway?" Whitworth demanded.

"Let's just say that I'm the man who's going to take you back to clear up this situation you've created."

EL MACHETERO SPOKE enough English to follow what was being said. He couldn't let the Yankees take Jordan away with them. The man had betrayed him and he had to pay for it. He couldn't allow anyone to live long enough to brag that he had bested El Machetero.

Since he had been injured when the Yankees had captured him, they hadn't searched him well and they hadn't discovered the throwing spikes in the pocket sewn into the top of his boots. Even though his right hand was gone, he could throw the deadly weapons almost as well with his left.

As the two Yankees talked, he slipped his hand to his left boot top and freed the eight-inch triangular spike from its sheath. The last-ditch weapon was sharpened on both ends to a needle point, and the triangle's edges were razor-sharp. With the weapon concealed in the palm of his hand, he slowly reached over his shoulder as if to rub his neck.

"Señor Jordan," he called out.

When Whitworth turned, the spike flashed through the air, turning one-and-one-half times before embedding itself in the hollow of his neck. Unlike a round spike, the triangular edges of this weapon sliced, instead of pushed, through flesh. On its way to embedding itself in Whitworth's spine, one of the spike's edges nicked his jugular. He gagged on the blood that rushed into his windpipe, clawed at his neck and crumpled to the floor.

Chicino spun on El Machetero, the AK in his hands spitting fire on full-auto. The burst caught the mercenary where he sat. Four of the six rounds tore through his chest, one of them ripping his heart open. He toppled to the floor, twitched and was dead.

Bolan and Hawkins both swung their pistols to cover Chicino, but held their fire as he carefully laid his smoking AK on the floor.

"Outside!" Bolan barked at him, gesturing to the door.

Chicino walked out.

Hawkins knew that the CIA man was dead, but he

knelt down to check his pulse anyway. "Do we take him back with us?" he asked as he looked up at Bolan.

"No. It's best we leave him here. I'll pay the villagers to bury him in an unmarked grave."

"Won't that cause problems in Washington? He's a high-ranking CIA officer, and someone is bound to ask questions about him."

"It'll be better if he just disappears. His James Jordan persona will surface when they clean house at Langley, and they'll just figure that he made a run for it. Plus, it won't hurt them to spend a while trying to find him. It'll remind them of what they're supposed to be doing for a living."

"You've got a point there."

"Striker," McCarter spoke over the com link, "we have the low end secured. It looks like our man brought in some of his cartel chums. They didn't know enough not to mess with real soldiers."

"The woods are cleared," Manning reported. "There were half a dozen of them up here, and they looked like drug troops, too."

"We're done in here, as well." Bolan glanced down at Whitworth one last time. "It's time to go home."

OUTSIDE THE TAVERN, Juan Chicino was talking to a courageous villager who had come out of hiding to see what was happening in his backyard. The man called out in the local dialect, and several other men came out of hiding and slowly approached.

"I told them that it is okay to come back now,"

Chicino explained to Encizo. "But they want to know what they should do with the bodies and the trucks."

"Tell them they can have everything here if they will bury the dead," Bolan said. "And you, where will you go?"

Chicino met Bolan's eyes squarely. "Now that the butcher is dead, I will go back to my people and live in peace."

"You can take one of Jordan's trucks if you want," Bolan offered.

"No." Chicino shook his head. "Leave it for these people."

"Vaya con Dios."

"Grimaldi's inbound," McCarter reported, "and he says he has enough fuel on board that we can go straight back to Panama."

"Damned straight," Hawkins said in his best down-home accent. "I gotta go shuck these here duds for a spell. I 'bout got all the good outta them I can stand."

McCarter's faced blanked as he tried to follow Hawkins's Southern idiom. "Bloody hell, man. I wish you'd speak English."

"But I do, old chap," Hawkins said in his best Eton accent. "I do."

CHAPTER THIRTY-ONE

Stony Man Farm, Virginia

Barbara Price found Aaron Kurtzman hard at work in his electronic kingdom. Two weeks had passed since Bolan had trapped Whitworth in Colombia, and things were almost back to normal. Now that they had restored their complete cybernetic capability, he was working overtime to ensure that no one would ever be able to break their security codes again. Hunt Wethers and Akira Tokaido were also putting in long hours revamping the entire system.

"Hal called," she told him, "and he said that the Man is cleaning house at Langley."

"About damned time," Kurtzman growled.

"He says that the President has appointed a new director and that several of the old Cold War Warriors are being quietly put out to pasture early. He doesn't want to risk having anything like this ever happen again."

"What about the computer techs Whitworth had working with him on this?"

"They've all had their security clearances pulled, and they've been reassigned to clerical duties. Even though they were just following what they believed were legitimate orders, they'll be lucky to get promoted past GS-9. They're finished in government."

"I'd rather they stay there where they can be watched," Kurtzman said. "I sure don't want them out there hacking for some private company."

"They'll be watched for the rest of their lives," she reassured him. "Hal made a point of that."

"Good."

"How soon will you be done with the new security system?" she asked.

"These things take time, you know."

"Hal wants us to get up and running ASAP. He's got another hot one waiting for us."

"What is it this time, a Vatican plot to overthrow the UN?"

She looked grim. "He says that he's not going to tell us until we're completely ready to deal with it. He says he doesn't want us doing a half-assed job of it."

That got Kurtzman's fullest attention, and he spun his chair around. "What in the hell is he talking about, 'half-assed'? We saved his butt this last time, didn't we?"

"That's not the way he sees it, and as you know, we're only as good as our last job."

"I have half a mind to tell him to stick this whole thing and retire. Maybe he'd like to try to run this damned place without me."

"Well," she said, "he did mention something to the effect that maybe we should look into having a shake-up around here, as well. Get a little new blood in, was how he put it."

"You tell that—" Kurtzman said before he saw the big grin on Price's face.

"Dammit, Barbara, don't do that to me."

"What he said was 'Thanks for a job well-done,' and he's sending you a new coffeepot."

As always, Kurtzman took offense at any reference to his coffee. "What's wrong with the old one?"

"He says that the Energy Department wants to borrow it for their alternative-fuel program."

"Over my dead body."

Take
4 explosive books
plus a
mystery bonus
FREE

**After the ashes of the great Reckoning, the
warrior survivalists live by one primal instinct**

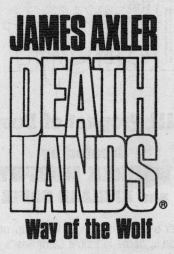

JAMES AXLER
DEATH
LANDS.

Way of the Wolf

Unexpectedly dropped into a bleak Arctic landscape by a
mat-trans jump, Ryan Cawdor and his companions find
themselves the new bounty in a struggle for dominance
between a group of Neanderthals and descendants of
a military garrison stranded generations ago.

Where there's smoke...

THE Destroyer™

#111 Prophet of Doom

Created by
WARREN MURPHY
and RICHARD SAPIR

Everyone with a spare million is lining up at the gates of Ranch Ragnarok, home to Esther Clear Seer's Church of the Absolute and Incontrovertible Truth. Here an evil yellow smoke shrouds an ancient oracle that offers glimpses into the future. But when young virgins start disappearing, CURE smells something more than a scam—and Remo is slated to become a sacrificial vessel....

Look for it in April 1998 wherever Gold Eagle books are sold.